Ebook ISBN: 978-1-956335-13-2

Paperback ISBN: 978-1-956335-14-9

Audiobook ISBN: 978-1-956335-15-6

Ebook and paperback cover design by Molly Burton at Cozy Cover Designs.

Chapter header and scene break drawings by Etheric Tales.

Axia map designed by Sarah Waites at The Illustrated Page Design.

First published in 2024 by Ringtail Press.

www.melissajacksonbooks.com

Created with Vellum

MELISSA ERIN JACKSON

Summary

Deandra Hendricks works her fingers to the bone at two jobs to keep her Los Angeles apartment. With a rapidly dwindling savings account, the prospects for her future are bleak. So when her cousin invites her to visit Axia—the hidden magical hub their grandparents retired to—she agrees. Deandra doesn't possess a stitch of magic herself, but a long weekend vacation in a strange new town might be just what she needs.

Her first day in Axia is so bizarre, though, she wonders if her bleak life in Los Angeles hasn't been so bad after all. And just when she thinks her day can't get any stranger, she finds a baby dragon trapped in a dumpster. At a loss, she takes a trip to the vet, hoping they can help find the little guy's owner.

The dragon, it turns out, only appears in its true form to her, while everyone else sees a dire wolf puppy. She and the vet discover that, as long as the dragon wears his bespelled collar, his true identity is hidden. Someone went to great lengths to keep this supposed-to-be-extinct animal a secret.

Then the "dog" is accused of arson and is seized by authorities. Determined to help him, Deandra searches for the real arsonist. She catches wind of a thriving black market that's populated by those who would stop at nothing to claim an animal this rare. She must work quickly to clear her dragon's name, because if he falls into the wrong hands, she could lose him forever.

Corly Land Management
Wheeler Ave
Heather's Elixirs
Telepost
Welcome Center
Pizza Place
McClaren
Axia

Mythic Pet
Kitchen
Purl Way
Caddel's
Office
Drug
Store
Art
Gallery
Burned
Building
Dumpling
Hut
Cottage
Hogarth's
Hoagies
cery
ore
Telepad
Station
Zombie
Cactus
Unusual
Claims
ZOMBIE
CACTUS
POLICE
Police
Station
ra Sensory
Pastry
Oracle
Park
Grandparents'
House

Chapter 1

A bright blue light pulsed off the circular pendant on the counter in a slow, rhythmic pattern. Deandra cocked her head as she watched it. It wasn't doing anything else—no humming, buzzing, or shooting flesh-melting laser beams, so her initial alarm over the strange object had lessened considerably over the last five minutes.

Lips pursed, she picked up the accompanying card to re-read the note.

Hey, Dee!

Our gossipy mothers got to talking, and I may have overheard that your life is in "upheaval." I figure it's not as bad as all that, but Grandma and Grandpa (heavily) suggested I send you a travel talisman anyway. Visiting a magical town is a terrifying idea, I know, but Axia is a great place to start. It's basically a retirement community for people like them.

I'm going to keep bugging you to come see this place until you cave. And now, thanks to the aforementioned gossipy mothers, I have new information to use against you. Being new(ish) single is as good an excuse as any! Get your butt over here already. I bet you won't be able to leave once you see it.

If you decide to come, let me know, and we'll inform the Welcome Center.

- Wendy

Deandra sighed, placing the card back on the counter. The travel talisman still pulsed blue. She knew Axia wasn't some creepy cult commune straight out of a dystopian sci-fi movie, but it sure sounded like it. The capital letters of "Welcome Center" screamed "once you're here, you'll be microchipped and stripped of your ability to make your own decisions."

But as impulsive as her cousin Wendy could be, Deandra knew exactly what Axia truly was: a hidden magical "hub" in a rural part of

Northern California. Deandra and Wendy were both fully human—much to Wendy's chagrin—but their grandparents were "magic-touched." They were wind elementals who had retired to Axia several years ago. As elementals aged, so did their magic. An errant sneeze could cause a miniature gale-force gust. In Axia, they could live out their golden years in a community where life was slower—and magical mishaps were treated as a natural part of aging.

Deandra cautiously touched a finger to the circular disc on the counter. The center was hollow, making the talisman resemble a flat metallic donut. The metal was a soft gray and cool to the touch. No magical zaps singed her fingertip. While the disc was thin, when Deandra picked it up—the attached chain sliding along the counter—there was a definite heft to the metal. The blinking blue light had been emanating from the center of the disc, but now that the talisman was in Deandra's hand, the light went from flashing to swirling. Her eyes widened as a whirling vortex whipped into a frenzy.

She gasped, dropping the disc with a clatter. What if the magic sucked her in like a portal?

Yet, when the talisman hit the counter, the vortex immediately returned to a calm, pulsing blue light.

Shuddering, Deandra scooped up the disc long enough to shove it *and* the note from Wendy back into the small cardboard box they'd come in. Tucking the box under her arm, she hustled across her small dining-slash-living room to her desk wedged into a corner. In a drawer, she found tape to seal the offending box back up. She might have used the entire roll. Simply writing "return to sender" on the box and shipping it off from whence it came wouldn't work, since the mail system in Axia was some complicated closed system. Stuff could get out just fine, but getting it in required several hoops to jump through. For now, Deandra would keep it stowed in the very back of her closet until she could figure out what to do with it.

Once the talisman was securely tucked away, and the closet door was shut tight, she glanced at the clock on her bedside table—and cursed. She had only ten minutes to get dressed for work if she had any hope of getting there on time.

She was out the door in eight.

After four grueling hours, Deandra flung herself into the back seat of her car. She slammed the door shut and flopped onto her back, an arm thrown over her eyes. She worked an absurd number of hours each week as a barista in a wildly popular coffee shop in downtown Los Angeles. Since living in Los Angeles was ludicrously expensive, she also worked as a ride-share driver when she needed to help make ends meet. Which was ... often.

Deandra was reliable, had the mental fortitude to deal with the clientele, and had no life whatsoever, so her boss gave her all the hours she wanted. The turnover rate with students was astronomical, but ninety percent of the time they were the only ones applying for the job. So, while new employees dropped like flies, Deandra picked up their shifts left and right. Her entire existence had become working her fingers to the bone just to keep her apartment—an apartment she'd shared with her boyfriend, with his well-paying job in the medical field, until five months ago.

She tossed and turned on her back seat, trying to get comfortable. She'd only needed to supplement her income with ride-share gigs once this week, which was good because the pay at the shop was better, but it also meant she was exhausted, her back ached, and her feet throbbed. This was technically her lunch break, but she was so tired, she wasn't sure she'd have the energy to eat anyway. A nap was more vital.

She'd been screamed at no less than three times today, all for things decidedly inconsequential. She'd listened to a diatribe about the cost of a cup of coffee being both "exorbitant" and "highway robbery" by a woman wearing Louboutin heels and an honest-to-God pearl necklace. A new coworker had been reduced to a puddle of tears after a man had berated her for putting vanilla creamer in his drink that wasn't sugar-free as he'd "explicitly requested." Her coworker had remade the drink for him, which the man had promptly taken to the condiment table—and then proceeded to dump in four packets of sweetener.

The tips were decent—sometimes great—but Deandra wondered if any amount of money would make this level of exhaustion worth it.

After ten minutes, when a power nap still eluded her, she gave up and rolled onto her side to rummage around in the purse she'd tossed haphazardly on the floorboard. Her unearthed cell phone told her it was just after five in the evening. She dialed her mom, then flopped onto her back again, staring at a black speck on the dark fabric ceiling, unsure if it was a stain or not. She longed for it to be a venomous spider. A ballooning bug bite would get her out of the rest of her shift—and possibly into a hospital, which was less ideal. But they'd let her sleep and would bring her Jell-O, so already this option sounded better than going back into Urbean Edge.

"Hello ..." her mother answered cautiously. "How's it going?"

"I have lost the will to live."

The black speck on her dark ceiling scuttled forward a few inches.

Deandra added, "I'm currently awaiting the sweet release of death via arachnid."

"Ah," her mother said, unfazed. "This is a lunch-break call."

Deandra knew her mother wasn't unsympathetic to her weekly plight—after all, Deandra's parents were restaurant owners and dealt with just as much daily nonsense as she did. Since it was after five p.m.—after six for her mother—she was probably bone-weary, too. Their restaurant served breakfast and brunch at an establishment that had grown into an institution in Denver, Colorado. Her mother's day started at four a.m.—so six p.m. was practically midnight for her.

But her mother, as usual, took on her "I'm listening" tone, even if she was drained. "Did that woman pretend to find broken glass in her veggie wrap again?"

Deandra grimaced at the week-old memory. "I actually don't want to talk about work."

"Oh?"

"I ... uh ... got an interesting gift from Wendy today. Grandma and Grandpa told her to send it. The middle swirls around. The whole thing glows blue. I wasn't sure what to do with it, so now the terrifying thing is buried deep in my closet."

"I don't need to know the details of your sex life, Dee."

"Mom!"

"Sorry." She cracked up. "What is it? A travel talisman?"

"Yeah. That's what she called it."

There was a long beat of silence, and when her mother spoke again, her tone had lost all traces of humor. "Are you thinking of using it?"

"I don't know," Deandra said, sighing. "I've never been to a hub. And Grandma and Grandpa travel less now that they live in Axia. It sounds like they're doing great there, but they aren't getting any younger. I don't want to regret not seeing them."

"Sounds like you've made up your mind," she said. "Axia sounds much more relaxed than the hub I grew up in. I'm sure you'd be fine."

"You could come with me," Deandra said, wincing slightly in preparation for the response she knew was coming. "I'm sure they'd send some for you and Dad, too."

"Did they put you up to this?" her mother asked, sounding more resigned than angry. "Guilt me into going by using my favorite daughter as bait?"

"I'm your only daughter."

Her mother didn't even laugh at the bad, oft-used joke. "It's not a good time. Business at the restaurant is hectic. We couldn't leave the place unattended."

They had a full staff more than capable of holding down the fort for a few days, but Deandra knew there was no point in arguing. Her mother—and all her siblings—had grown up in a hub. It hadn't been easy for her mother to live in a city teeming with magic when she didn't have any herself, despite both of her parents being elementals. Of her mother's three siblings, only one had been born with magic. He was practically a prodigy, as if, instead of their parents' magic being equally distributed to the four children, Uncle John had gotten all of it.

John was the eldest, too. He would have lorded it over his siblings anyway, as that was the way of older siblings, but for him to also be blessed with magic? It hadn't been pretty. As soon as the younger siblings were old enough, they'd fled the hub system and vowed never to return.

Deandra didn't blame her mother for wanting no part of that life. Nevertheless, she'd always been curious what a hub city would be like. She imagined it like a movie, but instead of the fantastical things she saw being the product of green screens and robotics, they'd be powered by *real* magic.

Deandra had been living in the city of Hollywood magic for three years now. The city of glitz and glamour. Heck, she'd served coffee to Zac Efron just last month. She'd almost suffered heart failure at the sheer excitement of it. Fifteen minutes later, however, a man who was upset about his scalding coffee not being hot enough had called her an "incompetent nincompoop," which had killed the Efron high.

Maybe what Deandra needed was a little dose of *actual* magic. It was possible she'd find Axia just as overwhelming as her mother thought all hubs were, and after a weekend, Deandra would come running back, arms wide, to embrace her too-expensive, pollution-laden, traffic-clogged city.

"I think I'm going to take them up on the offer," Deandra said. "If the place is as chill as Wendy says, maybe you and Dad can join me."

"Maybe," her mother said unconvincingly, stifling a yawn. "When do you think you'd go?"

"I have Thursday off this week. Is that ... oh, that's tomorrow. Joe could cover Friday, and Marcy could probably cover Saturday and Sunday. I'll make a long weekend of it."

"I'm sure everyone would love to see you. You'll be in good hands there," she said. "Probably."

Deandra sighed softly to herself. "I'll be fine."

"I know. This is my issue, not yours." There was a slight smile evident in her voice when she added, "I wonder how long it'll take them to set you up on a blind date."

"Did you *really* have to tell them Mark and I broke up?"

Deandra hadn't even told Wendy about the break-up yet. Her feelings about her failed relationship were still a tangled mess that Deandra hadn't had the energy to unravel just yet.

"Sorry, baby girl. I absolutely threw you under the bus," her mother admitted. "Gayle was getting on my case about going to one of those wellness retreats with her, and I needed to deflect."

"Well if I end up going on several disastrous dates with a bunch of weirdo wizards, I'll report back so you have more things to gossip about with Aunt Gayle."

Her mother laughed. "Pro tip? Wizards aren't a thing. There are witches or sorcerers—two very different things—and both terms are gender neutral."

Deandra's brows smashed together. "Then what are Grandma and Grandpa?"

"Wind witches."

"Is there a handbook I need to pick up first?" Deandra asked.

"There should be several pamphlets in the Welcome Center when you get there," her mother said without a hint of mirth. "Oh, and it's common for Centers to employ avian shifters, since birds are so gregarious. They often have an odd look to them, as the shift from avian to human isn't seamless. The uneven shift only afflicts avians for some reason—the other animal shifters don't have that problem. Try not to stare. It's offensive."

Deandra wondered if she should take notes.

"I *would* like to be a fly on the wall to see your reaction to experiencing the world inside a hub for the first time," her mother added wistfully. "Culture shock isn't a strong enough term."

Oh boy.

This would no doubt be a very, *very* weird weekend.

Chapter 2

Deandra left at five a.m. the next morning, the sky still dark and the air chilly. She'd already been awake for two hours, too amped up to sleep. Stocking up on caffeine when she finally set out had become imperative.

The drive from Los Angeles took the better part of eight hours, partly because of several bathroom and snack breaks. During those long eight hours, Deandra had wished, not for the first time, that it wasn't an overnight bag lying on the back seat, but a dog. A dog would have made for a great road trip companion. Someone who wouldn't complain about her music or the stretch of time she'd listened to a historical romance audiobook that had gotten so unexpectedly racy, she'd missed several minutes over the sound of her own embarrassed laughter. Mark had been allergic to animals in general and had refused to even consider hypoallergenic breeds.

Maybe when she got back to LA, she'd look into getting a dog. She probably also needed to relocate. The ability to keep her apartment on a single salary and a rapidly depleting savings account wouldn't last much longer. She wouldn't be able to keep a roof over her head *and* keep a new pup fed.

The directions Wendy had provided eventually led Deandra to what could only be described as "the middle of nowhere."

"*You have reached your destination*," her GPS informed her.

Deandra slowed to a stop. A cloud of dust rose around the car, gravel crunching under the tires. There was nothing here but empty fields, a highway off in the distance, and the dirt road she idled on.

"The heck I have," she muttered.

She tapped at her phone propped up on her dashboard and called Wendy.

"Hi!" her cousin replied so quickly, the phone had barely rung once. The din of voices sounded in the background. "Are you here yet?" She was a little out of breath.

Deandra squinted through the wafting dust cloud. "I'm ... somewhere. This can't be right. I must have taken a wrong turn."

"Do you see a barn anywhere? I think that entrance has a barn. Or was it a shed ..."

Deandra questioned her decision to do this. A slight breeze kicked up another thick cloud of dust, reminding her that, despite how often people thought of California as the land of perfect weather, it was a desert state.

As the dirt settled, she saw it: way out in the distance, in the middle of a field of yet more dirt, stood a dilapidated structure. It was still up for debate whether it was a shed or a barn. "I think I see it."

"There should be a road that leads directly to its doorstep," Wendy said.

Deandra took her foot off the brake and eased forward. A short chicken-wire fence, no more than two feet high, hugged either side of the road for as far as she could see. Uneven metal spikes poked into the air from the top of the crudely cut fence. She supposed she could try to gun it and drive over the fence, but the tires might not make it—the car's paint job surely wouldn't. No road, paved or otherwise, led to the falling-apart structure in the distance.

"You're *wearing* the talisman, right?" Wendy asked when Deandra hadn't given her an update in over a minute.

Deandra most certainly wasn't.

She glanced toward the passenger seat, where the small cardboard box sat among a scattered array of snack bags. The talisman was still inside the box. In fact, the box was still sealed tight.

It wasn't that Deandra feared the talisman ... okay, that was a lie.

"Ugh. Give me a second," Deandra said, putting the car in park. "In my defense, you never said I had to put it on."

"It's a *necklace*, Dee. What else would you do with a necklace, other than wear it?"

"Don't sass me. I'm starting to freak out here."

Wendy chuckled. "*Starting* to?"

Be best friends with your cousin, they said. It's even better than having a sister, they said ...

Deandra gave her mirrors a cursory check to make sure the deserted dirt road remained deserted. A literal tumbleweed rolled by behind her, but she saw no other signs of life other than the lone songbird warbling from its perch on the wire fence.

After getting the box unsealed with the aid of much finagling and even more cursing—why had she used so much tape?—Deandra stared down at the box in her lap for a long moment. The memory of the swirling vortex was fresh in her mind. If she got sucked into some alternate universe, she'd never forgive Wendy. She said as much out loud.

Wendy snorted. "I know it's been a minute since we've hung out, but you're way more dramatic than I remember."

Deandra opened the box. The talisman still lay innocently at the bottom, giving off the ever-present blue glow. Steeling herself, she reached inside and pulled out the metal disc. She marveled again at the heft of it in her palm, despite the material appearing no thicker than a few pieces of tin foil squeezed together.

She held the disc up by the attached chain. It was gaudy when considered as a piece of jewelry, rather than a quirky bit of art.

"Here goes nothing," she muttered, clasping the chain behind her neck.

The disc rested against her chest, the coolness of the metal seeping through the fabric of her shirt. Despite the "necklace" not being her style at all, it didn't look half bad lying against the peach hue of her blouse.

The vortex housed in the hollow of the disc had kicked up speed as soon as Deandra pulled the talisman from the box. It was disconcerting to have the contained tornado of magic so close to her body, but so far it hadn't sucked her organs out through her chest, so she hazarded a glance away from it and out the window.

She gasped.

A few feet ahead, the road she was on curved slightly to the left. The wire fence had parted, seemingly to allow her passage. From what she could tell, the newly formed road *did* lead straight to the lone structure waiting in the field beyond.

"Told you," Wendy said, but she didn't sound smug. She sounded ... hopeful. A fondness for her cousin softened the edges of Deandra's anxiety. Wendy loved Axia, and she wanted Deandra to love it too.

As apprehensive as Deandra felt, it wasn't only nervous butterflies winging erratically in her belly. She was excited. She was practically thrumming from head to toe. Wasn't this what every child wished for—to find a secret key that granted access to a hidden magical world?

Well, who had decided magic was just for kids?

She put the car in drive, took her foot off the brake, and inched forward, slowly turning left onto the newly revealed road. The tires met no resistance as she drove past the wire fence. She lightly pressed her foot on the gas and accelerated past barren fields. This wasn't a hallucination. This was actually happening.

"I'm on my way," she said, noting the giddy trill in her own voice.

"Awesome!" Wendy said. "I'll meet you at the Welcome Center. See you soon!"

The call disconnected.

As she got closer, Deandra noted that the dilapidated shed sat directly in the middle of the road. Even from a distance, she could tell there was no parking lot. Was she supposed to stop outside the shed and wait for assistance? Would an unseen trap door open beneath her car, where she'd plummet onto an Axian road? The idea of an entire town existing under this field was doing a number on her brain, but she kept going.

The shed was more like a small cabin, the walls weatherworn and leaning dangerously to one side. Shingles were missing from the sagging roof, leaving a few gaping holes open to the elements. The door hung precariously from its hinges, revealing a few snatches of black from inside the dark, small house. Deandra half expected a goblin or some other small magical creature to scurry out onto the rotting porch to greet her.

But even when she was close enough to be sure the few windows on the front of the house held no glass, no one emerged from inside the cabin. No one rounded a corner from behind it. Nothing came scuttling out of the broken roof.

Suddenly, the entire cabin *shimmered*. Deandra slammed on the brakes, and the car skidded to a stop, the back tires fishtailing. A fresh dust cloud kicked up, wafting about the car. Her heartbeat pulsed in her throat.

The cabin's edges went soft, like water dripping onto still-wet paint, the colors running and bleeding. The house slowly melted into the air like mist. A blink later, the scene snapped into sharp focus again, revealing a series of obelisk-shaped posts that stretched out in either direction. They reminded her of fence posts, only there was nothing connecting them to one another, as if someone had given up on the project right after installing them. Each one was covered in unfamiliar markings.

Directly in front of her were two larger obelisks, each at least eight feet tall, while the others stood closer to five feet. Between the pointed tips of the larger posts stretched a metal sign. Metal leaves and flowers wove around each other from either end of the arching sign, where they met in the middle to form the letters of "Axia." While it was easy to read the word, it also seamlessly blended into the metal plant life; something beautiful hidden in plain sight—perhaps like the town of Axia itself.

All that lay beyond the obelisks were more barren fields, though.

Telling herself that the cabin *hadn't been* real, and these obelisks were, she slowly lifted her foot off the brake. The car rolled forward, the occasional rock crunching under a tire. As she passed under the arch, she squinted one eye closed, bracing for the impact of the car crashing—albeit slowly—into the old cabin.

She fully passed under the arch without incident, then stopped several hundred feet beyond it, eyeing the back side in her rearview mirror. Nothing but the unfinished fence and dirt in all directions.

Then, all at once, an entire street lined with businesses popped into existence around her.

She froze, her eyes stuck open.

She screamed bloody murder.

Holding on to the steering wheel of her idling car for dear life, she gazed left and then right, screaming her head off all the while. Human brains were not equipped to process such a thing, Deandra decided, as she switched to creative strings of obscenities that would have made her foul-mouthed boss blush.

The road below her was a normal-enough looking road. From where she sat screaming, she noted the normal-looking sidewalks. There were a handful of buildings that looked normal, too. They had brick façades, shiny glass windows, and there was even a very normal-looking woman walking her normal-looking dog. It honestly looked no more magical than any of the handful of towns she'd stopped in on her drive here.

What strolled around the corner of an ice cream shop, though, was so baffling to Deandra's malfunctioning human brain that her screams and curses dried up in an instant. Because now, clomping down the sidewalk ahead of her, was a centaur.

A freaking *centaur*!

She lurched forward, hugging the steering wheel to her chest like a life raft. The body of the centaur was a sleek chestnut-brown horse, and where the neck and head should have been was a man's torso. The man-half was shirtless, his skin a golden brown a few shades lighter than her own. He had the face of someone who belonged on the cover of GQ. He slowly clopped forward, covering the distance between his original location and Deandra's car in a matter of seconds—what with the *horse legs*.

Craning his neck to peer through the windshield, he flashed her a grin. Her stomach swooped. He was far too good-looking for his own good—for *anyone's* good. Men that easy on the eyes were capital-T Trouble. She involuntarily bit her lip as he offered her a flirtatious wink.

His tail swiped left and right in her peripheral vision, likely instinctively swatting away flies.

Get it together, Dee!

This place had broken her in a matter of seconds. She was ogling a man with a freaking *tail*.

A very gorgeous man who needed both a brush *and* a currycomb. She gave her head a very hard shake. This was what insanity felt like, she was sure of it.

The centaur laughed—the sound muted—then he continued on his way. She watched him in the passenger-side mirror. He waved at someone across the street, and given the way he started swishing his equine hips, Deandra figured he was flirting with that individual too.

Knock, knock.

She flinched so hard, the car rocked, punctuated by another wave of wildly ribald curses. Whipping her head to the side, she peered out her driver's side window toward the source of the sound—and shrieked.

Her arms flailed, knocking her rearview mirror askew. The strangest-looking woman Deandra had ever seen squatted there. When all Deandra did was stare at her wide-eyed, the woman angled her pointer finger toward the ground a few times.

Swallowing hard, Deandra hit the button to lower her window, even though her instincts told her to throw the car in reverse, slam her foot on the gas, and accelerate right the heck out of this whacky place.

"Hello!" the woman said, her voice melodic. The pleasantness of her tone was a sharp contrast to her abnormal appearance.

"H-hi," Deandra said, swallowing. She was going to need a defibrillator soon.

"I'm Allegra," the woman said, sticking her hand through Deandra's open window.

Deandra shook it, finding the woman's delicate hand cool to the touch. Her fingers were long, pale, and thin, which matched her tall, willowy frame. Even her neck was long—perhaps *too* long.

"I'm the curator of the Welcome Center."

Deandra blinked dumbly at her, taking her hand back. Much like her reaction to an entire town snapping into existence, Deandra's mind couldn't reconcile the oddity of Allegra's features.

Her nose was a bit too big for her face, her eyes spaced too far apart, and her head moved in quick, jerky movements as she observed Deandra. A slight breeze swept past Allegra, and Deandra realized that the woman's stylish blond pixie-cut hair wasn't hair at all but *feathers*. The tips of the feathers were black. It was the kind of cool, edgy hairstyle Deandra admired on others but could never pull off herself. If it weren't for the incongruous way Allegra's features resided on her face, Deandra could picture her working the runway as an androgynous model—someone who could make any fashion style work.

Her mother's warning suddenly careened into place, pushing out Deandra's plethora of jumbled, half-formed questions. "*It's common for Centers to employ avian shifters ... they often have an odd look to them ... it only afflicts avian shifters for some reason—the other animal shifters don't have that problem. Try not to stare. It's offensive.*"

Deandra quickly diverted her attention. "I'm so sorry."

Which likely earned her even fewer favors, but she was floundering here. She really should have asked more questions before she embarked on this impromptu adventure.

Allegra's laugh was even more melodic than her speaking voice—a cheerful, warbling sound that eased the knot of anxiety squeezing Deandra's chest like a vise.

"Between you and me," Allegra said with a conspiratorial edge that made Deandra glance over at her, "I took this job specifically for the look on humans' faces when they visit a hub for the first time. As shocking as it might be to see a centaur or faun, I find it's often the avian shifters whom humans find the most unsettling. Humans search for human-like faces in everything—it's an instinctual reaction when presented with something alien, for lack of a better word. Humans try to find order in chaos. I am well aware that an avian shifter's face, to a human, looks like chaos. I figure it's good to give newcomers a shock to the system when they get here. They'll know fairly quickly if it's too much to handle."

Deandra wasn't sure what to say.

"I went to an all-avian high school," Allegra added. "I was voted 'most beautiful' four years in a row. Beauty is in the eye of the beholder, no?"

Deandra nodded, hoping she one day possessed the confidence of an avian shifter living among humans.

"The Welcome Center is a few buildings ahead—between the

telepost office and the sandwich shop. Looks like you're going to need *all* the welcome pamphlets."

"I might need a welcome encyclopedia," Deandra muttered.

Allegra's melodious laugh made another delightful appearance. "There's a parking lot around the back." She stood to full height. "See you inside."

With no warning, Allegra gave her arms a quick flap and turned into a swan twice the size of an ostrich. Deandra nearly swallowed her own tongue.

Allegra squawked with the force of a bullhorn, then waddled down the middle of the street. She waved a massive white wing—tipped with black—at a couple walking down the sidewalk. The couple smiled and waved back.

The couple in question just happened to be a pair of four-foot-tall, green-skinned beings with pointy ears. Goblins, maybe?

Good grief.

Deandra allowed her heart a full five minutes to stop trying to pound its way out of her chest before she forced herself to decide whether to move forward or hightail it back to Los Angeles.

Curiosity, as always, won out.

Blowing out a long, slow breath, she eased the car into drive and followed her feathered welcome committee.

She really hoped Axia had a well-stocked liquor store.

Chapter 3

The Welcome Center was a wide-open space decorated like a cozy living room. Several plush sofas in forest green and navy blue were scattered around the room, accented by low tables. Shiny pamphlets were fanned out on the tables' surfaces as well as stacked into neat rows in the large shelving unit pressed against the wall beside the front door. Deandra didn't see Allegra anywhere.

A counter stretched along the back of the room where more pamphlets and flyers lay carefully arranged on the worn wood. A second avian shifter—this one male—stood behind the counter with a phone pressed to his ear. At least she knew now that avian shifters were easily identifiable on sight.

While Allegra was long and thin, this man was stout—wide in the shoulders and not an inch over five-foot-five. His hair, while much longer than Allegra's, was composed of feathers as well. Most were deep chocolate brown, but a few were stark white.

His voice was just as pleasant as Allegra's, and he was patiently relaying directions to the location of the town hall to the person on the other line. When his laser-sharp, beady eyes swiveled in Deandra's direction, she froze. Her gut told her he had to be an eagle in avian form. The idea of a five-foot-tall bird of prey nearly made her pass out right there on the shiny hardwood floor.

A door just beyond the counter opened and out stepped Allegra —thankfully back in her human body. Smiling brightly, Allegra elegantly swept forward, skirting the end of the counter, weaving around a few of the love seats, and stopping before Deandra, blocking her view of the eagle man.

"You have that glazed-eyed look newcomers get," Allegra said, her chipper tone suggesting she found this deeply amusing. As far as bird personalities went, Deandra thought Allegra should have been a corvid—smart, cunning, and mischievous. Swans had an aggressive streak that Allegra appeared to lack, at least, so Deandra supposed she could have done worse, as far as guides went.

At a young age, Deandra had been chased by a rather ornery goose through a park. When she'd tripped over her own untied shoelaces with the murder bird approaching fast, her short life had flashed before her eyes. Her dad had snatched her off the ground before she'd become goose chow, and her mother had chased the bird off, a battle cry on her lips and a purse swung in her grip like a military flail.

Smiling softly at the memory, Deandra suddenly wished they were here. Her mother would get a kick out of watching Deandra and her father have a total meltdown. He'd never been to a hub, either.

"How are you holding up so far?"

Deandra snapped out of the memory and offered Allegra a weak smile. "Umm ... fine?"

A laugh bubbled up behind her. "Liar."

Grinning, Deandra spun to find her cousin Wendy standing in the doorway. She was such a welcome, familiar sight, Deandra almost burst into tears. Though they talked often, it had been nearly a year since she'd last seen her cousin in person, so the joy she felt wasn't wholly over the top. But it was close. She flung her arms around Wendy. Deandra had to stoop a little to do it, as Wendy was a good six inches shorter, but Deandra held on tight, her chin on her cousin's shoulder.

At first glance, most people wouldn't think Deandra Hendricks and Wendy Choo were related. Deandra was tall and dark, while Wendy was petite and fair skinned. Their grandparents and mothers were African American, but Wendy's mother, Gayle, had married a Chinese American man. Like Deandra's own father, Wendy's dad was fully human, sealing the deal that Wendy had no chance of ever wielding magic.

Wendy wrapped her arms around Deandra. The travel talisman was wedged between their chests. Though Deandra was sure the magic in it had winked out once she'd crossed into the town, a faint chill from the metal still seeped through Deandra's shirt.

Deandra's mid-back length waves hung around her shoulders, and Wendy petted her hair as if Deandra were an animal who needed soothing. That wasn't far off.

Wendy addressed Allegra over Deandra's shoulder. "What did you do to her? Did you shift in front of her? You know that freaks newbies out!"

"And *you* know how I feel about giving the fresh-faced ones a crash course."

"You thrive on chaos," Wendy said.

The sweet warble of Allegra's laugh would have better befit someone who shifted into a cute, fluffy songbird—not a swan the size of a Clydesdale.

As Deandra held on to Wendy for dear life, Deandra had a clear view of the street. Wendy and Allegra were still talking, but Deandra wasn't listening. She was currently too distracted by the same centaur from earlier on the other side of the road. He vigorously rubbed his equine backside on a tree. Deandra assumed it was to relieve an itch, and if it was for any other reason, she didn't want details. He must have sensed Deandra's eyes on him because he angled his bronzed torso toward her, continuing to scratch his backside on the tree so hard that he knocked several leaves loose. He pounded his fists against his chest as if he were a mountain gorilla, then made a very dramatic show of winking at her. Done with his manly centaur display, he strutted down the sidewalk and out of view.

Deandra moaned pitifully. "This place is *so weird*!"

Wendy laughed again and broke the hug, keeping hold of Deandra's shoulders. She stared up at Deandra for a beat. "I promise you'll be fine. It's just culture shock."

Her mom had been right: it wasn't a strong enough term.

"We're going to a pastry shop," Wendy said, looping her arm through Deandra's and spinning them away from the street. "It's run by a brother and sister. He's an empath. She's a witch. He can sense what you're feeling, and she can make you something to eat or drink based on that to give you a boost for the day."

"Oh, good idea," Allegra said. "I had an upset stomach, and the cinnamon bun I picked up this morning cleared it right up. I love my husband, but his foray into cooking isn't going well. He made an acorn hash last night that was absolutely dreadful." She leaned toward Deandra a fraction. "He's a squirrel shifter."

Of course he is ...

Though Deandra would likely never admit this to her mother, she was beginning to understand how her mother could choose to live in the "normal" world over a magical one. She hadn't even been here an hour yet, and Axia, despite being a small town, was already ... a lot. Her mother's hometown had been a large city. Deandra tried to imagine a bustling place like San Francisco or Las Vegas or Chicago, and then adding magic and mythical creatures to the mix.

She gave a little head-clearing shake. This was a small town that largely catered to the retirement crowd. Deandra could handle a small town. Rolling her shoulders and standing taller, she said, "A pastry sounds great. And coffee. I'm going to crash soon without more caffeine."

"I got you, girl. Don't worry. You'll be in love with this place in no time," Wendy said.

Allegra got Deandra outfitted with a map of the town as well as a small, full-color booklet titled *A Beginner's Guide to Axia*. The image below the cheery lemon-yellow title featured a group of people huddled together: a human lady, a green-skinned orc man who stood two heads taller than the human, an equally tall woman who looked human enough but who must have spent a minimum of eight hours a day in the gym, and the same centaur Deandra had seen earlier. His face now lived rent-free in her mind for all of time. Unless, of course, the centaur had a twin. Perish the thought.

In front of the group of four, standing no taller than four feet, were a goblin and a gnome, complete with a pointy hat atop her head. Everyone in attendance appeared to be in stitches over something the orc had said. The gnome's eyes were closed, her laugh lines prominent and her cheeks a rosy pink from laughter.

A brief flip through the booklet revealed what looked like character sheets from a video game: things to know about the various species, including social faux pas that could enrage—or, at minimum, deeply offend—an Axian resident. Deandra assumed it was only a matter of time before she got herself in serious trouble for inadvertently sticking her foot in her mouth.

Toward the back of the booklet, past pages about various businesses—with accompanying coupons for newcomers—was a glossary. She'd have to commit this whole dang thing to memory tonight when she got a quiet moment to herself.

Deandra offered Allegra a genuine smile. "Thanks for this. This actually makes me feel loads less overwhelmed."

"Then my work here is done," Allegra said. "You're in good hands with Wendy, but if you need anything at all while you're in town, don't hesitate to stop by." With a wink that was especially off-putting with her too-far-apart eyes, she added, "I promise to keep the shifting to a minimum."

Deandra decided, as she left the Welcome Center with Wendy, that Allegra hadn't meant that last part one bit.

Chapter 4

Deandra fetched her purse from her car parked in the Welcome Center lot and discarded her dormant travel talisman on her passenger seat. Wendy informed her that the Welcome Center was walking distance from Axia's downtown area, so Deandra locked up her car and the pair set off down the sidewalk.

"Allegra is great," Wendy said, "but she really *does* thrive on chaos. That's more of a swan characteristic than a general avian thing. You can fully trust her to behave when she's working, but in social situations?" She chuckled. "Let's just say she can drink nearly anyone of any species under the table, and she's absolutely ruthless at billiards. She almost got into a fistfight with an orc at a bar a few weekends ago. He was visiting from another hub, so he didn't know Allegra is a pool shark. Allegra pretended to be clueless for the first two games, losing a couple hundred dollars to the guy. Then she went all-in on a bet for the third game. She *destroyed* the orc. He was hopping mad. She narrowly missed getting flattened into a pancake. Security guards saved her. Apparently, the orc went completely bonkers afterward and trashed the place. It's still closed for renovations."

Deandra winced. "Were you there?"

"Nah. I work with Allegra's brother-in-law. I heard *all* about it the next day. Word spreads quick in Axia," Wendy said. "If you get into any mischief while you're here, Grandma and Grandpa will know about it by noon the next day."

"And then they'll call your mom, who will in turn call mine," Deandra said.

Wendy laughed. "Yep."

Mischief was not on Deandra's to-do list while in the strangest place she'd ever been in her thirty years.

Thankfully, the walk to Extra Sensory Pastry was no stranger than anything else Deandra had experienced so far. By the time they reached their destination, her heart rate had settled, and much of the tension had left her shoulders. And, better yet, when they stepped inside the cozy café, Deandra was hit with the decadent scents of sugar, baking bread, and coffee, dispelling the rest of her nerves.

Casting a glance up, Deandra marveled at the latticework on the ceiling interwoven with vibrant green vines and delicate fairy lights. Vines snaked from the ceiling in a few places, clinging to the walls as they crept toward the tall windows that let in a wealth of early afternoon sun.

Tabletops came in shades of green—sage, olive, emerald, and mint—and were ringed by mismatched chairs. Some were high-backed and elegant, some were plushy and soft, and others were built for two. All were upholstered in green or brown, and even though the haphazard nature of the décor should have made the place feel like a muddled mess, it was somehow even more inviting. The café owners clearly wanted their patrons to be comfortable and to stay awhile.

As Deandra and Wendy wove around tables, Wendy told her that, even though the café's special pastries were the primary draw, salads and sandwiches were on the menu, too. The café seated thirty or so but was currently only half full. Deandra figured they'd just missed the lunch rush.

Behind the counter stood a man and woman in their forties. Deandra wasn't sure if they were twins or not, but there was no doubt they were related. They were short and unassuming-looking people—the kind of people Deandra would have passed on the street back home without cataloging them to memory. The fact that they both had powers made Deandra wonder how many magical people she'd seen and interacted with in the "normal" world, oblivious to the magic coursing through them. Magic-touched weren't required to live in a hub like Axia, after all. They just had to hide their abilities while living on the outside to avoid revealing one of the world's great secrets: that magic existed. In hubs, the magic-touched could unapologetically be themselves.

When Deandra and Wendy reached the counter, Wendy laid her folded hands on the smooth wooden surface but didn't speak. Deandra stopped awkwardly beside her. The male half of the sibling duo made his way over. His name tag introduced him as Sebastian, while his sister's said Isabel.

Sebastian the empath—according to Wendy—had pale skin, brown eyes, light brown hair that had started to go a little gray at the temples, and a kind, soft smile. A flicker of blue sparked in those plain brown eyes, like a spark of lightning, when he made eye contact with Deandra. It was there and gone so quickly, she wondered if she'd seen it at all.

Sebastian held her gaze long enough to tip the interaction into the "too long to be polite" category. Especially since the longer he stared, the more his expression slackened. Deandra's cheeks heated.

She knew "empath" didn't mean "mind reader," but an irrational part of her felt exposed, as if he were reading her diary.

When he finally broke eye contact—turning toward his sister who waited patiently a few feet away—Deandra let out a whoosh of breath.

"Axia's newest arrival will have a large coffee with two pumps of vanilla and a dash of Serenity. She'll also take a ... hmm ..." Sebastian said, hand to his chin as he regarded Deandra again. "You came to Axia in search of something—something intangible. But what you *truly* seek might not be what you think you want. A Clear-Sighted Éclair will help you find the path to what you *need*."

How cryptic.

In a tone far less ominous, he asked, "Which flavor filling would you like ... pastry cream, mocha, vanilla, or strawberry?"

Deandra blinked twice, thrown off by the subject change. "Uhh ... mocha?"

"On it," Isabel said, then got to work preparing Deandra's order.

Wendy's coffee would have a surprise additive, Sebastian said, but her pastry for the day would be a Bear No Malice Bear Claw. He stared at Wendy defiantly, as if he expected her to protest. Her expression said she wanted to, but she merely nodded once. Wendy paid for their food, then made her way to an empty table in the middle of the café. Deandra trailed after her.

They sat in companionable silence for all of three seconds before Deandra cracked. "Who do you 'bear malice' toward?"

Wendy gusted a dramatic sigh. "Like I said, it's impossible to have secrets here for long. My fault for visiting an empath, but honestly, the pastries are so worth it," she said. "The malice is toward Madison Arbuckle. She's a witch I work with."

"Is that a figure of speech, or is she literally a witch?"

Wendy laughed. "Both. We got into a fight before I left on my lunch break to come meet you."

"Wait, what? Lunch break? I didn't realize you ditched work for me," Deandra said. "Sorry. I could have—"

Arching a brow, Wendy asked, "You could have what? Navigated this place on your own? You would have panicked and fled, screaming the whole way home."

"I was *going* to say that I could have gotten here later in the day. You said to aim for early afternoon," Deandra said, cheeks heating.

Wendy held up a hand, still smiling. "It's fine. I promise. My boss is cool with it. I asked for a shorter shift *days* ago so I could run around town with you. Everyone knew you were coming and that I was excited about it.

"When you first found the entrance and called me, I'd been trying to get out of the shop so I could be the first one to meet you instead of Allegra. I was on the way out the door when *Madison* threw some kind of spell at me, and I crashed into a talisman display by the door."

Wendy held up her arm, revealing that the underside of one forearm bore several small scratches. "I had to clean up the mess before I could leave. Plus, I took Mr. Peabody down with me when I fell. He's a dwarf and ornery as all get-out. We'd already had words earlier that day because he accused me of mis-shelving talismans and said he'd mistakenly picked up a nickel-plated one instead of a nickel-free one 'because of my blunder.'" She added finger quotes for extra emphasis. "He had an allergic reaction, and his hand was covered in welts. While he was screaming at me, I figured out *Madison* had been assigned to that section yesterday. She's the one who put the talismans in the wrong place, not me. When I told him that, he kept saying I shouldn't blame others for my mistakes.

"Madison timed the spell just right, so that when Mr. Peabody came back later in the day to wave his doctor's note and bandaged hand in my boss's face, I knocked him over. He was so furious. Heather ran over and fussed over Mr. Peabody, offering him discounts on his next order, like he knew she would."

"And Heather is your boss, right?" Deandra asked, trying to keep the names straight. Wendy hadn't been working at Heather's Elixirs long. Plus, when Wendy got going on a story, she had a tendency to leave out pertinent details.

"Oh, right. Sorry. Yes, my boss. She's a brilliant witch—an absolute master with poultices and potions. She's basically a walking encyclopedia of herbs. She's even a trained welder, so she hand-makes a lot of the metal talismans we sell. But she's shy, doesn't like confrontation, and believes Mr. Peabody every time he threatens to sue." Wendy rolled her eyes. "Threatening to sue is his go-to move for everything. Everyone is pretty sure he's all bark and no bite, but there's always a worry he'll make good on his threat one day. His daughter is apparently some big-deal lawyer in Luma."

"What's Luma?" Deandra asked.

"Biggest hub in California," Wendy said. "Anyway, while Mr. Peabody was tearing my boss a new one, *I* was yelling at Madison for purposefully tripping me *and* getting me in trouble because she can't do her job properly. She would never admit it, but I know she was mad I got time off. She's going to be the only employee on the floor for a few hours today. She just turned twenty, and good grief, Dee, that girl is so incredibly lazy. She uses magic for the most basic tasks because she can't be bothered to get off her butt. She doesn't even need the money. Her parents are trying to *instill a work ethic* in her."

It didn't sound like her parents' plan was working.

"Does she only act lazy when your boss isn't around?" Deandra asked.

"Oh, Heather is quite aware of Madison's plethora of shortcomings. She's Heather's niece. Heather would have fired her on day one if the little brat wasn't related to her."

Deandra winced.

"Then Madison yelled at *me* for accusing her of things she didn't do. Heather eventually told me to just go—but she was mad at everyone by that point. It was a mess." Wendy frowned. "All *that* is why I got to the Welcome Center a little later than I'd planned. I knew Allegra was going to try something to give you a 'crash course.' I wanted to get there first."

Isabel deposited their coffees on the table. "Pastries will be right up, ladies. One tincture needs a few more minutes to cure."

Deandra watched her walk away, wondering what in the world was going to be in that pastry. But another thought crowded that one out, and Deandra refocused on her cousin. Wendy took a long sip of her coffee.

"Back up a second," Deandra said. "You said Madison *threw* a spell at you? Isn't that enough of a reason to fire her if she's trying to hurt employees? Is that ... is that like throwing a *knife* at someone? Shouldn't that be illegal?"

Being a normal human in a town like this could get very dangerous, very quickly. Deandra grabbed her coffee cup and wrapped her hands around it, enjoying the warmth seeping into her palms.

"Oh, there are strict rules about using magic against others to cause harm," Wendy said dismissively. "There are eight levels of magic, and anything over a 4 can be harmful to humans. It's forbidden to use anything over a 4 here, especially since a lot of people in Axia are seniors with aging magic. Even glitchy Level 5 magic could cause real problems. I can't even process the idea of Level 8."

And yet Madison had *thrown* a spell at Wendy, a human, and there didn't seem to be any consequences for it. What would stop Madison from using a stronger spell next time?

Wendy eyed Deandra over her cup. "Somehow I freaked you out even more than Allegra did." She put her coffee down. "Okay. This is all explained in that booklet you got, but every hub—which is what we call a hidden magical city or town, like Axia—has a ruling council called the Collective. They're the sorcerers who keep the veil intact because only sorcerers have veil magic."

"And veil magic is what makes the town invisible, unless you have something like the travel talisman to get you in?" Deandra asked.

"Exactly," Wendy said. "An intact veil means the town stays hidden, and magic can be out in the open. In bigger cities, the

Collective can be made up of hundreds of sorcerers. They run the hubs, make laws about how magic can be used, stuff like that.

"Since Axia is so small, we only have three Collective sorcerers, and their primary job is to maintain the veil. We don't get a ton of outside visitors, and it's in a remote location, so maintenance is pretty minimal, from what I hear. Which makes sense, 'cause these sorcerers are basically retired, too. But they can sense magic use, so if someone was gearing up a Level 5 attack spell or something, they'd know."

Deandra had her doubts about how fast a trio of aging sorcerers could move if they needed to stop someone clear across town from throwing a spell.

"There are also werecat guards who—"

Deandra held up a hand. "Excuse me. *Were*cat? Like a were*wolf*? Do they shift on the full moon, too?"

Sebastian showed up right then to deliver their pastries. He chuckled at Deandra. "Oh, don't be silly. Everyone knows werewolves don't exist."

Little truth bomb detonated in his wake, he walked away.

Wendy huffed a laugh. "Sorry. Everyone is going to mess with you a bit—both because you're new and because you're my cousin. What he means is, werewolves went extinct a while ago. They were the only magic-touched people who were affected by the full moon. A werecat is just a person who can shift from human to cat. Mostly big cats—like lions and jaguars."

"So ... Allegra is a wereswan?"

Wendy choked on a bite of her Bear No Malice Bear Claw. "I guess technically, yeah. But no one calls them that."

Deandra heaved out a breath and sat back hard against her chair. By the time she learned even a fraction of this place's rules and quirks, she'd have to leave again. Her brain might explode before then. Wendy had only lived here for eight months or so, and she already seemed so at home. Deandra wondered if Wendy had felt as out of her depth when she'd first arrived as Deandra did now.

"As I was saying," Wendy said, after giving Deandra a few moments to stare blankly into space, "werecats work for the Collective. They're the magical police force. Axia also has a mayor and human police. All mundane and magical issues are covered between those two groups. It's safe here, I promise. Madison's little stunt was a Level 1 spell that was the equivalent of sticking out your foot to trip someone. It was childish, but the bright side is that Madison is going to have to get off her butt and work for once this afternoon. She'll be stuck with Heather, who was already in a foul mood when I left because of Mr. Peabody. Either Madison is going to have to step up, or Heather is going to finally lay into her for taking advantage of the position her parents bullied Heather into giving her. Win-win for me."

Deandra arched her brows. "That's very ... big of you."

Wendy let out a little gasp, looked down at the coffee cup in her hand, and said, "Sebastian, you sneak! You put Bright Side into this, didn't you?"

When she and Deandra turned toward the counter, Sebastian had a phone cradled between his ear and shoulder and a notepad and pen in his hands as he presumably took an order, but he offered Wendy a wink of acknowledgment.

Wendy scoffed good-naturedly as she turned to face forward again. "How dare he make me take the moral high ground instead of letting me stew in petty feelings for half the day."

Deandra laughed. "The horror."

Sighing, Deandra glanced down at her own cup. She knew she'd stalled long enough on trying her Serenity-infused coffee. She took a tentative sip. The coffee was somehow the most perfect cup she'd ever had—which was saying a lot for her. She knew it wasn't because of the magic tincture; it was just really good coffee. The Serenity didn't kick in until the fifth sip, and it wasn't a hit so much as a gentle easing of her neck and shoulders. She didn't feel impaired or drowsy. The Serenity additive had just taken the edge off her nerves.

The newly arrived mocha cream-filled Clear-Sighted Éclair was also excellent, but if its magic had affected her, she couldn't tell.

The caffeine and sugar gave Deandra the jolt of energy she needed to continue her tour of Axia. They wandered around for an hour, peering in shop windows and strolling through a park where a gaggle of water pixies put on a show in a massive three-tiered fountain. It was like a miniature version of Cirque du Soleil. The small crowd that had formed around the fountain cheered as the show ended, tossing items into the water. Deandra would have expected coins to be thrown in as payment. Instead, people threw things like safety pins, loose buttons, and acorns. Did people here walk around with acorns in their pockets, or had they brought them specifically for the pixies? Deandra decided she liked the mystery of not knowing, so she didn't ask Wendy for an explanation.

Needing something more solid in their stomachs than pastries, they decided to grab a proper lunch next. They plopped onto a bench at the park near the fountain while Wendy figured out where to go. Deandra let the warm sun bake into her skin as she watched the pixies collect their spoils from the water.

Deandra's grandparents were going to be at a Mermaids Club meeting for most of the day, so she probably wouldn't be able to see them until the evening—assuming she could stay awake that long. She'd been quite disappointed to learn that actual mermaids weren't part of the festivities. It was similar to the mundane Lions Club, of which lions played a role in name only.

Wendy leafed through Deandra's welcome packet, stating that she hoped to find a steep discount on a meal from one of the fancier dining spots in Axia. She muttered out loud to herself as she perused the options. She had narrowed it down to either Axian Delights, which would require them to change clothes, or Hogarth's Hoagies, which would not, when her phone rang.

Wendy groaned when she pulled her cell out of her pocket. "Sorry. It's Heather."

"Maybe she murdered Madison and needs your help hiding the body," Deandra offered brightly.

Wendy snorted. "I'm pretty sure assisting with the disposal of corpses was in my employment contract, so I'd be duty bound to help her."

Deandra picked up the welcome booklet from where Wendy had deposited it on the bench seat. Personally, Deandra preferred the idea of Hogarth's Hoagies, solely because it sounded like less work. She knew she'd packed at least one dress, but she couldn't remember now if she'd brought decent foot attire befitting the likes of Axian Delights.

After a minute, despite only being able to hear Wendy's side of the conversation, Deandra got the impression she'd end up having lunch on her own.

By the time she'd hung up, Wendy's cheeks were pink. "Ugh! Now I wish Heather *had* murdered her." She tossed her head back and stared up at the clear blue sky.

Deandra closed the booklet and propped a leg on the bench to face her cousin. "What happened?"

The glare Wendy fired at her was so fierce, Deandra was glad that ire wasn't actually aimed at her. "Madison apparently got so overwhelmed about needing to work the floor on her own that she quit! She burst into tears, said the customers were too demanding, and just ... left."

"Wow ..."

"Epitome of spoiled brat, I swear," Wendy said. "So now I have to go back and help Heather because she's running the place by herself. I'm really sorry. You could come with me! But you'd be stuck on your own in the back for a few hours. Heather is teaching a potion-making class to some witch kids who are coming to the store for a field trip. She totally forgot about it, and they'll be showing up within the hour. She's trying to get Devon to come in today too, even though it's his day off. It's going to be a madhouse. Witch kids plus potions usually equals a few minor explosions."

Part of Deandra was intrigued, but the majority of her thought it would be better for her sanity if she got herself a hoagie and laid low until her grandparents got home. "It's okay. Take care of what you need to. We'll meet up later."

Wendy eyed her dubiously. "You sure? You wigged out pretty hard earlier."

"Yeah, I'm sure," Deandra said with more conviction than she felt. "I've got my trusty map and a coupon for a discounted sandwich. I'm all set."

Wendy's phone pinged. She sighed at the screen, then turned it to face Deandra: an "SOS" message from Heather. A new one popped up a moment later—one that consisted entirely of crying emojis.

With another apology and a quick hug, Wendy set off at a brisk pace. Though Axia wasn't a huge place, Wendy said the emergency nature of the situation meant she'd have to take a telepad ride.

When Wendy was out of sight, Deandra looked up "telepad" in the glossary of her welcome booklet and learned that telepads were essentially teleportation tubes. Most cities had dozens, if not hundreds, of telepads, but Axia only had four, allowing you to jet from one end of town to the other in a blink. While that sounded very cool in theory, the booklet recommended that those new to hubs take a class to help acclimate them to what they'd experience during a ride. It made Deandra think of the high-G training classes that pilots and astronauts took to get used to the forces on their bodies during acceleration. Passing out and vomiting weren't uncommon—both of which were mentioned in the booklet as symptoms of teleportation travel. The booklet included the terrifying tidbit that "traveling too-far distances in a telepad, or taking a ride in a malfunctioning tube, can cause the loss or misplacement of limbs and/or organs."

"That's a solid nope," Deandra said to herself, flipping back to the page with Hogarth's Hoagies.

After consulting her map and getting oriented, Deandra rolled back her shoulders and stood. She was an adult, and she could walk to a sandwich shop all by herself—*without* an escort, thank you very much. She worked in the service industry in downtown Los Angeles, for Pete's sake! She could handle this.

With a definitive nod to herself, she set out into Axia's downtown.

Chapter 5

The map assured Deandra that the hoagie shop was only five blocks away. Other than spotting a pair of young, blue-skinned children with short curved black horns protruding from their temples, the walk during the first few blocks was uneventful.

At the corner of Wheeler Avenue and McClaren Way, Deandra stopped to check for oncoming traffic so she could continue on McClaren to the sandwich shop. Just before stepping off the curb, she spotted a large group of people milling about on a sidewalk down Wheeler Avenue. They formed a semicircle around the front of a building. Curiosity getting the better of her once again, Deandra made a left on Wheeler and quietly joined the back of the group.

The storefront before them had a large window on either side of a closed wooden door. Both windows had **Large & Wide** stenciled in golden, looping letters. Vertical blinds were drawn shut, hiding whatever lay inside.

"Phew! I made it," came a voice beside Deandra. "My uncle's never on time, though, so I shouldn't be surprised it hasn't started yet."

Brow cocked, Deandra eyed the young woman beside her.

"Oh, gosh!" the newcomer said, hand to her chest. "I'm so sorry. You look just like my friend Rae from behind. She said she's wearing a peach-colored top today." She thrust out a hand. "I'm Callie, the weirdo who strikes up conversations with total strangers."

Deandra laughed, channeling her friendly barista persona. "I'm Deandra. You can call me Dee."

"Well, nice to meet you, Dee. Are you new to town?"

Deandra wondered if it could be *that* obvious. Axia presumably had visitors often; Callie couldn't possibly know every person who called the town home, even if it was small.

Grinning, Callie said, "My ability is a mix of aura-reading, empathy, and clairvoyance, but saying I can read auras is close enough. Yours is tinged with a shade of blue that usually implies a low-grade fear, which is pretty common for people who aren't used to hubs."

Clearly, in a hub, announcing your abilities was as natural as saying hello. Deandra was sure it was a refreshing way to live, since in the "normal" world one had to keep such things to themselves for fear of being ridiculed or violating a secrecy law. Still, it was going to take some getting used to for Deandra.

Heaving out a breath, she said, "Just got here today."

Callie nodded. "Your aura says you're handling it better than you think, if that helps. I've seen grown men bolt out of here after only a few hours."

It *did* help. A little.

"So your uncle owns this store or something?" Deandra asked, gesturing to Large & Wide.

"Oh! Yes, the oversharing-with-strangers thing. My uncle is a co-owner of this place. Large & Wide is a chain of clothing stores—like Big & Tall, but for the magic-touched. Orcs, trolls, draken ... they got tired of needing to get their clothes custom-made or tailored, since finding mundane shops geared toward people over six feet is difficult. My uncle and his business partner struck a deal with the tourism board here to get a store location. They're hoping it'll drive more folks to Axia to shop since there aren't many Large & Wides in smaller hubs. The ones in the big hubs, according to my uncle, are overpriced." Callie shrugged. "He's really excited about it."

Deandra subtly gave Callie a once-over. She looked human, was an inch or two shorter than Deandra's five-foot-eight, and had reddish-brown hair, bright green eyes, and a "girl next door" friendliness that had made Deandra warm to her immediately. Was her uncle the opposite of that? Some giant, eight-foot-tall, green-skinned man with tusks?

Callie sensed the questions swirling in Deandra's head, either from her expression or aura, because she flashed another bright, friendly smile. "My uncle is a mundane. Magic skipped his generation. A cousin is dating a draken guy though, and during a family dinner a couple of years ago, the topic of shopping for clothes when you're, well, large and wide, came up and my uncle saw the business idea for what it was. Now he's the proud co-owner of three of these stores. Today is the soft opening."

Deandra made a note to look up "draken" later in the welcome booklet's glossary.

"Why are you out here instead of in there?" Deandra asked.

Callie winced slightly but recovered just as fast. She shrugged. "I love my uncle, don't get me wrong, but he's a high-strung mess whenever a new store is opening. His aura is so wild during these things, it gives me a headache. He's like a disco ball. So I'm here to support him—just from a distance."

Deandra wondered if Wendy and Callie knew each other. Wendy would like her, too. She supposed Callie could just be visiting, though, and then would jet—or telepad—off to another hub once the soft opening was over. Before Deandra could ask where Callie hailed from, the piercing cry of a siren sounded. Like a school of fish, the crowd turned just as a small fire truck, its lights flashing, zipped down McClaren Way.

A murder of crows, cawing loudly, flew in the opposite direction of the screaming fire truck. A pair of orange cats bolted down McClaren next, and a jet-black dog—or maybe a coyote?—with a fluffy tail followed close behind. It probably wasn't a good sign when animals started fleeing.

A few moments later, another fire truck roared by in the opposite direction from the animals.

A great plume of black smoke shot into the air a block or two away. The smell of burning wood wafted toward Deandra on a breeze. It was curious that she hadn't smelled it before, with the fire so close. Someone clearly had called the fire in before the smoke had even crested the roofs of nearby buildings. The color of the smoke suggested it was burning hot and fast. Had something exploded?

Deandra hoped no one had been hurt.

"I wonder if that was Landry's place. That building's as old as Axia itself. The wiring's no doubt faulty," someone nearby said.

"Bet it was that potion shop over on Talbot," someone else mused. "Unnatural smells seep out of that place at all hours."

"Musta been one of those lightning pixie gangs," an old man muttered. "Always causing trouble."

"Oh, for Goddess's sake, Harold! For the last time, there are no lightning pixies in Axia! There aren't even any in this realm."

Harold grumbled. "That's what they *want* you to believe ..."

"Ladies and gentlemen," a deep voice called from the front of Large & Wide, causing the school of fish to shift again.

Deandra expected to see a man bearing a familial resemblance to Callie standing in front of the store, but instead, it was a pair of officers. While they both were in uniform, one was in black, and the other was in blue. Deandra could tell with one glance that, while they were members of law enforcement, they were from different branches. She recalled what Wendy had told her about Axia having both a human—or mundane—police force and a magical one. Was it possible that one of these officers was a *werecat*? Her mind spiraled as she tried to guess if it was the dark-haired man or the blond woman who could shift into a lion, puma, or ocelot.

"Who was it?" someone called out, snapping Deandra out of her thoughts.

The tension in the crowd had grown exponentially. Clearly she'd missed something.

The male officer had his hands up in placation. "We can't release the individual's name until next of kin is identified. The public will know as soon as we're able to share the information."

Next of kin? Had someone died? She peered over her shoulder toward the still-thick cloud of black smoke. The scent of burning wood had morphed into an even stronger stench of burnt plastic.

"Please, again, we need everyone to clear out," the female officer said. "The fire is magical in nature, so for now, it's staying contained in the building where it started. But, while we don't believe the fire will jump to other buildings, since we don't know the cause of the fire, we don't know if there's anything hazardous in the smoke. Please get somewhere safe. The soft opening will be postponed until further notice. Check the town hall's website for the new date."

The crowd dispersed, albeit reluctantly.

Deandra offered Callie a small smile and a "nice to meet you," then started back down the sidewalk. She pulled the map out of her pocket as she walked, figuring Hogarth's Hoagies was too close to the possibly hazardous smoke, so she'd need a new place to eat. Her nerves were starting to fritz out again, though, and she considered camping out in the back room at Wendy's work, or on her grandparents' porch, or even in the back seat of her car that was still parked in the Welcome Center's lot. She wondered if her aura was a disco ball now, like Callie's uncle's.

"Hey, Dee?"

Deandra came up short; Callie sidled up next to her.

Callie said, “If you’re trying not to look like you’re the new kid in town, walking around with your nose in a paper map isn’t the way to do it.”

Deandra chuckled awkwardly. “Got any recommendations on where to get lunch?”

“There’s a great dumpling place a few blocks that way,” Callie said, angling her thumb back down McClaren, in the opposite direction of the sandwich shop. “Happy to join you if you don’t mind a bit of a walk to get there.” She laughed. “The sunshine yellow that just flooded your aura says you’re relieved by the suggestion.”

“That’s a little unsettling, but also accurate.”

“That pretty much sums me up, yeah,” Callie said. “Shall we?”

The Dumpling Hut was a bustling restaurant that catered mostly to takeout orders, but there were a handful of tables for dine-in customers. Deandra and Callie sat at a tiny table in the corner of the small dining area and ordered four kinds of dumplings, each one more delicious than the last. Deandra told Callie about living in Los Angeles, which, from the glint in Callie’s eye, sounded as magical to her as Axia did to Deandra. Callie told her about growing up in a small hub town and of the harrowing experiences she and her friends had when they’d traveled to one of the big hub cities for the first time ten years ago, when Callie had turned eighteen.

Stuffed with dumplings, Deandra sat back, throwing her chopsticks on her plate as a sign of defeat. “Are telepad rides as scary as my welcome booklet suggests?”

Callie popped the last dumpling in her mouth and then threw in the proverbial towel as well. “As long as you’re not trying to get from here to, I don’t know, New York in one jump, it’s not scary at all. Disorienting for a few seconds, and it feels a little strange, like your whole body is being stretched like a piece of taffy. But you can't beat traveling hundreds of miles in a blink."

"Which hub is your favorite?"

Callie said, "Hmm. Luma, probably. I haven't been to them all yet—there are forty-three in the US. But Luma is a lot of fun. That's where I went for my last birthday."

Callie took out her phone and swiped across the screen as she talked. "I was with a group of friends who know all the non-touristy spots. There's a night club whose location changes every few weeks, and you can only get in if you have the right password—assuming you can find the club to begin with. I tried elfin wine for the first time, which, let me tell you, was a mistake. Drink enough of that stuff and it's like absinthe. The next morning, we woke up in my friend Gordo's apartment. Someone was draped over the side of the couch, I woke up *behind* the couch, and someone else was found fully clothed in the shower stall." She shook her head. "It's a miracle we all survived. I'll never touch the stuff again."

Deandra reeled from the realization that "elfin wine" might suggest elves existed. She wasn't sure if those were *Lord of the Rings* elves, the cookie-making kind, or both, but she decided she didn't want the answer either way. There was only so much information a girl could ingest in a day.

Callie turned her phone to show Deandra a picture of five laughing people. Callie had her arms draped across the shoulders of two ladies. The three of them and two guys were splattered with what appeared to be neon-colored paint.

"The weirdest thing wasn't that we don't remember getting covered in paint that night, *or* who took the photo, but that we somehow had gotten all the paint *off* again before we got back to Gordo's." She shook her head again. "If you learn nothing else from today, let it be this: do not drink elfin wine."

Deandra grinned. "Noted."

One of the ladies in the picture had long, dark hair like Deandra's, and her skin was a russet brown.

Deandra pointed at her. "Is that Rae?"

Callie angled her head to study the photo. "Yep, that's her. There's a definite resemblance, right?"

Deandra didn't see it. But she also wasn't well-versed in what she looked like from behind. She wondered how Callie could have mistaken her for Rae, though, when Callie could supposedly read auras. "Did you ever hear from her?"

Callie scratched the side of her nose. "Uh, yeah. I, uh, got a text from her just after I met you. She said she wasn't able to make it. Her dad got sick, so she had to go pick up some medicine for him." Her gaze roved Deandra's face, her expression pinched. Deandra got the impression she was struggling with how to best phrase what she wanted to say next. She spoke slowly at first, in a measured tone, but eventually warmed to the topic. "Rae grew up here, like me. We were best friends all through high school, but after we graduated she moved to a big hub for a job opportunity she couldn't pass up. We don't see each other as much anymore. One of the hard parts about growing up, right? Friends and family move on and scatter in the wind."

Deandra could relate to that all too well. She'd been slightly devastated when Wendy had moved to Axia, if only because it'd felt like she'd been cut off from one of her closest friends. "I'm sorry Rae couldn't make it."

Callie waved it away, smiling brightly. "There's always next time, right? Besides, fate clearly wanted me to meet you today. You're definitely better company than my anxious uncle. He's probably even twitchier now that the soft opening has been pushed back."

Deandra was in the middle of figuring out how to make Wendy and Callie become best friends when someone approached their table. She expected to find their waiter there. Instead, it was the blond officer who had been standing in front of Large & Wide earlier. She was such a striking woman—Hollywood starlet beautiful, but with the intimidating air of a Secret Service member—that Deandra recognized her immediately.

Deandra swallowed nervously, some primal part of her wanting to run away screaming. Humans no longer had as many instincts as their prehistoric ancestors did, but they were still there, lying dormant. Deandra's were wide awake now, clearing away the dregs of her happy food coma. This was the instinct to flee in sheer terror when faced with a predator that she had no defenses against—a prey animal running from a saber-toothed tiger.

Oh gosh. What if that's *what this officer can turn into?*

Deandra sat up, back ramrod straight and hands folded primly on the tabletop. That move had been fueled by instincts, too—an instinctual fear of authority figures.

Now that the officer was right in front of her, Deandra noted the symbol stitched in white on the breast pocket of her uniform. Encased in a circle were the silhouettes of several hands all reaching upward toward a ball of glowing light. The foreign symbol confirmed that this was a werecat, even though Deandra's caterwauling instincts had already told her as much.

Callie reached across the table and gently wrapped a hand around Deandra's forearm. "Relax, Dee. Your aura is giving me a headache. I understand that experiencing magic for a mundane can be stressful, especially on your first day, but there's no need to be scared of Officer Sutter. I went to school with her little brother. She's good people."

Deandra blew out a slow, shaky breath. Callie retracted her hand.

The werecat smiled down at them—a genuine, kindhearted smile that warred with how jarring Deandra's initial reaction had been. "I'm sorry I frightened you," Officer Sutter said, her voice smooth and pleasant. She turned to Callie. "Miss Tobin, would you—"

Callie crossed her arms and sat back hard against her seat. "*Miss Tobin*? What's with the formality, *Shannon*?"

The werecat offered Deandra a pained, tight smile. A sinking feeling in Deandra's gut warned her that some unpleasant news was coming even before Callie presumably registered the fluctuating colors of the officer's aura. Maybe werecats were harder for Callie to read.

"It's your uncle, Callie," Officer Sutter said gently.

Callie's playful haughtiness slipped off like a coat dropped to the floor. "What about him?"

"We should talk outside."

"*Shannon*," Callie said, standing up so suddenly that her chair skidded into the wall behind her. "Tell me right now."

Officer Sutter pursed her lips, and though she lowered her voice and turned away from Deandra as much as possible, Deandra still heard every word. "He was in that building that caught fire earlier. Callie, I'm so sorry, but your uncle is dead."

Chapter 6

Deandra only heard snatches of what was said between Officer Sutter and Callie after that. Her mind did strange things when faced with traumatic news. Sometimes all she could hear was buzzing—like a swarm of angry bees or too-loud television static. Sometimes her mind shut down entirely and she zoned out, not processing anything for minutes at a time.

Her mother was the type to shunt all emotions when confronted with terrible information, like the body cutting off blood to the extremities in exceedingly cold temperatures. Her mother became practical to a fault, handling the nitty-gritty of what needed to be dealt with. When the logistics were taken care of—when there was proof the core of the body had survived the worst of the trauma, and hot blood had sent thawing heat back into limbs—*that* was when her mother broke down. Deandra and her father, however, were both known to burst into sobs first and ask questions later.

Callie, at first, had gone into a sort of zombie-like state, as if she'd instantly rejected what the officer had told her and had stopped listening. But it was soon clear Callie was like Deandra's mother. Emotional channels were being dammed up to be dealt with at a later date. When Callie finally spoke, her tone was calm and reserved, almost robotic.

"I will need to inform my parents and Uncle Brian's family," Callie said.

"They've already been contacted," Sutter said. "They're taking telepads here as soon as possible and will meet you at the police station."

Deandra wanted to ask why they'd meet at a police station. But more than that, she wanted to ask why Callie's uncle had been a block away in another building when he'd been scheduled to attend the soft opening of his own store. Deandra still had no idea what kind of building had burned down—a store, a restaurant, a residence? It wasn't her place to ask. Heck, she shouldn't be here listening to this very private conversation at all, but Deandra bolting from the Dumpling Hut probably wouldn't make Callie feel any better.

"Okay," Callie said with a nod. Turning to Deandra, she said, "I know this is a strange request, Dee, but would you walk with me over there?"

Deandra opened her mouth and closed it half a dozen times, like a beached fish.

"I'm more than capable of escorting you to the station, Callie," Sutter said. "My squad car is parked out front."

Callie swallowed hard and took a moment to speak, the first sign that she was an absolute wreck underneath the hardened exterior she was doing her best to keep in place. "Dee has a calming aura. She—"

"So you're *using* her?" Sutter asked.

Deandra cocked her head at that.

Callie clenched her jaw. "This is exactly why I want to be in the company of *someone else*, Shannon. Dee's got sympathy pouring off her right now, and frankly, you don't. You're draining when you're like this."

"When I'm like what?" Sutter asked, arms crossed. "Doing my job?"

"Yes." Callie let out a sharp quick breath, and in a rush, added, "It's the whole werecat thing, okay? You exude very intense energy all the time, and my nerves will be absolutely shredded if I'm trapped in a car with it."

Heat colored Sutter's pale cheeks. Deandra considered crawling under the table.

"I just need a friend right now." Half a second later, Callie groaned. "Not that you're not. Ugh ... sorry. I just—"

Sutter held up a hand. "It's fine, Callie. It's hard when something like this affects a family friend. Being objective is ... rough. But I'm okay with whatever will make you feel better." With a small smile, she added, "If that means rejecting years of friendship for the companionship of a person you clearly just met, that's okay."

Callie rolled her eyes, but she was smiling too. "Thanks, Shannon."

Sutter gave Callie's arm a quick squeeze. "You bet. I'll see you over there." Addressing Deandra, she said, "It was nice to meet you, Dee. Sorry it wasn't under better circumstances. Don't let this one get you into any trouble, all right?"

If the playful comment spoken in a very serious tone hadn't been enough to make Deandra even more uncomfortable, the murderous look in Callie's eye as she watched Officer Sutter stride for the exit surely did. These two clearly had a fraught history.

"Well," Callie said, offering Deandra the most heartbreakingly sad attempt at a smile. "I guess we should go?"

They quickly collected their things, paid the bill, and headed for the door. As they stepped out onto the sidewalk, Callie looped her arm through Deandra's, just as Wendy had done earlier that day.

Deandra asked, "Do you need a sympathetic ear, to talk about something unrelated, or silence?"

"Something unrelated."

So they talked about nothing in particular while Callie led them in the direction of the police station. It was back the same way they'd walked earlier in the day, up McClaren Way, which Deandra was realizing must be one of the major thoroughfares in town. A burnt-plastic smell, with a touch of something chemical, like ammonia, grew stronger the closer they got. Instead of turning left on Wheeler Avenue toward Large & Wide, Callie guided them to the right. This stretch of Wheeler was lined with well-tended homes on both sides. The occasional small café or boutique was nestled among the houses, which Deandra was sure made the business owners of Axia feel like they were truly part of the community.

The pair eventually arrived at a small shopping center that housed a few shops and the police station, the façade matching the cottage-like feel of most of the town, rather than a hulking, industrial, glass-and-cement station like those she'd seen in larger cities.

They stopped in the parking lot, in clear view of the station's main entrance. Callie still held tight to Deandra's arm.

"Did you want me to go in with you?" Deandra asked.

Callie said, "The flare of red in your aura says you're hoping I'll say no."

Deandra's face warmed.

"No, I'll be okay. My family's probably been here for several minutes now," Callie said, finally letting Deandra go. "But let's swap numbers, okay? I'd like to meet Wendy and grab dinner or something before you leave."

As much as Deandra would like to hang out with Callie again, she figured the woman would be occupied with the aftermath of losing a loved one. The grief would hit her like a freight train sooner rather than later, and grabbing dinner with a near stranger would shoot to the bottom of her priority list, but Deandra took out her phone to program Callie's number into it all the same.

After a quick hug, telling Callie to call her if she needed anything, Deandra watched as her new friend stiffly walked to the police station and then disappeared inside.

Heaving out a breath, Deandra turned back the way she'd come. She was going to sleep like a log tonight after all this walking. At least she'd burned off some of the dumplings.

She texted Wendy, asking for an update on how work was treating her, but after ten minutes, she still hadn't gotten a reply. Deandra once again came to a stop at the corner of Wheeler and McClaren. The path straight ahead would lead to Large & Wide. To the left was downtown Axia and the general direction of her car, and to the right was where the fire had raged. She chewed on the inside of her cheek, taking in the still lingering scents of ammonia and burnt plastic. Was the peculiar smell because the fire had been "magical in nature"?

Deandra couldn't see the burned building in question from here, but it was close. There were no officers posted on street corners waving away looky-loos. No crime scene tape blocked off the street. No orange cones warned curious residents to stay away from the area because of the toxic air.

She pulled her phone out of her back pocket. Still nothing from Wendy. Which meant Deandra had some time to kill. Her grandparents wouldn't be home for hours yet.

Before she'd realized she'd made the decision, Deandra turned right onto McClaren. Though Deandra had very little information about the fire, Officer Sutter had said "the *building*" Brian had been in had burned down. Not "a *house*." Deandra's curiosity about the type of building Brian had been in when he was supposed to be at his own store had been eating away at her. She'd just take a peek, then head for Wendy's shop. Maybe she could take a nap in the break room.

The scent of burning plastic made her eyes water the closer she got. Large cottage-like homes lined the street beside her, each one boasting a bright green lawn. A swing hung from the thick branches of an oak in front of one house, and on the grass of another lay a discarded beach blanket covered in abandoned dolls. No one was outside enjoying the summer sunshine here—the pungent, cloying scent proving to be a deterrent for most.

A one-story brick building loomed ahead on the corner, the words "ART GALLERY" stamped along a side wall in thick gold lettering that was visible even from halfway down the street.

She'd just reached the last house before the art gallery when a flicker of blue drew her attention to the neat row of hedges separating the lawn from the sidewalk. An odd tingle skittered over her limbs, as if they'd all just woken from a deep sleep. She stopped in her tracks, gazing down at the low hedge. The tidily kept bushes didn't sport any color other than green, now that she was staring at it head-on. And yet, instead of shrugging and assuming her eyes were playing tricks on her as she normally would, she took a few steps closer. One of the bushes gave a little rustle.

While her mind said, *Oh, it must have been a bird*, her body seemed to move of its own accord. Hands on her knees, she bent closer to the bush, her nose an inch away.

A tiny face popped out from between two leaves. Deandra shrieked and stumbled back. Suddenly she was nose-to-very-tiny-nose with a winged human-like creature. The pixie was bedecked in blue from head to foot. Even her hair was blue. She looked much like the pixies Deandra had seen in the fountain earlier, performing their Cirque du Soleil act.

"How would you like it if I stuck *my* face into *your* living room!" the pixie shouted.

"Oh gosh! I'm sorry. I didn't realize someone, uh, lived in there," Deandra said.

"Of course you didn't," the pixie said, blissfully moving back a few inches so Deandra no longer felt like she was going cross-eyed from the proximity. Her wings moved at the speed of a hummingbird's. "Flightless giants are oblivious!"

Deandra had been about to say, "*Well,* that *was uncalled for,*" when a hissing sounded somewhere to her right. She had no idea why her gut told her the hiss sounded more reptilian than feline. Glancing down, she found a small, black gecko covered in the barest hint of yellow spots on its back and head. It stood beside her shoe, its head cocked so it could stare up at her. Deandra resisted the urge to kick it into the hedges. She wasn't particularly fearful of lizards or amphibians or whatever the thing was, but there was a calculating intelligence in that round, dark eye and she didn't trust it.

The gecko hissed again and, with frightening speed, latched onto her tennis shoe and chomped down on Deandra's big toe. She *did* react then, frantically kicking her foot to dislodge the psychotic pest.

The pixie stuck her fingers in her mouth and let loose a series of piercing whistles. "Scatter, Clarions! Predator!"

In the same moment that Deandra managed to shake the gecko loose and fling it into the bushes, a burst of blue exploded from the leaves. At least two dozen pixies shot into the air and took off in different directions, shouting obscenities as colorful as their hair. When the gecko started hissing up a storm from somewhere within the depth of the bushes, Deandra took a cue from the pixies and hustled away.

Even the wildlife here is enough to stress a girl out...

Her heart was still racing when she reached the corner of McClaren and Purl Way. A quick glance over her shoulder didn't reveal the gecko charging down the sidewalk, so she hoped that meant the tiny beast had decided to pursue a meal better befitting its size. And, as grouchy as that pixie had been, Deandra hoped the Clarion family could go home later without finding a gecko lying in wait to rip off their wings.

The art gallery was to her back now and was currently closed, if the dark interior was any indication. Directly across the street was a drugstore. On her side of the street, down the length of the rest of the block, was a three-story apartment complex with a matching one across the road.

Between the drugstore and the apartment building stood the blackened husk of what might have once been a business, but the fire had so thoroughly destroyed it that nothing remained but a few scorched chunks of cement and the charred remains of the foundation. Somehow neither the apartment complex nor the drugstore that had shared walls with the burned building bore any scorch marks. Not even soot or ash dotted their sidewalks. Deandra had to assume there couldn't have been much to shield anyone from the unnatural stench of the fire, though.

Deandra wasn't the only one who had come to gawk. Several people stood outside the drugstore, chatting among themselves and periodically eyeing or pointing at the destruction next door. A trio of young men stood on the curb on Deandra's side of the street, staring at the blackened rubble. The few cars that drove by did so at a crawl.

"Shame, isn't it?" a woman asked.

Deandra started, finding a pair of middle-aged women standing beside her. She hadn't even heard them approach. "Yeah. At least it stayed contained, though. Can you imagine how much worse it could have been if it had jumped buildings?"

The two women muttered their agreement. The one closest to Deandra was at least six feet tall and very pale, her hair so blond it was nearly white. The second woman was dark-skinned—darker than Deandra herself—and was short with a head of poofy, tight black curls streaked through with gray.

After a moment, Deandra asked, "Do you know what the building was before it caught fire? A shop, a restaurant? Can't even tell what it used to be ..."

The taller woman eyed Deandra curiously. "Not from around here?"

"Just here for the weekend visiting my cousin. The whole town is a mystery to me."

"Ah," she said, and angled her focus back across the street. "That might be the strangest part of this whole thing. That spot's been empty for months. Would you say it's been six months now, Bea?"

The dark-skinned woman, Bea, hinged forward to peer around her friend and offered Deandra a polite nod. "At least that."

"It's like the spot is cursed," the first woman said. "Six different restaurants over the course of ten years tried to make it there, and they all folded. Most restaurants don't make it, but it seems like being in that spot cuts one's already bad odds in half."

"That last place ... the pizza joint?" Bea added. "That one was great. Very unique atmosphere. I really thought that one might make it. But after it tanked like all the others, no one's been willing to lease the spot."

"Even if they clean it up and get a new build in there, no one's going to want it. Not after that poor man was found dead in there," the first woman said. "Cursed *and* haunted."

"Edna!" Bea admonished her friend, but she was holding back a laugh as she swatted her arm.

"It's true!" Edna said. "It's a wonder they were able to identify him with a fire that burned that hot. Hot enough to burn bones and teeth, that's what Charlie said."

Bea scoffed. "Oh, Charlie doesn't know anything of the sort."

Edna rounded on her friend, hands on hips, and peered down at her. "Charlie's daughter is dating a boy who lives in 3F; 3F shares a wall with that burned-out building. Her daughter's boyfriend was escorted out of there by some firefighters, and he heard *them* say that—that the fire was so hot it burned bones to nothing."

"No kidding!" Bea said, mouth forming a little O of surprise.

"How *did* they identify him, then?"

It wasn't until the question was out of her mouth that Deandra realized she'd spoken the question out loud.

Edna and Bea glanced at one another, having what appeared to be a silent conversation. Their close friendship was immediately evident in the way they shared mannerisms and the ability to speak using nothing but pointed facial expressions. The pair reminded Deandra of herself and Wendy.

"Are you a mundane, dear?" Edna finally asked.

Deandra nodded.

"Thought so," Edna said. "There's a witch on the force whose specialty is death magic. Oh my, your eyes got so big! It doesn't mean she can cause death with her magic. It just means her magic gives her details *about* death. From what I hear, death witches have to be on the scene right away to get any real concrete details, otherwise they have to use boots-on-the-ground police work just like everyone else. The death witch was able to get over here fast enough to get an ID off the location where a bit of the ... uhh ... remains were. But not fast enough to know what—or *who*—started the fire."

"You hear all that from Charlie's daughter's boyfriend in 3F, too?" Bea asked.

"*That* I heard from Tony," Edna said smugly.

Bea whistled, then leaned toward Deandra conspiratorially. "Tony is Edna's neighbor who works as a receptionist at the police station. Tony cannot keep a secret to save his life. He's also sweet on Edna, so all she's gotta do is bat those baby blues and he starts flapping his gums."

Edna fluttered her lashes at Deandra to prove Bea's point. They *were* a striking blue.

Deandra laughed. Wendy herself had said that secrets didn't stay secrets for long in Axia. It had only been a couple of hours since the fire, and Deandra already knew more about the incident than possibly even Callie did.

The thought of Callie sobered Deandra up. She couldn't forget that, as intriguing as this bit of gossip was, the man who had perished in the fire across the street had been someone's uncle. Callie had said Brian had a family—were there young, grieving children, a heartbroken wife, devastated parents? She swallowed hard.

"Thanks for the chat, ladies. It was nice meeting you two,"

Deandra said. "I should probably go track down my family. Stuff like this makes you realize how fleeting time is, huh?"

Edna groaned. "Oh, don't make us think about how sad this actually is, young lady! Let us be callous monsters for a few more minutes."

Deandra laughed again, unable to help it. "I hope you monsters have a good rest of your day."

Bea and Edna grinned at her.

As Deandra walked down McClaren, away from the growing crowd, Edna's words replayed in her head. "*The death witch was able to get over here fast enough to get an ID off the location where a bit of the ... uhh ... remains were. But not fast enough to know what—or* who *—started the fire.*"

Who had started the fire?

Was it possible someone had set the fire intentionally? Had Brian been in the wrong place at the wrong time, or had he been the victim of foul play? Deandra supposed it wasn't wise to take Bea and Edna too seriously. They were a hoot, but she guessed they were also gluttons for drama. Hopefully nothing sinister had gone on beyond a freak accident—if only for Callie's family's sake.

Axia might have been a quiet, retirement-friendly town, but this weekend was already turning out to be more eventful than Deandra had bargained for.

Chapter 7

Deandra had just passed the art gallery and was crossing the mouth of the alley that ran behind it when she heard a muted crash. She came up short, peering down the cement path that ran between the back of the gallery and the cinder-block wall that edged the property of the cottage next door—the same cottage with hedges inhabited by the Clarion family of pixies.

Clang!

It sounded like something large slamming into a metallic surface, which hopefully ruled out the demented, shoe-biting gecko. She glanced up and down the sidewalk, but she was alone here.

The crash came again, followed by what sounded like a cry of distress. A dog, maybe?

Had that been ... a bark?

Another thud sounded, followed by a whimper.

Deandra crept into the alley, stepping lightly as she waited for another sound. She didn't hear anything else until she was fully in the back parking lot of the gallery.

Is this wise? she asked herself. *The last time you investigated something in this area, you got yelled at by a pixie.*

She decided to ignore herself.

The lot was small, allowing for maybe fifteen cars. A green dumpster sat in a back corner made by the connecting walls of the cottage on one side and the apartment building across from the burned building on the other.

Thud.

The sound had definitely come from *inside* the dumpster—and it was also definitely an animal's whimper.

Without thinking, she ran toward it. The two black plastic flaps were closed, and she shoved a hand under one, intending to flip it open. It only occurred to her then that she was in Axia, and a dog here might be something decidedly more dangerous. It could be a creature *pretending* to be a trapped dog. Or a drunken centaur. Or any number of other horrors her unimaginative brain couldn't dream up.

She considered backing away, but the fear-filled whimper from inside the dumpster made the decision for her. With a great heave, she thrust one of the flaps up. The stench from inside wasn't any more pleasant than the ammonia and burnt plastic smell lingering in the air. She wrinkled her nose. On tiptoes, she peered inside, searching for any movement among the two-thirds-full dumpster piled with tied-up white trash bags. A swarm of angry pixies *hadn't* come flying out, so this experience was already better than the last.

"Hello?" she asked, hoping none of the animals in Axia could talk, because that would really be the final straw.

Woof!

The bark was so loud—echoing off the metal walls of the dumpster—that Deandra yelped and stumbled back. The flap slammed back into place with a crash. The whimper came again.

"Oh, good grief," she muttered, hand to her chest.

Placing her purse and phone on a large stone that sat by the cinder-block wall, she glanced around the parking lot, searching for anything she could use to better see into the dumpster. Dumpster diving wasn't on her agenda, but with a better vantage point, she might be able to help get the pup uncovered if he was buried under a heavy piece of garbage. Thinking of what might be housed behind the dark windows of the art gallery, she imagined a defenseless puppy stuck under a discarded marble statue. Why would someone toss a statue in the trash? She had no idea. She was starting to go loopy. Maybe it was the fumes. Or maybe the gecko that had bitten her shoe had been venomous and the poison was eating away at her brain.

No matter.

She had a puppy to rescue.

She *had* put it into the universe that she'd wanted a dog, hadn't she? She thought of Sebastian's empathic reading, how he'd told her that she was searching for something, and that the Clear-Sighted Éclair would help her see the path to what she sought. Was that path leading her to a new puppy? To companionship?

Spotting a few plastic crates by the back door of the gallery, she hustled over to grab two, then ran back to the dumpster. She hoped no one in the apartment building was watching her erratic behavior right now. Anyone who lived on the second or third floors of the building near the gallery would have a perfect view of the parking lot.

She flipped the lid of the dumpster back open, using enough force that it swung wide and came to a rest against the wall behind it. Stacking the crates, she carefully tested their stability, blowing out a relieved breath when the pair held firm under her weight. "Dog?" she asked, her stomach resting against the rusted edge of the dumpster. Grimacing, she grabbed the nearest bag and heaved it to the side.

Woof!

She flinched hard, but didn't tumble off her crates, which she considered a win. "Can you follow my voice, pup?"

She flung aside another bag. It was unexpectedly light. The end of what looked like a crepe-paper streamer poked out of the cinched-closed bag, like it was sticking its tongue out at her.

The bags on the far left—under the second plastic flap of the dumpster—jumped. Sighing, she climbed off the crates, flung the second flap up to rest against the wall like the first, and re-stacked her crates.

She tossed a couple more bags out of the way, one of which snagged on something, the bottom tearing open. Crushed Styrofoam containers spilled out noodles, wilted vegetables, and thick, congealed sauces.

The bags jumped once more. Deandra caught sight of a mass of thick black or gray fur shifting under the garbage—a mass that seemed much bigger than a puppy. One more thrown-aside bag revealed the remains of a broken piece of furniture. An end table, maybe. The dog seemed to be stuck beneath it.

Steeling herself, she took a deep breath and leaned forward as far as she dared. Her fingers grazed the nearest wooden leg of the end table. The crates under her feet wobbled dangerously. She really hoped she didn't pitch headfirst into this thing. "Can you hear me, pup? Gotta help me out here."

The trash gave a great heave, the mound surging toward her like a tide. She got a solid grasp on the table leg and tossed it away. The crates rocked wildly, and she grabbed hold of the lip of the dumpster to steady herself. Another heave, and a giant furry head broke free from the garbage pile. A head that was so big, Deandra's panicked brain screamed *wolf!* She finally lost her balance then. Thankfully, she tumbled backward and not into the dumpster. She hit the pavement hard enough that her breath expelled from her lungs in a whoosh. She'd covered her head, avoiding hitting her skull on the ground, but she still managed to give her brain a good rattle. Oil spots swam in her vision, and her tailbone ached.

Groaning, she stared up at the blue sky for a moment, then pushed herself into a sitting position, assessing the damage. Other than her bruised tailbone, a mild headache, and a banged-up elbow, she was relatively unscathed. There was a dark, oily stain on the thigh of her jeans, but she chose not to think about that.

She eyed the dumpster, not hearing any sign from within that the dog had fully gotten free. The crates had fallen over but still looked intact. Sighing, she got to her feet.

Time for round two.

By the time she'd gotten to her feet, though, her charge was peering at her over the lip of the dumpster. Except it wasn't a furry wolf face staring at her. It was an orange *dragon*. A baby one, too, if she had to guess.

Deandra completely froze, her eyes stuck open. This couldn't be happening. Was this actually happening? Maybe she had hit her head after all.

The creature woofed, but somehow it turned into a happy chirping sound instead, as if the noise had decided halfway during its journey to her ears that it wanted to be something else.

She blinked rapidly.

Burnt-orange ridges ran down the middle of its skull, and the start of tiny pink horns poked from either side of its head, as well as cone-shaped ears. Its irises were a bright pink that matched its horns. She couldn't say why she instantly knew this was a dragon, but when the creature flew-slash-fell out of the dumpster, semi-helped by its pink wings, she got confirmation.

She took a cautious step back.

This was quite possibly the strangest thing that had happened to her in Axia yet. A barking baby dragon stuck in a dumpster. Had it crawled in there and gotten stuck while rummaging for scraps? Maybe they were the raccoons of the magical world—trash lizards. It was roughly the size of a raccoon, anyway. A very *large* raccoon.

The little thing got its four feet under it and gave itself a shake, much like a dog, dislodging a slimy pile of noodles that had gotten stuck on its back ridges. Without warning, it galloped awkwardly toward her, its pink-hued claws clicking on the asphalt. She froze. It tripped over its own feet just before it reached her and stumbled, sliding on its chin and crashing into one of her shoes. She thought belatedly that the little dragon might be a threat to her—what with the breathing fire thing—but before she could back up farther, the dragon was upright and had launched itself at her.

She fell backward again, giving her brain another good jostling. She tensed, wondering if this was how she'd die: disemboweled in an alley by a dragon. As it stood on her torso with all four paws, she noted that its claws hadn't torn into her shirt. In fact, she thought the dragon might have retracted them.

And then the tiny dragon was licking her face and neck, chirping and snuffling like a piglet. Tension leached out of her like a burst dam. She laughed, swatting him away.

"You're welcome, you're welcome," she said, still laughing, knowing somehow that he was thanking her for freeing him.

She had no idea how she knew the dragon was a boy—there were no readily visible, uh, bits to suggest a gender either way—only that she knew.

Wrapping her arms around the squirmy lizard, she sat up. He had retracted his ridges, too, and had tucked his wings close to his back. As he sat in her lap gazing up at her, his giant pink eyes made something twinge in her chest. This was puppy-dog eyes on overdrive.

She probably should have been more freaked out by the fact that a *dragon* was in her lap. She supposed her threshold for weird had been exceeded already, and now she was numb to it. Allegra had been right to try to scare the bejesus out of Deandra earlier. Either you accepted this place with all its quirks, or you hightailed it out of here immediately.

Plus, despite the fact that there was a *dragon* in her lap, he had the biggest, sweetest eyes she'd ever seen ... *anyone* would have fallen victim to them.

A thick white collar ringed his neck, complete with a tag hanging from a metal loop. "Oh, you're someone's pet!"

With one arm wrapped around the dragon to hold him still, she grabbed hold of the tag with her free hand. An etching of what appeared to be a ball of flame decorated one side of the circular metal tag, but the other side was blank. Frowning, she examined the collar. Strange designs that might have been letters ringed the leather, but the symbols weren't anything she recognized. Gently removing the collar, she checked the underside, hoping a name or phone number would be written there, but no dice.

Reattaching the collar, she stared down at the gentle dragon. "Who do you belong to, huh?"

The dragon chirped.

A moment later, those big pink eyes went glassy, and smoke began to waft from his nostrils. As cute as the creature was, and as much trouble as she'd gone through to free him from the dumpster, she had enough sense left to get the dragon out of her lap and to dart several feet away from him. She tucked herself into a ball and threw her arms over her head, knowing she couldn't outrun whatever was coming next. She had no defenses against a fireball or whatever fate was to befall her. Her fight-or-flight response had settled on freeze —again.

Instead of being barbecued alive by a dragon, she heard a sound that was no doubt a sneeze. She uncovered her head to find the little dragon sitting in the same place she'd left him, his face contorted. He sneezed once more. A fireball the size of a basketball launched out of his mouth and hit the dumpster dead center. The metal box jerked back several inches, and the standing-open lids slammed back into place.

Deandra flinched.

The dragon sat on his rear, his back feet stuck out in front of him, and his front feet propped on the ground. He looked over at her, clearly miserable. He was Eeyore in dragon form. Smoke poured from his nose.

"Aw, buddy. Do you have a cold or something?"

He chirped, but with much less enthusiasm.

The dragon was clearly well taken care of—the cold or allergies notwithstanding—and presumably belonged to someone. Maybe he was microchipped. Was it even possible to microchip a dragon?

Making her way to her belongings she'd left by the cinder-block wall, she fished her welcome booklet and map out of her purse. After consulting both, she learned that Axia boasted three veterinarians. The nearest one was the only one listed as an exotic animal specialist. "Dragon" was as exotic as it got, she thought.

"Wanna take a walk, buddy?" she asked, hoping the dragon would walk alongside her without too much trouble. She could carry him, but probably not for very long.

The dragon scrambled to his feet and trotted over, smiling up at her. Despite having been trapped under trash and the heavy end table, he didn't seem to be injured, at least. She wondered why he wasn't using his wings, but the brief sight she'd gotten of them implied that their length didn't match his body mass. If she was right that he was a baby, maybe he hadn't grown into the wings yet.

She strapped her purse onto her shoulder. Checking her phone again for texts from Wendy, but finding none, she stowed the cell in her back pocket, then headed toward the alley and the sidewalk beyond. The dragon waddled beside her. There was an occasional sniffle, but otherwise he was back to being cheerful enough.

When she rounded the end of the alley and headed toward the direction of the vet, the dragon kept pace with her, content to stay by her side. Even when a woman on the other side of the street walked by with her barking German shepherd, the dragon didn't stray or react. She glanced down and he looked up, offering her another grin, as if he thought she was the best thing that had ever happened to him.

When she'd thought about how nice it would be to have a dog, this was definitely *not* what she'd meant.

The dragon peeped happily.

She couldn't help the fond smile that spread across her face. He might have been a fire-breathing lizard, but he was stinking cute.

She sighed. This continued to be the strangest day of her life.

Chapter 8

A few minutes into her walk to the veterinary office, Deandra began to question how hard she'd actually scrambled her brain when she'd fallen off those crates. Though the dragon stayed trotting by her side, like the well-trained, overgrown lizard he was, anyone who saw them coming quickly crossed to the other side of the street. The few dogs they saw either barked furiously at the dragon or cowered in fear. A cat that had been sunning itself in the middle of the sidewalk had woken with a start, hissed furiously, and then darted up a tree, continuing to offer disgruntled commentary from the safety of the branches. The dragon paid it all no mind. The humans accompanying the dogs eyed the dragon warily, but their line of sight was often up near Deandra's hip, rather than down by her calves.

She further questioned her own mental stability when she and the dragon finally made it to the vet office. As she approached the reception counter, the tech peered over the edge, smiled warmly at the dragon sitting by Deandra's feet and asked, "Well, who is this handsome pup?"

Was "pup" another word for a baby dragon?

The question was apparently rhetorical, because the vet tech plopped back in her seat and smiled at Deandra. She had big brown eyes and a demeanor that was almost as cheerful as the sea of smiling animal faces that dotted her mint-colored scrubs. Deandra relaxed a little, confident bringing the dragon here was the right choice.

The tech tucked a lock of short brown hair behind her ear. "Is this your first time here?"

"Uhh ... yes," Deandra said. "I'm new to town. Just arrived today, actually. Longest, weirdest day of my life. First a centaur flirted with me, and then a building caught fire, and—"

The vet tech's brows hiked. It was like a stranger asking the obligatory "How are you?" and instead of the customary "fine," got an earful they hadn't wanted.

Deandra coughed. "Sorry, yes. This is my first time here. Do you take walk-ins? I guess I should have called first, but you're the only exotic animal vet in town. The, uh, pup is really friendly and well-behaved, all things considered, so I figure his owners are missing him. Hopefully he's chipped."

The vet tech continued to stare curiously at Deandra. Was microchipping pets not a thing in Axia?

Instead of acknowledging any of that, the tech asked Deandra's name and number. "Any guesses on the breed? I just need to put something in the box." She stood again to peer over the counter. Deandra guessed she couldn't have been an inch over five-two. "Husky mix, maybe? I can't tell if he's gray or just dirty. German shepherd? I suppose it could be a very young dire wolf, but even for a runt, I think this one is too small. My gut says it's a mundane breed."

Now it was Deandra's turn to stare. She glanced down at the dragon. Between the honey-orange scales, ridges along his spine, and rose-colored eyes, Deandra wasn't sure if he could be any further from a "mundane" dog. And yet, hadn't Deandra initially thought he was a wolf when she found him thumping around in the dumpster? Maybe Axia had officially broken her tired human brain, and this was, in fact, a dog.

Swallowing hard, she looked back to the tech. "A German shepherd-husky mix might explain the shaggy fur."

The vet tech nodded as if this made perfect sense and quickly typed away on her keyboard. "Any guesses about it being a boy or a girl?"

"Boy," Deandra said without hesitation.

"That was my guess, too. That's all we need for now. Dr. Caddel will be with you shortly. Just have a seat."

Deandra thanked the tech, then turned away from the counter. The dragon padded along beside her. He still hadn't used the tiny pink wings folded across his back since he'd taken that initial tumble out of the dumpster. What was she supposed to do if he did? Were *flying* mundane dogs a thing here? She supposed if she really was starting to lose it, this "dog" might not have any wings at all. When she sat on the bench seat in front of the lobby's windows, the dragon parked himself by her feet, rather than floating up to sit on the bench with her.

After a few minutes, another tech called her name, and she and her dragon-dog shuffled through a side door and down a short hallway to an exam room at the end.

Deandra took a seat on yet another navy-blue bench seat that ran along one wall, while the tech took up a position in front of a computer. It was deathly quiet in the room; the sound of Deandra's jeans rubbing against the plastic seat was nearly deafening. She swallowed. What if she had a concussion? She didn't even know what the symptoms of a concussion *were* …

The tech asked Deandra the same set of questions she'd been asked earlier, throwing a puzzled look over her shoulder at the notion of Deandra's "dog" being microchipped.

"I'm sure Dr. Caddel can help you with that." With a tight-lipped, borderline patronizing smile, she added, "His father is a mundane," as if that was relevant to the conversation in the slightest.

The tech left the room, closing the door quietly behind her.

The dragon, who had been sitting very patiently by Deandra's feet, tipped his head back to look up at her. His blue-black tongue lolled out the side of his mouth. His pink eyes glittered—literally—like gemstones.

But soon that glazed-eyed look took over his expression again and his yellow-ribbed chest contracted a fraction. The sparkle went out of his eyes as he sucked his tongue back into his mouth.

"Buddy?" she asked slowly, inching away from him on the bench. "You all right?"

His face contorted in a now-familiar grimace. Deandra pitched over sideways, fueled solely by instinct.

Sneeze!

A ball of fire shot over her head and hit the wall behind her. Five long seconds later, she unshielded her face, half of which was smashed against the antiseptic-smelling bench seat, to find the dragon's little face peering at her. His grin was back, tongue lolling and smoke billowing from his nostrils. He sniffed.

With the threat seemingly past, she righted herself. The wall behind her now bore a scorch mark the diameter of a soccer ball. If she scooted over an inch, she figured her head of wavy dark hair would cover the mark, but she wasn't sure how she could explain where it had come from.

"*Oh, this? My dog breathes fire. Why? Is that unusual?*"

She returned her attention to the dragon. Maybe something foul from the dumpster had been sucked into his nose while he was rummaging for snacks.

He heaved a breath out of his nose, smoke expelling in two puffs of white. He shook his head, trying to paw at his face, but his forelegs kept missing their mark by an inch. Reluctantly, Deandra gave his muzzle a scratch. The dragon hummed his thanks, then more aggressively rubbed his warm nose on her palm to really get a good scratch going. She thought of bears standing upright as they rubbed their backs against a tree.

The dragon let out periodic chirps of delight as he kept rubbing his nose on her hand. She laughed despite how damp her hand had gotten.

A soft knock sounded on the door. The dragon started and turned toward the noise, while Deandra sat back to block the scorch mark on the wall. She discreetly wiped her fingers on her pants.

Deandra had expected a middle-aged woman to step into the room, but instead it was a thirty-something man with light brown skin, brown eyes, and closely shaven dark hair. He wore blue scrubs and a polite smile.

"Deandra Hendricks?" he asked, stepping inside. "Sorry for the wait. Mrs. Jacobs's baby pegasus got loose again, and I had to chase her down the block. Thankfully, she loves flowers."

She stared at him, unable to process most of what he'd just said. "The pegasus or the owner loves flowers?"

He chuckled. "Both, I suppose. But I meant Starshadow."

Deandra still wasn't clear on who they were talking about here, so she changed the subject before the pulsing behind one eye turned into a full-on migraine. Headaches were a symptom of concussions, weren't they? "I found this ... little guy today. He seems well cared for—other than the sneezing—so I figured he's got an owner. Can you scan him to see if he has a chip?"

"A, uh, chip of what?" he asked, sounding even more puzzled than she felt about Starshadow and her penchant for flowers.

The dragon peeped.

"There was some debate up front about his breed," the vet said, laughing. "Since he likes to offer commentary, I'm leaning toward husky."

Deandra idly massaged her temple. What if all of this was an elaborate fever dream and she was still in her apartment in Los Angeles, thrashing around under her sheets while ravaged by the flu?

The vet walked over and dropped to his knees in front of the dragon. "You okay with me doing a quick exam, boy?"

The dragon chirped again.

Dr. Caddel chuckled. "I'll take that as a yes."

Checking the dragon's temperature via rectal thermometer was loudly vetoed by the patient, but the vet was able to check the dragon's heartbeat by way of a stethoscope with little fuss. Dr. Caddel peeled back the dragon's lips to check his teeth and peered into his ears with a small penlight. While prodding the dragon's neck with gentle fingers, the vet's eyebrows hiked. "Did you know he was wearing a collar? I missed it under all this fur."

She pursed her lips as she stared at the stark-white collar sitting around the dragon's neck in sharp contrast to its orange scales. Coughing awkwardly, and spoken with all the confidence of an actress who had forgotten her lines, she said, "I cannot believe I missed that."

The vet offered another polite smile. "The owner's name might be printed on the collar ... or on the tag ..."

The dragon grew increasingly frustrated with the vet's efforts, and let loose a low, menacing growl while the vet hovered over him. "Sorry, buddy. Having a hard time finding the clasp with all this fur. Maybe you should ask your mom if you can take a trip to the groomer."

The dragon's growl deepened.

"*Oookay,*" Deandra said, simultaneously calming the dragon down and making the vet sit back.

Instead of telling the vet she'd already checked the collar and tag, she decided to humor him. He was a smart guy, right? All that book learnin' and whatnot. Maybe he'd recognize the symbols etched on the leather. She easily unhooked the collar from the dragon's neck.

The moment the collar was off the dragon and held out toward said smarty-pants veterinarian, the man issued a high-pitched shriek like a little girl on the school yard who'd just had her pigtails yanked. Deandra clapped her hands over her ears. A puff of smoke wafted out of the dragon's nostrils in a short burst, his orange scales warming to a muddy brown. That only made the vet scream louder.

The vet hit the floor, hard, on his backside, then scrambled backward like a crab. His yelp was abruptly cut off when he crashed into the wall. "That's ... that's a *dragon*!"

Deandra sat up straight. "So I'm *not* going cuckoo?"

The vet blinked rapidly. "Holy. *Realms*."

Placing a hand on the dragon's head, she shushed him. "Easy, boy. It's okay. Easy, easy ..."

The smoke subsided, and his color slowly returned to normal.

A knock sounded on the door. The vet jumped.

"Dr. Caddel?" came a muffled voice from the other side of the door. "Everything okay in there?"

Eyes as wide as dinner plates, the vet gestured wildly at Deandra. "Get that collar back on him right now. Quick!"

The urgency of his tone made her comply without question. Deandra had just affixed the collar back in place when the door flew open.

Two techs came tumbling in. The cheerful one from earlier held a wicked-looking pole with a sparking blue light dancing off the end, and the other inexplicably held a butterfly net—if butterflies were the size of small cars.

"We ... uh ... heard screaming," the woman with the net said, taking in the scene.

Both women panted heavily, ready to go to war. Deandra's heart slammed in her rib cage.

Her "dog" was on his back currently, quite unperturbed as he swatted in the general direction of his own muzzle, trying to dislodge a tuft of gray fur that was stuck to his nose. She hoped he wouldn't get frustrated and decide to incinerate the fur. His little feet were angled toward the ceiling. Deandra noted that the pads of his feet were a delightful shade of yellow.

"Everything is fine here, ladies," the vet said, managing to sound a fraction less hysterical than he had a few seconds ago. "Miss Hendricks's dog seems to be at least partly dire wolf after all. He's not more than a few months old, I'm guessing. You know how rambunctious they can be."

The tech armed with the net noticed the scorch mark on the wall behind Deandra. "Been a while since I've seen a dire wolf with a connection to fire magic ... that's a pretty rare trait for them, isn't it?"

"Very," the vet said, noticing the scorch mark for the first time, too. "He also seems to have a cold. I'll just finish up my exam, and then I'll send Miss Hendricks on her way with some medication. I assure you, we're fine. Just got knocked around a bit. I think I'm still winded from chasing Starshadow."

The two techs laughed politely, but even Deandra could tell they had their doubts about the vet's story. The one with the net shot an unfiltered glare at Deandra. Maybe most of her doubts were about Deandra herself. After all, what was a clueless mundane new to Axia doing with a rare fire-breathing dire wolf puppy?

Would the tech use that net on Deandra if she found out the puppy was actually a dragon?

Not even the vet wanted his assistants to know that much.

Reluctantly, the techs backed out of the room and closed the door. After five long seconds of total silence, the vet scrambled onto his hands and knees and crawled back toward the dragon. When Dr. Caddel reached him, the vet sat back on his haunches.

"Can you remove the collar again?" he asked.

Deandra cocked a brow at him.

"I promise not to scream this time."

She did as he asked.

Though he kept his word about not screaming, he still released a shaky exhale. "Incredible. Truly. Where did you say you found him again?"

"He was stuck inside a dumpster near that building that burned down earlier," she said, shrugging. "I thought it was a trapped dog."

"Brave of you to attempt a rescue mission by yourself instead of getting help."

"Or stupid."

He laughed. "There's a fine line."

A thought occurred to her then. This dragon, who lacked full control of his fire, had been found near the site of maybe-arson. Could this sweet creature somehow be responsible for Callie's uncle's death? "You don't think ... I mean the fire ... could he have accidentally—"

The vet held up a hand. "I heard it was a magic-based fire, and while the dragon *is* magic-touched, his fire is very natural."

Deandra thought she and Dr. Caddel had very different opinions about what constituted "natural."

After several moments of watching the vet watching the dragon, Deandra asked, "Doesn't the sign out front say you specialize in caring for exotic animals? You chased down a pegasus earlier. You and the techs aren't fazed by the idea of fire-breathing wolves. That one lady was carrying the biggest net I've ever seen. Why is a dragon such a big deal?"

He tore his gaze away from the dragon, who had dozed off sitting up, his chin propped on Deandra's knee.

"Up until five minutes ago, I was operating under the assumption that they've been extinct in this realm for nearly a century."

Deandra wondered how much of her time in Axia was going to be spent staring blankly at people. "This realm as in Earth?"

"Yes," he said. "Magic-touched, fae, and mundanes traveled between the realms once. But the portals between this realm and the fae realm unexpectedly closed permanently a century ago. A few dragons wound up marooned here after the portals were suddenly no longer accessible. Mundanes ... humans, I mean ... drove dragons and other large ancient beasts into extinction. At least, that's what I've always been taught."

Deandra glanced down at the dragon. She no doubt knew less about dragons than the vet did, but it was clear this one was a baby, which meant, at least in the very recent past, there had been more than one on Earth. Were his parents somewhere? Had they passed away before the little guy hatched?

A soft, squeaky whistle issued from the dragon's nose every few seconds. Her heart ached. Not only was he possibly an orphaned dragon, he had a stuffy nose. She'd never thought of herself as someone with strong maternal instincts, but she currently wanted to scoop him into her arms and protect him at all costs.

She mentally shook her head. She was only in Axia to visit family. Her apartment back home was too small, and the complex didn't allow pets. Her hours at the coffee shop were too unpredictable for her to take on the responsibility of a "puppy." On days when she had to add ride-share gigs into the mix, she was sometimes taking jobs until after ten in the evening. She *would* feel safer at night with him in her passenger seat, though. Drunk men and aspiring robbers would think twice about messing with her if they saw a dire wolf riding shotgun.

She could just imagine trying to walk her "dog" in downtown Los Angeles, especially if he ever figured out how to fly. What if the collar broke and fell off, revealing his true nature? People would lose their minds.

Maybe she could create an account for him, and they could become internet famous. That was one thing she could say about LA and the internet at large: The potential for creating ridiculous careers was endless.

If celebrity dogs could be kidnapped for ransom, though, she could only imagine the kind of riffraff who would come crawling out of the woodwork if it became public knowledge that she had a *baby dragon*.

"Deandra?"

She snapped out of her musings to find the vet staring at her, getting the impression that hadn't been the first time he'd said her name. "Sorry. What did you say?"

He had the collar in his hand. "I was saying that there's some complicated spellwork etched onto this. I'm rusty on runes, but my best guess is that this is imbued with a glamour spell."

Deandra only knew of glamour spells from TV shows and movies, but even that scant knowledge lined up with what seemed to be going on here. "Why would someone want him to look like a dog instead of a dragon? Wouldn't the discovery that dragons still exist be a good thing? People would be stoked if the dodo made a comeback."

He smiled ruefully at her, but his expression soon slipped back to something more serious. "It depends on who crafted the collar and why. There's a thriving black market for magical items. A dragon is as rare as they come. An interested buyer might pay hundreds of thousands for *part* of a dragon egg. But a fully intact one that then hatched?" He whistled. "Such a find would be priceless to some."

Deandra glanced down at the dragon with his head still propped on her knee.

"I think it's best to keep that collar on him at all times unless you're around those you trust," he said, handing the collar back. "There's no way to know if the previous owner—or the creator of the collar—had merely purchased the dragon to have as an exotic pet, or if they had money-making plans for him. Keeping him might be dangerous for you if a criminal-type comes looking for him."

"Well, this took a dark turn."

He laughed. It was an easy, genuine sound that lightened her mood a fraction. "Axia isn't exactly a criminal hotbed, so I'm leaning toward eccentric exotic-pet owner."

She decided it said a lot about Dr. Caddel that he hadn't tried to convince her to leave the dragon with him. The rarity of the animal had clearly been a shock, but it didn't seem like it had even crossed his mind to manipulate the priceless dragon out of this clueless mundane's hands.

"What should I do?" she asked, running a finger back and forth across the dragon's forehead. "Post 'found dog' flyers?"

The dragon's nose gave a loud whistle, like a tea kettle, and they both chuckled softly.

"I'll send you home with some meds to treat his cold first," he said. "Frankly, I need to clear my head a bit, and then I can possibly come up with a more practical solution."

Deandra frowned down at the sleeping dragon, wondering if he'd truly been abandoned.

"I've been thinking ..." Dr. Caddel said. Deandra braced herself, worried he'd changed his mind and now wanted the dragon for himself. "Were you able to see him as a dragon from the start?"

Initially, when the dragon had been buried under garbage and debris, she *had* thought he was a wolf. Had that been because she'd seen snatches of the glamoured dragon beneath the debris, or had she always seen a dragon? Had her brain assigned a more palatable label to the creature in order to, as Allegra had suggested, bring order to chaos?

"I'm not sure. By the time I freed him, he appeared as a dragon," she said.

Dr. Caddel bobbed his head thoughtfully. "It's been a long time since I studied dragon lore—it was part of my studies when I decided to specialize in exotics—but a fairly established theory is that dragons imprint on those within their inner circle. You see this in mundane animal populations, too. A duckling imprinting on a human who raises it, for example."

"So, what, he thinks I'm his mom?"

"Not exactly," Dr. Caddel said. "Dragons form something like pods or packs. Their pod is their family unit. Blood relation isn't a requirement. Those who are part of the unit share a kind of telepathic bond. It's more of a link of souls than the ability to speak in each other's minds. If a dragon was on the other side of the planet and needed assistance, it could send a warning down the psychic link to let others in the pod know. It's been described as a feeling more than a communication with words."

He paused to study the dragon for a few moments. "I believe this little one has looped you into his inner circle. There's literal magic in a dragon's trust, and that trust overrode the glamour magic of his collar. With his collar on, all *I* see is a shaggy puppy. I think *you* can see him for what he really is simply because he wants you to."

Renewed affection for the dragon washed over Deandra. She really had no idea what she was supposed to do with him, though. She couldn't uproot her life in Los Angeles and move to Axia simply because a baby dragon adopted her. And even *that* nutty idea was more plausible than taking him back to LA.

Maybe Wendy was in the market for a new pet.

Dr. Caddel asked, "Did you give your number to the ladies up front?" When she said she had, he nodded. "Good. I'll do some research and get back to you tomorrow. Fridays are notoriously busy here, so it might not be until the end of the day, if that's all right. I'll want an update on how he's doing with his medication, too."

"Yeah, that would be great. Thank you." She bit her lip. "I, uh, have a stupid-slash-obvious question that I should have asked a while ago, but what do dragons eat?"

Please don't say "people," please don't say "people"...

The dragon was adorable, and Deandra was attached to him already, but she *would not* commit homicide for him. Every lady had her limits, and murder was hers.

Dr. Caddel appeared amused by her distress. "That's part of the research I want to do. It all depends on the type of dragon he is."

There were *types*?

"Like dinosaurs, he might be an herbivore, a carnivore, or an omnivore. As alarming as you might think it would be to have a strict carnivore for a pet, an herbivore might be more of a hindrance, especially once he's older. The sheer amount of vegetation he'd have to eat while in his adolescence would be … astronomical. Here's to hoping he's an omnivore."

Deandra ran a finger back and forth over the dragon's forehead. He hummed softly in response, almost a purr. "If I can't keep him and his owner doesn't show up before I have to leave town at the end of the weekend …" she said, already feeling awful about voicing this out loud, so much so that she practically whispered it, "what would happen to him?"

The vet sighed. "I really don't know. There are a few zoos in the world who cater to mythical animals, but none are prepared to house a dragon. I'm sure any one of them would pay a large sum to have him, though. Any zoo that advertised having a thought-to-be-extinct dragon would triple its attendance overnight."

Deandra pursed her lips. As much as some of the smaller mundane zoos could bum her out to no end, she knew how much good zoos could do in the name of education and conservation. If anyone in this "realm" could care for the little guy properly, it would be the staff of a mythical zoo. Yet the idea made her want to cry.

"Just think about it," Dr. Caddel said. "Taking on a new pet is always a big decision—even more so in this case."

Understatement of the century.

Deandra wondered how in the world she'd gotten herself into this situation. If she'd never used that travel talisman, none of the whacky things that occurred today would have happened. Actually, had she moved to Boston with Mark when he got transferred there for his new job at the research hospital, none of this would have happened. But somehow, as much as she'd cared about Mark, taking that step—moving forward in their relationship and moving to a new state, *again*—had felt wrong.

He hadn't proposed, but she figured that would have come down the line eventually. She wasn't sure when during her three-year relationship the entirety of her personality had become "Hi, I'm Mark's girlfriend." They'd moved from her hometown of Denver to Los Angeles after only a handful of months into their relationship.

She'd left her parents and friends behind for the greener pastures of a bright new future.

Once they'd settled in LA, Mark was usually so busy that Deandra spent most nights alone on the couch. She'd befriended coworkers from the coffee shop and tagged along on bar crawls and game nights, but Mark was either too busy to join her or made excuses not to attend.

Deandra had never thought Mark was a snob before, but being in Los Angeles had pulled some of his dormant snobbery to the surface. On the rare occasions he agreed to go out, it was often to wine-and-cheese parties thrown by his acquaintances. She inevitably ended up in a corner with only someone's pet for company while everyone else talked shop. Artists and aspiring actors would be sprinkled among the guest list, and she could at least commiserate with them over what it was like working in the service industry. But she could tell there was a level of pity aimed her way when she voiced that her job as a barista wasn't a temporary stepping-stone to something better. She didn't have a dream job floating in the distance, tempting her ever forward like a donkey lured by a carrot. Her own plans had dried up because her decisions had become so firmly tied to Mark's.

It was at one of those awful parties, while she hid in the den with someone's golden retriever, that she'd realized she'd lost herself somewhere along the way.

So when Mark asked her to move with him to yet another new city, she'd been seized with an all-encompassing fear that if she told Mark yes, it would seal the deal. The Deandra she once knew would be gone forever. She'd eventually have financial stability with a doctor for a husband, but who cared about that when there'd be nothing of *her* left?

So she'd said no.

He'd been gone for five months now. He sent her the occasional "How are you?" text but not much else. She figured it was more out of guilt than from missing her. After all, when his offer to join him on the next step in his career adventure had turned into a breakup, he hadn't fought her very hard.

She wished she knew if the universe was rewarding her now for telling Mark no or if it was punishing her in an epic way.

Dr. Caddel cleared his throat.

Deandra winced slightly. She really needed to stop zoning out like this.

He asked, "Do you think you could keep him asleep while I get a blood sample? I want to make sure he doesn't have anything else wrong under the hood, other than the cold."

Deandra kept gently petting the dragon's forehead while Dr. Caddel expertly got a vial of blood from the dragon's haunch without waking him up. Dr. Caddel left the room long enough to deposit the blood sample somewhere and to fetch the cold meds.

Grabbing the dragon by the muzzle, Dr. Caddel pulled up the dragon's top lip and shot the liquid directly into his mouth so fast, the dragon woke with a snort. The dragon looked like he wanted to issue a protest, but got distracted by the flavor of the medicine, smacking his lips and flicking his tongue in and out in mild distaste.

Dr. Caddel instructed Deandra to give him his next round in the morning. The dragon would need the meds twice a day until the bottle was empty. Empty, she noted, would put her well into next week. She tried not to think about what would happen to the dragon after Monday when she left Axia.

Deandra, the dragon, and Dr. Caddel then said their goodbyes, and he promised again to call her the following day. Once Deandra confirmed the collar was snugly around the dragon's neck, they made their way to the lobby.

As she paid for the medication, the tech told her she could administer it directly into the dragon's mouth or add it to his food. Deandra was just relieved the meds came in liquid form. She'd had to pill cats before. She didn't want to learn how to pill a dragon.

The more cheerful, less suspicious of the vet techs lifted the lid off a ceramic jar on the counter and said the "good boy" could have a treat. Deandra picked one of the hard, bone-shaped biscuits out of the jar and held it out to the dragon. He tentatively sniffed it and then very gently took it with his front teeth.

Deandra waited, hopeful, as the dragon slowly chewed. He froze, screwed up his face, then spit a spray of chewed-up dog treat all over the floor and Deandra's shoes. He darted over to the wall and proceeded to lick it vigorously. Considering the fact that the dragon liked to eat garbage, it didn't say much about the quality of the treats.

"Sorry!" Deandra said, kicking one of her feet to dislodge a large, soggy bit of biscuit.

The vet tech merely laughed. "At least he's honest. Don't worry about it. I'll clean it up. I hope the meds help him. Dr. Caddel will give you a follow-up call tomorrow."

With a wave, Deandra and the dragon left the office. He immediately flung himself onto the small lawn outside, rolling around as if he could get the stink of the place off him. That, or he just liked grass.

Deandra's phone rang. Glancing at the screen, she grinned and quickly answered the call. "Wendy! Thank all that is holy ..."

"You didn't get spooked and flee town, did you?" Wendy asked, breathless. "Sorry I abandoned you, but I'm finally off work. You won't believe how weird my day's been."

Deandra eyed her dragon, who was now on his belly, army-crawling toward an unsuspecting butterfly on a nearby flower. The dragon wiggled his butt, then pounced, missing the butterfly by a mile, partly because he'd gotten distracted by the bright pink spade at the end of his own tail, and was now chasing it. "Bet you ten bucks mine was weirder ..."

Chapter 9

Deandra only got lost once on her drive to Wendy's apartment. The walk back to the Welcome Center had been relaxed, and the dragon had behaved himself, continuing to be oblivious to the stares and outright avoidance of anyone who crossed their path. To her relief, the dragon hadn't shown any signs of getting car sick. It would be just her luck to have a dragon with a sensitive stomach in her back seat, yakking up fiery bile on her upholstery. But he'd merely sat calmly and gazed out the window, watching the world creep by outside.

Granted, he was still sniffling periodically, his eyes were a bit watery, and the excitement of the day appeared to have zapped him of most of his energy. He might become a high-octane menace once he was healthy and well rested.

Wendy lived on the second floor of a ten-unit apartment complex. She'd arrived at home a few minutes before Deandra finally found the place, and she opened the door to #4 just as Deandra and her ungraceful dragon made their way up the stairs. The poor guy had slipped twice, his too-large paws doing him no favors on the steep stone steps. She had to carry him up the last four stairs. He twisted around to give her neck an appreciative lick just before she placed him back on solid ground.

She found Wendy staring open-mouthed at her from her apartment's doorway. "How ... what ... you ..."

"Like I said, my day was weirder," Deandra said.

Wendy stared down at the dragon sitting by Deandra's feet. Her eyeline, just like everyone else's, hovered closer to Deandra's hip. "How ... how did you carry him up the stairs? He looks like a puppy, but he's gotta weigh at least eighty pounds."

Deandra propped a fist on her hip. "Are you doubting my physical prowess?"

Wendy cackled.

"Rude! It wasn't *that* funny."

"Get inside," Wendy said, chuckling and stepping back. "We clearly need wine for this conversation."

"Clearly."

The dragon trotted along behind her, but once he crossed the threshold, he set about exploring the apartment, sniffing aggressively with his nose to the floor.

While the apartment was tidy, Deandra appreciated that it also looked lived in. A small plate with the crumbly remnants of a pastry sat on the round, wooden coffee table in front of the plush, teal-green couch. A wadded-up blanket was draped over the arm of the sofa, and a pair of slippers lay on the floor, one turned over. An open magazine was being used as a makeshift coaster on the end table, where a half-full mug of coffee still sat.

The wall above the couch had four gorgeous art prints hanging in simple black frames. The prints were clearly all made by the same artist, each featuring a witch performing a spell using one of the four elements—earth, air, fire, and water. Wendy had moved to Axia to be closer to their grandparents, but it had been a dream of Wendy's since she and Deandra were kids to one day wake up with the ability to wield magic. Magical powers weren't switched on by sheer will and desire, Deandra was sure, but she could admire Wendy's steadfast hope anyway.

The dragon trotted down the apartment's main hallway. The living room they stood in now gave way to the kitchen, with a modest dining room area in between. Wendy had created the illusion of walls by adding a TV cabinet just beyond the coffee table, bookending it with potted plants with thick green leaves. On the other side of the cabinet, she'd positioned a bookshelf of the same height and width.

Wendy said, "You sit. I'll get the wine."

Deandra eyed her dragon as he passed two doors on either side of the hall, then disappeared to the right.

By the time Wendy returned, Deandra had flopped onto the couch, and the dragon had wandered back into the living room. She hoped he didn't have another sneezing fit in here. Deandra couldn't afford to replace Wendy's furniture. The dose of medication the vet had administered seemed to have finally kicked in. The dragon still sniffled periodically, but his eyes no longer looked as watery.

Wendy handed Deandra a glass of red wine and settled on the other side of the sofa, sitting cross-legged and facing Deandra. "All right. Start at the beginning."

Deandra took a long sip, then launched into it—starting with meeting Callie and ending with rescuing the "dog" from the dumpster. Wendy, her now-empty wine glass sitting on the coffee table, had listened dutifully through most of Deandra's tale, only interrupting a couple of times to ask a question. She opened her mouth now, presumably to ask something else, but Deandra cut her off.

"This dog is not actually a dog," Deandra said, eyeing the dragon who had his head propped on her knee again, his gaze shifting between her and Wendy.

"Well, that much is obvious," Wendy said. "I'm not an expert in mythical animals, but I'd bet money that's a dire wolf. A puppy, probably. Which is alarming, given that it's basically already the size of a pony. You're only in town for a few more days. Are you planning to take a *dire wolf* back with you to LA?" She gasped. "Have you already decided to stay in Axia?"

"I haven't decided anything."

Wendy grinned. "That's not a no!"

Deandra held up a hand to calm her cousin's mounting excitement. "The vet told me to only share this with people I trust. You're on that very short list. But I need you to not freak out."

Cocking her head, Wendy stared at the dragon, her brow furrowed. "Freak out about what?"

"Just ... take a deep breath, okay?"

"You're freaking me out already!"

Deandra focused on the dragon, leaning forward a fraction to rub the spot between his eyes. "You have to stay calm too, okay? No breathing fire in here, all right?"

"*Fire?*" Wendy hissed.

The dragon sat up straight and held her eye contact. Somehow, Deandra got the impression he understood.

Deandra unclasped his collar.

"Oh, *holy* realms!" Wendy shrieked.

By the time Deandra turned toward her, her cousin was poised on the arm of the sofa like Catwoman. It was an impressive feat of dexterity, even if it had been fueled by fear. Wendy thrust a pointed finger toward the dragon. "That's a flipping dragon, Dee! It has ... it has *wings*! What ... how ... how is there a *dragon* in my apartment? Don't dragons eat, you know, *people*?"

"He's been in your apartment this entire time, and you never once felt threatened, right?" Deandra asked, trying to keep her voice calm and even, both to keep the dragon from getting too agitated and to offset Wendy's frantic energy. Deandra held up the white leather collar now clasped in her fist and relayed the information Dr. Caddel had shared with her about glamour spells and the magic inherent in a dragon's trust.

Wendy slowly climbed off the side of her couch. "He ... *does* seem friendly ..."

At that, the dragon bounded over Deandra's lap and onto the couch. Before Wendy could protest, he placed a paw on either of her shoulders and gave her face several slobbery licks. Wendy laughed and gently shoved him away. Deandra was grinning at her by the time she recovered and the dragon was back on the ground, looking rather pleased with himself.

Did he understand English, or was his understanding part of the supposed connection they shared due to the dragon imprinting on her? Either way, he'd managed to win Wendy over, even if she still looked shell-shocked. Deandra rehashed her concerns about what to do with the dragon, given her situation.

"I don't think I'm cut out for pets, period," Wendy said. "He's very cool, but I can't keep him. And as much as Grandma and Grandpa are trustworthy people, they would not keep *this* a secret." She gestured at the dragon, who had gone back to sniffing every inch of Wendy's floor. He vanished from view around the side of the TV cabinet. "Grandma would tell her book club. Grandpa would tell his golfing buddies. They'd both blab about it at the Mermaids Club. You'd have Animal Control banging down the door before the weekend was out. And Animal Control in Axia is no joke, let me tell you."

A plaintive howl sounded from the kitchen.

Deandra and Wendy stared at each other a beat, then scrambled off the couch and toward the sound. The dragon sat in the middle of the kitchen, back in his dejected Eeyore pose. He angled a sad-puppy-dog expression at Deandra. He tossed his head back and wailed, the sound so hauntingly sad, goose bumps rose on her arms.

"What's *wrong* with him?" Wendy asked, a fist pressed to her mouth.

Deandra couldn't blame her for the stricken look on her face. The dragon was carrying on as if he were dying, after all.

"I think he's ... hungry," Deandra said, wondering how she knew that. "Guess the dumpster-diving meal wasn't enough."

Wendy asked, "And you're sure he was dumpster diving, and not that someone *put* him in there? What if someone was trying to hide him? Or worse?"

Deandra frowned in the dragon's direction, unable to imagine anyone wanting to hurt him. His manners suggested someone had treated him well, but she supposed dragons could be well behaved naturally.

The dragon tipped his head back and howled again.

"All right, all right," Deandra said. "Don't be so dramatic about it."

For the next twenty minutes, Wendy and Deandra raided Wendy's fridge and cabinets, looking for anything the dragon would eat. He ate an entire head of lettuce like an apple, found cucumber even more detestable than dog biscuits, mildly tolerated carrots, loved plain yogurt—but hated the lemon-flavored variety so much that he whacked the cup across the dining room with his tail—and gobbled down an entire package of raw ground beef.

"Well," Deandra said, wincing at the mess on the floor once the dragon's hunger was finally satiated. "I guess I don't need Dr. Caddel to tell me whether or not the dragon is an omnivore."

The dragon, glutted, lay on his back, his limbs flung wide in four directions. He snored softly.

Wendy wiped up the lemon yogurt that streaked across the wooden floor between the kitchen and the living room, while

Deandra swept up the chunks of chewed-up cucumber and carrots off the tile. She stuffed the trash into the can below the sink.

"I'll pay you back for the groceries," Deandra said, tucking a flyaway hair behind her ear. "And replace them. I can stay in a hotel or something if this is going to be too much. I—"

Wendy held up a hand. "Stop stressing. I can't tell you how happy I am that you're finally here. A baby dragon is definitely an unexpected wrinkle, but it'll be fine. Sleep on it, wait for Dr. Caddel's call, and then we'll go from there. Get some sleep. It's kind of early, but your eyes are bloodshot and I don't think it's from the wine."

Deandra nodded, her brain feeling a little floaty. The alcohol had hit her bloodstream, and now that she was a little more relaxed, a yawn seized her. She wiped the backs of her hands across her eyes.

At Wendy's insistence, Deandra got her overnight bag out of her car, then took a long hot shower. Wendy had been on dragon-sitting duty, but even after Deandra emerged from the bathroom—clean, warm, and clad in her favorite pair of pajamas—the dragon remained where she'd left him: passed out and snoring on his back.

Deandra poked the dragon a couple of times, but he didn't stir. Hefting him into her arms like a deadweight toddler, Deandra followed Wendy to the guest bedroom. It was simply furnished, with a queen-sized bed covered in a teal-green comforter and topped with a trio of fluffy white pillows. A small dresser stood against one wall, while a nightstand rested against another.

Deandra gently laid the dragon on one side of the bed. He issued a chirping snore but didn't wake. Though she'd laid him down on his side, he soon flopped onto his back. She would have thought that would be uncomfortable on his wings, but he looked perfectly content.

"Hopefully he doesn't have a sneezing fit in his sleep and burn the room down around us," Deandra said, only half joking.

Wendy managed a shaky laugh. "Thanks for keeping it weird, Dee. See you in the morning."

Deandra shut the door, turned off the light, and crawled onto the side of the bed not occupied by a dozing dragon. The bed was comfortable, the comforter smelled clean and fresh, and the pillows were soft.

She was asleep in seconds.

Chapter 10

The dragon awoke Deandra at an ungodly hour by jumping up and down on the bed like an excited kid on Christmas. She tried to ignore him, but when he switched from bouncing on the bed, to pawing at the closed bedroom door, to howling something awful, she finally got up. Instead of beelining for the kitchen, he scrambled out of the bedroom and directly toward the front door. In her sleepy haze, she opened it for him, and he tore down the stairs. It registered to her a moment later that he could have wanted out for any number of reasons—like he'd heard a cat prowling around outside and wanted to eat it.

She stumbled, barefoot, down the stairs, letting out a relieved breath when she found him in the bushes near the stairwell. The semi-embarrassed look in his eye told her that he was using the facilities, so she diverted her attention until he was done. At least he was potty trained. The lake he left in the bushes would have been decidedly unpleasant to clean up had he decided to use one of Wendy's potted plants for a toilet.

When they made it back upstairs, Wendy was awake and making coffee. She looked even more haggard than Deandra felt, evidenced by the floppy bun on the side of her head and the dark circles under her eyes, but all hopes of going back to sleep were dashed when the dragon started up his sad "I'm starving and will perish immediately" yowling. He was worse than a hungry house cat.

The only raw meat Wendy had left was a pair of still-frozen chicken breasts. Deandra had been in the process of figuring out how to defrost the chicken quickly when something tugged on her pant leg. The dragon sat by her feet, a chunk of her pajama bottoms in his mouth. When she looked down, he let go, sat up on his haunches, and held up his front paws expectantly.

"They're still frozen, buddy," she said.

He peeped.

Shrugging, she managed to get the two chicken pieces broken apart, and hesitantly held one out to him.

Holding the frozen chicken in one taloned paw, he took a massive bite out of it, chewing happily. Chicken popsicles wouldn't have been her first choice, but to each their own. He devoured the chicken in seconds, then held out a paw for the second one.

Deandra put the remaining piece on a plate, dribbled some of his liquid medication on the chicken, and then placed the plate on the floor. The taste of the slightly cherry-smelling medication didn't dampen his enjoyment of the meal. As he licked the plate clean, she raided Wendy's fridge for more vegetables. He liked broccoli but sprayed little green floret bits everywhere as he chewed. While he'd enjoyed the head of lettuce last night, cabbage was so offensive to him that he recoiled after smelling the half wedge of purple leaves. Smoke billowed from his nose.

"Okay, okay, no cabbage," she said, quickly putting it back in the fridge to get it out of his sight.

Wendy offered him a large tomato, which he ate in one bite, and then he crunched reluctantly through the two remaining carrot sticks.

Deandra wondered how much of a disaster it would be to bring the dragon with her to the grocery store so they could work their way down all the aisles. Keeping him fed was going to be a challenge.

"Don't stress," Wendy said, echoing what she'd said last night. She handed Deandra a mug of coffee. "Caffeinate, get dressed, and then we'll run some errands. I was originally going to dump you at Grandma and Grandpa's for half the day, but Heather gave me the day off after yesterday's nonsense. Some fresh air will help."

Deandra wasn't sure how, but she took her cousin's advice anyway.

First, they stopped at Mythic Pet Kitchen, a pet shop on the north end of town that sold mythical animal food and accessories. Wendy told her that the term "mythical" was a bit tongue-in-cheek in hubs, as the animals and semi-sapient beings that the mundane population would classify as mythical were very much real in places like Axia.

The only mythical animals the Pet Kitchen had for sale were seven fire newts that were kept in individual cages because, like betta fish, they couldn't be housed together, or they'd wage battles to the death. The sign hanging near the terrarium displays assured prospective pet owners that a fire newt made a great pet as long as it was the only pet in the house, there were no children present, and the pet owner was single, because fire newts were possessive.

She stared at a very pretty honey-colored newt covered in red spots, its coloring strikingly similar to her dragon's. The little creature launched off a small log and onto the side of the glass enclosure, as if it meant to attack her face. She reared back. The amphibian burst into flame, all its terrarium décor catching fire. The flames winked out soon after, though, the cage clearly outfitted with fire-resistant decorations. Satisfied that it had properly scared her, the newt darted off to hide under some foliage. Its red spots had faded in the aftermath of its attack.

One of the terrariums was surprisingly empty. She couldn't imagine anyone in their right mind wanting a fire newt as a pet. As much as the dragon occasionally expelling fireballs was terrifying, somehow these little creatures were ten times scarier. It reminded her of that gecko who had attacked her shoe and scared the bejesus out of the Clarion pixie family. Had that gecko actually been a newt? She supposed she was glad now that it had only bitten her shoe, rather than incinerating it.

She hurried away, finding the dragon and Wendy in the reptile section. Deandra smiled to herself when she found the dragon sitting dutifully by Wendy's feet as Wendy read labels off bags of dried insects to him. Now that his collar was back on, he was in dire wolf form; the trajectory of Wendy's eyeline was just above the dragon's actual head. Deandra wondered if the dragon would ever loop Wendy into his inner circle, allowing her to see his true form, regardless of whether he wore the bespelled collar.

A few minutes later, Deandra dumped her plethora of new pet supplies on the conveyer belt of the checkout counter. She'd selected a sample pack of insect varieties; a few cans of "freeze-dried meat in gravy" meant for "your meat-eating lizard companion," which came in flavors that sounded gag-inducing; and a harness and leash. Even though the dragon didn't need a leash for behavior control, the harness and leash might make the general public feel less apprehensive about seeing him trotting down the sidewalk.

The cashier eyed the dragon and then the harness. The harness had fit the dragon perfectly when Deandra had tested several out in the dog aisle. To the cashier, though, it would appear that Deandra had chosen a harness that was much too small for the dire wolf sitting beside her. The cashier said nothing, only offering Deandra a friendly smile as he handed her the bag of purchased items.

Wendy drove them toward downtown next, where Deandra had spent a good chunk of her day yesterday. Since the dragon was feeling better and was full of pent-up energy, Wendy stopped at Oracle Park, which would put them within walking distance of the biggest grocery store in town as well as a handful of restaurants. She and Deandra took a slow walk around the circular walking path that surrounded the park. The dragon scampered around the middle of the green, still wearing his harness while Deandra held onto the leash, just in case. He tripped over his own feet while he was caught in the throes of the zoomies, chased a flock of aggrieved gulls, and unsuccessfully stalked several more butterflies.

She was dangerously fond of the menace already, further evidenced by how she wanted to give a piece of her mind to at least two people at the park who glared at Deandra for letting her wild puppy run loose. One woman was pushing a stroller, and while the dragon never came anywhere near her, she acted as if the dragon were seconds from tearing her baby out of the stroller by its feet. The second was an elderly man walking a little white dog that barked nonstop in the dragon's general direction no matter their distance from one another.

When Deandra and Wendy were approached by a man in a brown uniform who pointed to a sign that stated all animals had to be leashed according to City Ordinance 3-9KM, Deandra had to call the dragon over and attach the leash to his harness. The patch on the man's breast pocket said he worked for Axia's Parks Management.

The dragon had bounded over with little fuss, his tongue lolling and chest heaving after running around for half an hour. He sat by Deandra's feet, gazing up at the man. When the man finally looked down at the "dog," the dragon sprang to his feet, licked the officer's hand, then flopped onto his back directly on the man's shoes, his yellow-and-white belly angled to the sky.

The officer melted under the dragon's charms, giving him a generous rub. The dragon chirped, but given the way both Wendy and the officer flinched slightly, it had sounded like a loud, enthusiastic bark to everyone else.

The elderly man, some hundred feet away, called out, "Have some professional dignity, Mike! That dire wolf is a danger to Charles Barksley! Those wolves are banned as pets in most hubs for a reason!"

His dog yapped a few dozen times in agreement.

Mike stood and coughed, the tips of his ears reddening. He was a pleasant-looking man in his fifties who sported a dad bod and a receding hairline. What was left of his hair was a soft brown. "Oh, don't listen to old Chester. Dire wolves are a common-enough breed in the hubs, but because they grow to such a large size, they're better suited to rural areas. They're excellent guard dogs. It's the size of the adults that makes people the most nervous. A tiny scrap of a dog like Charles Barksley could get crushed underfoot by accident—as could a small child. Heck, even a large one! But contrary to what old Chester might want you to think, dire wolves *aren't* banned in Axia. There *will* be several folks who'll be wary of the breed. Your pup is a very good boy, but it's the law to keep him on leash. One call from one busybody too many and he could be seized."

Deandra frowned. "Got it. I'm new here so I don't know all the rules yet."

"Well, it's nice to meet you ..." he said, hand out and brows raised in question.

"Deandra, but everyone calls me Dee," she said, shaking his offered hand. "And this is my cousin Wendy. I'm visiting for the weekend."

Mike nodded, then addressed Wendy. "You're January and Morris's granddaughter, right? My aunt is part of the Mermaids Club, too."

Wendy shook his hand as well.

"And who is this?" he asked, gesturing to the dragon.

Deandra had purposefully been calling him "the dragon" in her head, knowing that she was in real trouble if she gave him a name. "No name yet. I just got him. New to puppy ownership, new to Axia's rules ..."

Mike smiled good-naturedly. "The city ordinance is fairly recent, so don't feel too bad for not knowing. Someone didn't properly restrain their basilisk last summer. It got too amped up during a game of fetch and destroyed both the rose garden and a fountain. The roses were planted by the mayor's wife herself, as she was competing for some rose competition or other, and let's just say she was *very* miffed."

The dragon was still on his back, draped over the officer's shoes, but he'd somehow caught the end of his own tail and was chewing on it. Did dragons go through a teething phase?

"Just keep him on that leash and you'll be fine," Mike said, carefully scooting his feet out from under the dragon.

With a final belly scratch for the dragon and a tip of his imaginary hat, Mike strolled toward a golf cart waiting in the parking lot. A black plastic trash can with a rake sticking out of it sat in the back of the cart.

"Day two was supposed to be more relaxed," Wendy said as they kept walking around the path that edged the park. "We've only been out and about for a couple of hours and you somehow managed to get in trouble with park authorities already."

"I'll take park authorities over werecats," Deandra said, recalling how off-putting the werecat officer she'd met yesterday had been.

Her thoughts drifted to Callie. She was glad that Callie's family would be together to weather the storm of grief in the wake of Brian's passing, at least. She debated sending Callie a check-in text but chickened out.

On Wendy's recommendation, they stopped by a café with an outdoor patio and got breakfast. The dragon, tuckered out from his romp through the park, flopped over on his side by Deandra's chair and dozed off in the sun.

Wendy regaled Deandra with the details of the wild day she'd had at work yesterday, the highlight of which had been when a young witch's potion had spilled onto a table, burning a hole through it and the floor below, which had then become a tripping hazard for one of the chaperones of the field trip. The young man had unknowingly stepped in the burned hole, fallen, and badly injured his foot. They were all worried he'd broken something. While he'd howled in pain, Mr. Peabody—the sue-happy dwarf—had just so happened to return to the shop to complain yet again about his own recent injury.

"He was practically frothing at the mouth at the chaos," Wendy said. "He kept trying to convince the witch to sue, but the poor guy was in so much pain, he wasn't really listening. I was trying to help the witch get more comfortable on the floor with his foot elevated. Devon was trying to keep the witch kids in line. Heather was doing what she could to diplomatically kick Mr. Peabody out while also calling for an ambulance."

Deandra winced. "Was his foot actually broken?"

"Just a really badly sprained ankle. It blew up like a balloon," Wendy said. "He promised he won't sue."

"Small blessings."

After they finished eating, they set off again to walk to the nearby grocery store. They planned to work in shifts—one of them staying outside with the dragon while the other shopped. Deandra opted to take the first wave of dragon-sitting, as the short nap had replenished his energy reserves, and he was currently spinning in a circle while hopping like a bunny on uppers. After Wendy slipped into the store, Deandra set off with the dragon. A brisk walk would hopefully calm him down. He didn't fight the harness and leash, but being restrained would mean longer walks for Deandra, as he could wear himself out in half the time if he were allowed to run free.

They'd only made it a few blocks—stopping for a moment so the dragon could literally smell the roses—when someone called out, "Miss? Excuse me, miss?"

Deandra glanced around, finding a pair of men in brown

uniforms similar to Mike's marching toward her. She glanced left and right, finding a handful of strangers peering over at her curiously as they walked past on either side of the sidewalk, or as they stepped into or out of nearby shops. Several bore the "*Ooh, you're in trouuuble*" grimace she hadn't seen since her elementary school days, when a fellow classmate would be summoned to the principal's office.

Turning back to the quickly approaching brown-clad officers, she jabbed a thumb toward her own chest, hoping somehow it wasn't herself they were after.

"Yes, you," one of them said when he finally reached her. Both he and his partner had utility belts on, like a mundane cop would. A few black boxy devices were strapped to their belts, as well as several pouches of various sizes.

The dragon sat by her feet, smiling his dragon grin up at them. He had a tiny white daisy stuck to the end of his nose.

The second man held a black tablet in his hand. He kept his focus on that, tapping away at the screen while he spoke. His partner stood stoically beside him, hands tucked behind his back. "We've had a few complaints about your dire wolf, ma'am. I understand Ranger Michael Isaacs let you off with a warning, but we need a bit more information. First, we need the wolf's registration number." When Deandra didn't reply right away, he glanced up from the device. "Ma'am? You *do* have a registration number for him, don't you?"

He couldn't have sounded more patronizing if he'd tried.

Deandra honestly wasn't sure if lying, telling the truth, or remaining silent was the best course of action.

"Perhaps we've gotten off on the wrong foot," the other parks ranger said. He was in his mid-fifties, had very tanned, almost leathery skin that spoke to long hours in the sun, and a thick head of black hair, the richness of the shade suggesting he dyed it to mask the gray. He stuck out a large, strong hand. "I'm Dancy, and this is Vicks."

She reluctantly shook it.

"Ranger Vicks," the second man corrected.

Ranger Vicks was younger, possibly as young as twenty-five, rail-thin, with a long, angular face, and dark eyes that made Deandra think of river rocks—flat and devoid of life.

The men each towered over her by several inches.

Ranger Vicks glared down his long nose at the dragon. His bushy caterpillar eyebrows nearly met in the middle of his forehead. "Ah, it has a tag." The man reached for the dragon's collar with too much force and not enough permission, causing the dragon to shrink back. His scales turned a murky shade of brown.

Uh-oh.

She had no idea what he looked like in ticked-off dire wolf form, but as a dragon, smoke began to waft from his nostrils.

Ranger Vicks snatched his hand back, then resumed typing on his screen. "A dire wolf with fire magic," he said in disgust, as if he'd just stepped in the dragon's excrement. "Isn't this *most* interesting, Dancy?"

Dancy didn't appear particularly moved by this development either way. "Easy, boy," he said to the dragon in a calm tone, then produced a bit of jerky from one of the mystery pouches on his utility belt.

The dragon caught a whiff of the treat, and his scales instantly returned to their usual honey-orange hue. He darted forward to gently take the offered jerky. He chirped his thanks. One of Ranger Vicks's eyes twitched at the sound.

"And your name, ma'am?" Dancy asked, his hands tucked behind his back again.

"Deandra ... Dee Hendricks," she said.

Ranger Vicks tapped at his screen for several long seconds. "I'm shocked not to find you in the system, Miss Hendricks." He cocked a shaggy brow. "Are you a resident of Axia, Miss Hendricks?"

"No," she said more forcefully than she'd meant, wishing he'd stop saying her name.

"We might be a small hub, Miss Hendricks, but that doesn't mean we don't have rules just as strict—if not more so—than the larger hubs," Ranger Vicks said, finally giving his handheld device a break from his constant tapping. "Is your ... wolf ... registered elsewhere? I'll make a note of it and cross reference its registration number against the dire wolves cataloged into the main system."

Jeez, this guy was relentless. Wendy *had* said Animal Control in Axia was no joke.

The dragon nuzzled his head against Deandra's knee, and she glanced down. His large pink eyes searched hers, clearly able to tell that these two men were making her uncomfortable. She gave his head a quick scratch. He made a sound somewhere between a whimper and a howl, then leaned against her leg. "I just found him yesterday. I don't know anything about registration numbers."

Ranger Vicks leaned toward his partner. In a stage whisper, he asked, "Don't you love it when they lie, Dancy?"

The quiet, long-suffering sigh that escaped Dancy's nose was the only clue that he found Ranger Vicks as taxing as Deandra did. "Just show her the video, Vicks."

Ranger Vicks sniffed, then tapped away at his device again. "Dire wolf puppies are notoriously badly behaved and reckless. They're banned because they're dangerous."

"That's extreme and you know it. They aren't banned here," Dancy said. "People are just scared of how big they are. In adolescence, they're roughly the size of a mundane Irish wolfhound. Puppies are clumsy. Clumsy puppies that size are like a bull in a china shop—especially when they get the zoomies. But in the right environment, with the right owners, they're gentle as lambs. Gigantic lambs, to be sure, but they're not dangerous by nature."

Ranger Vicks stared at Dancy as if he'd just slapped his mother. Tightly, he said, "They are not compatible with this realm."

Dancy sensed the shift in the dragon's mood even before Deandra did, discreetly offering him another piece of jerky without alerting Ranger Vicks.

Deandra snapped, "Is *realm compatibility* an official violation of some kind or do you just personally hate dire wolves?"

Somehow Ranger Vicks appeared even more scandalized. "I operate by the book, Miss Hendricks, not my *feelings*. I would appreciate that you do not imply otherwise." He sniffed. "Based on my *knowledge* of dire wolves that I've obtained by *research*, it is *highly* unlikely that you stumbled upon this creature and bent him to your will in twenty-four hours. You're no witch. I *especially* doubt you possess animal telepathy."

Deandra was offended, even if he was right. She crossed her arms, keeping the dragon's leash loop grasped in her fist.

After a few more taps, Ranger Vicks swung the device around to face her. It was a video of her in the alley behind the art gallery. The angle of the video suggested the person who had recorded it had been on the top floor of the apartment building next door. The person had started recording well after Deandra had freed the dragon from the dumpster.

It was bizarre to watch an event she remembered vividly, but for it to be shown here in a way that wasn't wholly accurate. She learned three things while watching. First, Dr. Caddel had been right, in that regardless of what magic was in the dragon's collar, the magic of the dragon's trust overrode the glamour magic for Deandra. Second, recorded footage picked up the glamour, not the dragon's true form. Was that because the glamour magic was strong enough to trick technology? If *Deandra* had been the videographer, would the dragon have appeared in the footage as a dragon or a dire wolf?

And third, her dragon was a bit terrifying as a fire-breathing wolf. When the dragon sneezed and inadvertently shot a fireball at the dumpster, knocking it closed in the wake of the powerful blast, the video showed the wolf's shaggy gray fur turning a molten shade of reddish orange, as if the animal had become fire itself. When it opened its fiery maw, a veritable hose of fire sprayed out—like a flamethrower. Deandra's eyes widened in surprise.

The flames engulfing the wolf winked out almost immediately once the fire had been expelled from its body. The transformation was so fast, Deandra's mouth dropped open. No wonder people were fearful of these animals.

"She's a good actor," Ranger Vicks muttered to Dancy. "I'll give her that much."

Dancy didn't reply.

Ranger Vicks pulled the device away. "This behavior is simply unheard of for this breed, especially when they're this young, unless they've been trained since birth. Dire wolves are expensive—prohibitively so. This one is either unregistered because you or your associates stole it, purchased it on the black market and are using it for furthering your criminal enterprise, or both." He stared at her with his dark, dead eyes. "Which is it?"

"None of the above," she snapped. "I told you the truth. I found him in that dumpster. He was trapped in there, I freed him, and he bonded to me out of gratitude."

Even Dancy scoffed at that.

"Where were you yesterday afternoon around three p.m.?" Ranger Vicks asked.

Deandra cocked her head, thrown off by the sudden change in topic. She worked her way back through her day. The time stamp on the video had placed her in the alley around four thirty. At three, she would have been heading to Hogarth's Hoagies. She said as much, mentioning her impromptu detour to investigate why a gaggle of people loitered outside Large & Wide.

"The canine wasn't with you while you just so happened to be attending the grand opening of an establishment that doesn't cater to your demographic?" Ranger Vicks asked.

"Yes," Deandra said through gritted teeth. "*The canine* couldn't have been with me because I didn't even know he existed at that point."

"Hmm," Ranger Vicks said, tapping his chin with a long finger. "So there you were, standing in the crowd of a grand opening where you'd be viewed by a large number of people. My, it is convenient such an event was happening so close to the site of a fire, isn't it? A fire that burned so hot, it defies explanation. It's so curious that just across the street, a rare fire-breathing dire wolf was hidden—"

"*Trapped*," Deandra said.

Ranger Vicks glared at her, whether for the interruption or for her continued "lies," she couldn't be sure.

"All right. Enough, Vicks." Dancy reached into yet another pouch on his utility belt and produced a sheet of folded paper, then handed it to Deandra. Ranger Vicks started to protest, but Dancy held up his free hand, effectively shutting Ranger Vicks up.

Deandra took the paper with shaking hands and unfolded it. An official-looking seal—identical to the ones on Vicks' and Dancy's uniforms—graced the upper right corner. While there was a bit of confusing jargon interspersed in the page-long document, she got the gist: Her unregistered dire wolf was under suspicion of committing arson. He was to be seized by Axian Parks Management effective immediately until he could be cleared of the crime. If he were found innocent, he would be returned to her, only if she were able to produce the proper registration paperwork that declared him as hers.

Her stomach bottomed out. "How can an *animal* be accused of a crime? He doesn't have the mental capacity necessary to execute a plan to commit arson."

The dragon let out a sound that sounded very much like a harumph.

She shot him a glare that said "*You're not helping our cause by acting as if you can understand me.*"

He bunched up his muzzle, as if to say, "*Figure out a way to plead our case without insulting my intelligence.*"

Ranger Vicks offered his own noise of frustration. "Clearly you're not up to date on your ordinances."

Deandra resisted the urge to say, "No normal person is."

"Dire wolves fall under Animal Control Ordinance 14-2Z8. You *should* know that several mythical animals—because of the level of magic and intelligence attained by adulthood—are treated as sapient."

"What, like a juvenile being tried as an adult?" Deandra asked.

Dancy nodded. "Exactly."

"But he's a *baby*," Deandra tried. "It would be like punishing a toddler for *possibly* becoming a criminal decades from now."

"Rule are rules," Ranger Vicks said.

She clenched her jaw, looking down at the dragon. He stared up at her, his eyes wide and expression open and trusting. Her gaze snapped back to the two men. She flapped the paper. "You can't do this."

"We can and we will." Ranger Vicks had stowed away his device at some point while she'd read the letter. He held out a hand now. "We'll take him from here. There's a contact number at the bottom of your letter. You can call about his status on Monday."

"*Monday*?"

"Our investigative office is closed for the weekend," Ranger Vicks said.

Deandra took an involuntary step back. "So, what, he's just going to be in a *cage* all weekend?"

In a tone laced with more sympathy than Ranger Vicks had in his entire body, Dancy said, "He'll be taken to a facility right in town that caters to mythical animals. We have one of the better facilities in the entire hub system. He'll be well cared for there. I personally volunteer at the facility on Saturdays and will check in on him myself."

Tears welled in Deandra's eyes. Had freeing the dragon from the dumpster somehow resulted in a worse fate than if she'd just left him there?

The dragon tugged on her pant leg, and she glanced down to find a mouthful of her jeans hem in his mouth. He was on his stomach, glancing up at her. When their eyes met, he immediately rolled over, showing her his yellow-and-white ribbed belly. She choked out a laugh, squatting to give his chest a scratch. He chirped happily in response. He knew she was distressed and wanted to make her feel better, which somehow only made her feel worse.

"I promise he'll be okay," Dancy said.

"Until we nail the beast for arson, anyway ..."

The glare she shot Ranger Vicks was so venomous, he visibly swallowed and slightly shied away. She resisted the urge to sucker punch him in the family jewels.

Returning her attention to her dragon who remained on his back, that tiny daisy still affixed to his nose, she said, "Buddy, I'm gonna need you to go with these two, okay? I'll come get you on Monday."

She didn't think the dragon could understand everything she said, but he understood part of it. He scrambled to his feet, resting his chin on one of her bent knees. She gave his forehead a scratch.

Without looking at either of the men, she thrust the leash's loop toward Dancy. He took it and began to walk away, dragging the dragon a few inches. The dragon glanced between Dancy and Deandra, then grunted, flattening himself to the ground. Dancy tugged. The dragon hunkered down further, offering Deandra a wide-eyed look of panic that made her throat tighten.

When several more tugs yielded no results, Ranger Vicks lunged for the dragon. The dragon, so startled by Vicks's quick approach, flopped onto his side. Deandra thought Vicks meant to scoop the dragon off the ground. She saw the glint of metal a second too late. A needle plunged into the underside of one of the dragon's front legs before he or Deandra could react. The dragon cried in pain or confusion, and then the glittery light in his eyes went out. His lids slid shut.

Deandra screamed, lunging for Vicks, but Dancy got to her first, wrapping his arms around her from behind and hauling her backward. She kicked and screamed, watching in horror as Vicks scooped the limp body of the dragon off the ground and flung him over his shoulder like a sack of flour.

"*Deandra,*" Dancy hissed in her ear. She thrashed in his grasp. "He's alive, just knocked out."

Deandra slowly started to calm down, tears streaming down her cheeks as she watched Vicks cart her dragon away. "You said he'd be okay," she choked out. "You said you'd look after him."

"I will," he said, lightening his hold on her by a fraction. "I swear he's fine. I promise to be there when he wakes up, and I'll feed him jerky until he can't eat another piece."

Another choked sob slipped out. "That Vicks guy is the worst."

Dancy chuckled, finally letting her go. She spun to face him, wanting nothing more than to claw his eyes out, even if she did believe he'd do what he could to keep the dragon safe.

"He's a nightmare," Dancy said. "Got transferred here from a larger city a few months ago. I swear they sent him here because he's universally despised. Him hearing about a dire wolf puppy being found on the same day as a potential arson case nearly gave the guy apoplexy, he was so excited. Stuff like this doesn't happen in small towns often.

"Everything he's doing is by the book—aside from being a royal jerk about it. If he hadn't been here, I would have cut you some slack, for what it's worth. I can't say I know what's going on here, but you don't strike me as a criminal mastermind."

She sniffed. "Isn't that what all criminal masterminds want you to think?"

"I suppose so." Sighing, he added, "Just play by the rules as much as you can, and that'll keep Vicks from doing anything too drastic. He's a louse, but he's also a stickler for the law. Your boy will be safe until Monday."

Yeah, but what about *after* Monday? Deandra didn't even know the ins and outs of the legal system in the *mundane* world. She was more than clueless about the one in Axia.

"Get a move on, Dancy!" Vicks called from up the street. Deandra could barely make him out, but his voice carried. "We have paperwork to do!"

Dancy sighed. "He actually *likes* paperwork." He took several steps back. "Call the number on that letter tomorrow afternoon and ask for me. I'll give you an update. Try to have a nice weekend, Miss Hendricks."

When Dancy and Vicks disappeared around the corner, taking her dragon with them, her knees gave out and she sank to the cement.

Her dragon was gone.

Chapter 11

Deandra didn't know how long she'd been sitting on the sidewalk before Wendy found her. From the few snatches of conversation her shut-down brain could process, someone had witnessed Deandra's altercation on the street, had known Deandra's connection to Wendy, and had gone into the grocery store to find her. When Wendy plopped down in front of Deandra, she didn't have any bags with her. Deandra imagined a shopping cart full of food abandoned in an aisle.

Deandra couldn't seem to tear her gaze away from a disc of sunbaked, hardened gum on the sidewalk. The dragon's cry of pain as the needle sank into his underside replayed in her head. She kept seeing the glitter of his gemstone eyes go as flat and lifeless as Ranger Vicks's river-rock ones. She clenched her jaw. Was it too late to go after that guy? She pictured headbutting him in his giant nose.

Wendy gently placed a hand on Deandra's arm. "Hey. Can you at least look at me? Someone said you got in a fist fight with a parking attendant? I really can't leave you unsupervised, can I?"

Deandra choked out a laugh, glancing up with watery eyes. Wendy was a smudgy blur before her.

"Oh, Dee ... what the heck happened?"

Deandra's focus slid back to the petrified gum on the ground, but she recounted the event. Staring at a spot on the cement made it easier to concentrate, and it lessened her chances of bursting into tears.

"You're lucky I wasn't here," Wendy said when Deandra was done. "Then you'd also have to deal with me being arrested for homicide. Who does this Vicks guy think he is! That dra—wolf isn't even capable of hurting butterflies, let alone committing arson."

At the memory of her dragon unsuccessfully catching butterflies, Deandra *did* burst into tears.

"*Oh boy*," Wendy said. "All right. Up you go."

When Deandra had calmed down, she found herself sitting in a quaint restaurant with a giant salad on the table in front of her. She couldn't recall anything about her trip here. The salad was a Cobb piled high with fixings. A little bowl of peppercorn ranch sat beside a fork and napkin. Her stomach rumbled at the sight. She glanced up at her cousin, who sat before her own equally huge Caesar salad.

"Thanks," Deandra managed.

"Eat," Wendy said. "We'll strategize once you've plowed through at least half of that."

Deandra wanted to protest, but when her stomach growled again, she complied. The salad was gone in record time, and she *did* feel better. If she'd been with anyone else, except for her parents, she probably would have been a little embarrassed about sobbing openly. But Wendy had been there for middle and high school heartbreaks, friendship betrayals, and soul-destroying bosses. Wendy had seen enough over the years to know how to help Deandra cope, and vice versa.

Deandra asked, "So what exactly do we need to strategize? Breaking him out of animal prison?"

"How to figure out who really burned down that building," Wendy said, as if it were obvious.

"We're not exactly detectives," Deandra said.

"No, we're not, but Parks Management is serious business. A

friend has a registered pygmy phoenix, but the registration tag had fallen off at some point, and she hadn't realized it. A ranger—which, after your experience, makes me think it was that Vicks guy—stopped her during a walk and asked for proof of registration. It wasn't on the phoenix's collar, and my friend had left her phone in her car so she couldn't find the digital copy of the ID. The guy wrote her a ticket on the spot. Two hundred dollars," Wendy said.

"Jeez!"

"Dire wolves have the reputation of mundane Rottweilers, pit bulls, and Doberman pinschers. Combined. They very well could be gentle giants, but most people can't seem to get past the giant part. But, at the same time, they really *are* wild menaces as puppies. If there's a *hint* that they think the ...wolf ... is even a little dangerous, they'll find a way to keep him. And who knows what could happen to him then."

Deandra had to wonder all over again why the dragon's owner had chosen a dire wolf for a disguise. If they'd chosen something benign, like a large floppy-eared rabbit wearing a straw hat, things would be different right now. Though she supposed the choice had been at least partly due to the owner needing to select a mythical animal that could believably breathe fire. A fire-breathing rabbit hopping through the park probably would have given old Chester *and* Charles Barksley palpitations.

Deandra frowned. "Even worse? His actual nature is too friendly and trusting. All I did was free him from that dumpster, and he offered me his trust on a platter. I'm not someone who would exploit him, but what if he reveals himself to the wrong person while he's in Park Management's hands?"

"Exactly," Wendy said. "I have no doubt that Vicks is searching for some way to connect you to the black-market scene. Solving a big case could get him transferred back to a larger hub. We have the weekend to figure out what actually happened, or you *both* could end up in serious trouble."

Ranger Vicks *did* seem to have it out for Deandra as much as he did for the dragon. If the blowhard could take them both down, his ego would be even more out of control. He'd relish the promise of all the accompanying paperwork.

Resolve made her sit up straighter. "Where do we start?"

Wendy grinned.

They decided to head to the scene of the crime first. Deandra wished now that she'd gotten Edna or Bea's phone numbers—those two probably had the scoop on most of this by now. Wendy was assigned to the drugstore to strike up conversations with any of the clerks who might have seen or heard something odd yesterday before the fire broke out.

Deandra had originally wanted to knock on the doors of everyone who lived in an upstairs unit of the apartment complex that had a view of the art gallery's parking lot, if only to tear them a new one. There couldn't have been more than two or three viable culprits. But she figured if the resident was enough of a busybody to send that video to Parks Management, confronting them likely wouldn't go well. All she needed was someone to report her to the police or Ranger Vicks, and she'd be in even more hot water.

Instead, she would visit the art gallery, which was only open Friday through Sunday, and casually attempt to find out if they had security cameras. If they did, perhaps there'd be footage of how the dragon had gotten into the dumpster in the first place. If she could prove the dragon had been trapped well before the start of the fire, it would get them both off the hook.

Wendy parked on a residential street a block away from the art gallery. She claimed that if they appeared to "just be in the neighborhood," people would be more likely to talk to them. Deandra thought Wendy watched too many crime dramas.

They strolled up Purl Way, this section of the block flanked by apartments. The tall trees on Deandra's right were beautiful, but their canopy of leaves ensured anyone inside the units on the second or third floor likely wouldn't have been able to see what had happened across the street yesterday. Would the police question people up and down the street anyway, hoping someone had seen or heard something of note?

She and Wendy parted ways on the corner of Purl and McClaren, with Wendy setting off across the crosswalk. Deandra had donned a blouse and skirt to help pull off the lie that she was an art-gallery-perusing kind of lady. But as she turned to face the building, with its sleek floors and minimal décor to help showcase the artwork housed inside, she felt wholly underdressed.

Instead of walking inside right away, she rounded the corner and headed for the alley. She wanted to get a sense of how many cars were in the lot on a day the gallery was open. When she reached the back lot, though, it wasn't the number of cars that caught her attention, but the sight of the dumpster. Or, rather, the *lack* of a dumpster. A quick perimeter check of the lot told her what she'd immediately noticed: The dumpster was gone.

Brow furrowed, she scanned the eaves of the building, searching for cameras. She found the mounts for two—one above a back door that faced the parking lot, and one in the corner of the roof at the mouth of the alley—but the cameras themselves were missing.

Deandra made her way back to the front of the building. She shook out her hands and gave herself a little pep talk as she stood outside the entrance. She was a barista at a hoity-toity coffeehouse. She got berated on a daily basis over beverages. She hadn't cried on the job in ages. She was tough as steel when she needed to be. Being in Axia had thrown her off her game, sure, but she could get her mojo back.

Taking a calming breath, Deandra pushed open one of the tinted glass doors. A few people stood clustered around a painting in a back corner, but they were too engrossed in their hushed conversation to notice her arrival.

The décor of the gallery was dark—shiny dark floors, slate-gray paint on the walls, and small cone fixtures hanging from the ceiling to offer soft mood lighting. Glass vases and sculptures stood resolute on thin black marble stands. Photographs and oil paintings in elaborate, borderline-gaudy frames hung on walls with swaths of empty wall space between them. The artwork had small white placards with black text positioned on walls or on the fronts of stands. Soft, lilting classical music wafted down from speakers embedded in the ceiling.

"May I help you?" came a smooth, elegant voice.

Deandra tore her gaze away from the speakers and found a posh woman standing a few feet away. She wore a cream-colored cashmere top, a long black pencil skirt, and strappy black heels. Deandra couldn't be sure if her eyes or the dim lighting were playing tricks on her, but the woman's skin had a blue tint to it. Her hair, which she'd pulled into a sophisticated bun held in place by a pair of black chopsticks, was a deep violet. Small tusks protruded from her upper lip. How did those things not give her a lisp?

"Ma'am?" the woman tried again.

"Hi!" Deandra said a bit too loudly, her voice seeming to echo in this fancy, nearly deserted place. She coughed delicately. "Sorry. Hello." She desperately tried to remember the cover story she and Wendy had come up with, but her mind had gone blank. "I uhh … am here visiting from another hub. I'm … an assistant to an art teacher … and uhh … she tasked me with finding art galleries that allow field trips. The students are seniors in high school, and all have aspirations to study art."

"Oh, how wonderful," the woman said, unfazed by Deandra's fumbled introduction. "We don't cater to field trips, per se, but we hold a student-featured art fair in the parking lot out back once a month. Young artists are encouraged to bring their art, no matter the medium. A few of our local artists attend and offer advice to the budding artists. It's a beautiful, collaborative event, and attendance and participation are free. You just missed our last one, actually. It was on Monday. We finally got the lot cleaned up Wednesday morning, so it's empty now, but I have a few photos I can show you."

Deandra sidled up to the woman as she proudly swiped through a series of photographs on her phone, pointing out some of the more promising students. Deandra tried her hardest to appear interested. In several of the photographs, Deandra spotted the dumpster just where she'd last seen it—wedged into the back corner. A series of tables were pushed against one of the cinder-block walls that ringed the lot, the tabletops piled with metal catering dishes. One photo showed two people in the background chatting over plates of food. If Deandra had to guess, she would say it was Chinese cuisine. During her dragon rescue mission, she'd accidentally torn open a trash bag full of discarded noodles and vegetables.

"I'm sorry to have missed the event," Deandra said when the woman finally pocketed her phone. "Sounds like the timing was good for you, though. It would have been chaos if the fire had broken out during it."

"Oh, goodness, I know," the woman said. "When you first got here, I thought the police had come back. They'd left all of fifteen minutes before you arrived. They took the entire dumpster for some reason, downloaded footage from our security cameras from last week, *and* took the cameras themselves, too."

Deandra deflated a bit. If the police had already been here, she thought it very unlikely this woman would share the footage with her simply because she asked—especially when she already knew Deandra was here for a completely unrelated reason.

"They won't find much, I'm afraid," the woman said, gazing out the floor-to-ceiling tinted windows. Deandra turned to look, too. From the front door of the gallery, there was a clear view of a blackened foundation wedged between the drugstore and the apartment complex.

"They won't?" Deandra asked. "None of your cameras faced the street?"

"There was one positioned above the front door, and a couple out back facing the parking lot, but sometime between Wednesday night and today, all of the cameras were destroyed."

Deandra cocked her head. "Like in pieces on the ground?"

The woman kept gazing across the street, but her eyes seemed unfocused, like her mind was elsewhere. "They were still mounted on the walls, but their glass faces were pointed to the sky and smashed. The wires were all severed, too. It's awful to think that the fire was so premeditated that someone scoped out my gallery and destroyed the cameras beforehand. Because it *was* premeditated; that's what the police said. I've always felt safe in Axia, but after this week, I feel a bit violated. Is that terrible of me?" she asked, finally tearing her gaze away from the destroyed building and staring pointedly at Deandra. "A man died in that fire, and here I am worked up about some ruined security equipment."

"I don't think that's terrible. This place is your livelihood, and art is your passion," Deandra said. "Most people don't have many run-ins with police investigating a crime. That's enough to rattle anyone."

The woman huffed out a breath that whistled a bit as the air whizzed past her tusks. "Thank you. Sorry about the overshare. I'm sure this doesn't make you want to tell your boss about us. But I swear until this week, I never felt unsafe here."

Deandra felt awful about lying to the woman now, wishing she really *did* work for an art teacher. "Do you have a card I can pass along?"

The woman smiled brightly, then bustled off to fetch one.

Once it was tucked away in Deandra's purse, she bid the woman goodbye and slipped back out the door.

As Deandra stood on the corner, she eyed the drugstore across the street, hoping Wendy had fared better than she had. Deandra didn't know why they thought they could solve the mystery of the fire faster than the police. *Of course* they'd already visited the art gallery ...

Deandra was also quickly learning that law enforcement in Axia worked much faster than in the mundane world. The hub system clearly had its own rules and laws. In twenty-four hours, what essentially was a warrant had been issued for her dragon. She also remembered how Wendy said the Welcome Center would be informed of Deandra's arrival. Had her travel talisman been tracked or cataloged in some way? Had authorities been able to cross-reference her image on that video sent to Parks Management and the Welcome Center's records to find her? Deandra's full name had been on that official letter.

Axia's law enforcement was efficient and had magic among its resources. She had barely started her supposed investigation, and she was already outmatched.

Perhaps she had to tackle the problem from another angle. The police and werecats were looking for the arsonist. Deandra and Wendy were searching for someone else—the dragon's previous owner. Two separate people, most likely, whose actions were possibly being erroneously intertwined. Deandra just had to unravel them.

Her phone vibrated in her back pocket. The number on the screen wasn't one she recognized.

Walking down the side of the art gallery, back toward the alley, she answered the call. What if this was Parks Management calling to inform her that they knew the dire wolf was actually a dragon and that she would be arrested posthaste for participating in mythical animal smuggling? "Hello?"

"Deandra? This is Dr. Caddel."

"Oh! Hi."

He chuckled. "Everything okay? You sound ... flustered."

"In Axia, flustered is my default." It hit her then why he was calling her. "Parks Management took him from me," she blurted.

His tone shifted on a dime, flipping from collected professionalism to friendly concern. "What? When? Did they find out he's actually a—"

"No. They don't know. Yet. I mean, I don't think so. All someone would have to do is take that collar off, though." She halted on the sidewalk. Somehow in all her rehashing of "what-ifs," she'd forgotten how easily his true identity could be revealed simply by the removal of that collar. The glamour kept the collar mostly hidden under shaggy fur, but what if someone at the facility decided to give him a bath?

"Deandra? Dee ..."

"Yeah, sorry," she said, shaking herself out of her thoughts, then told Dr. Caddel what had happened a few hours ago.

Dr. Caddel groaned. "Vicks hasn't been here long, but he's crossed paths with everyone in Axia who has any connection to animals or the parks. Real piece of work, that guy." A door opened and closed on his end of the line. "I'll tell you what ... I'll stop by the facility myself today and drop off a new bottle of the ... wolf's medication. I'll let them know he's a patient of mine and that the collar has a magical suppressant in the runes. I'll tell them taking it off would actually make the wolf *more* dangerous."

In the chaos of everything, she'd forgotten all about the dragon's cold meds. "Wow. Thanks. That's very nice of you."

"Happy to do it," he said. "I only spent a short window of time with you, but I know a bond when I see one. I'm sorry Vicks wasn't more tactful."

An image of the dragon's giant sorrowful eyes flashed in her mind again. She sniffed, her throat tight. "Thanks, Dr. Caddel."

"You can call me Cruz. I feel like we're part of a secret club now. Secret clubs aren't formal. Not the fun ones anyway," he said. "Now, the reason I called ... I did a little research, and I believe your wolf comes from the Ruber clan. As you no doubt already learned, they're omnivores. They're loyal, smart, and gregarious. As a species, 'wolves' are leaders back in the fae realm, but the Ruber clan often held positions of protection, rather than leadership. Their loyalty meant you could rely on them to fight to the death for you, but it also meant if that trust was violated, they'd hunt you to the ends of the realm."

She hoped that when the dragon awoke from whatever knock-out juice Vicks had pumped into him he didn't think she'd betrayed his trust. She hoped he knew she'd do whatever she could to get him out of this mess.

"I'm ... uh ... a bit of a nerd when it comes to mythical animals," Dr. Caddel—*Cruz*—said. "I won't bore you-slash-embarrass myself with the details of that, but let's just say I'm part of several groups online dedicated to them. I've put out feelers for anyone missing a dire wolf wearing a collar marked up with runes. I figure anyone who is *actually* missing him would know the glamour that everyone else sees. It'll be easy enough to weed out people making a false claim on him if they don't know the collar's color or what the runes say."

She perked up at that. "Does that mean *you* know what the runes say?"

Deandra wondered if he'd taken pictures of the runes during one of the many times she'd zoned out during the appointment.

"Sort of," he said. "I've got a contact in Luma who's skilled at glamours. One of the best glamourers around, honestly. He's also well connected in Luma, so I know he'll be able to find the exact translation better than I could."

"Is it ... safe to tell other people about the wolf?" she asked, suddenly feeling a bit apprehensive about Cruz knowing the dragon's secret identity.

Wendy had said Luma was the biggest hub in California. There were doubtless dozens upon dozens of people who would resort to something shady to get their mitts on a thought-to-be-extinct dragon. Cruz himself had mentioned a black-market scene that would lose its mind at the promise of a dragon. Priceless, he'd said.

"The great thing about my contact is that he doesn't ask questions," Cruz said. "As long as he gets paid, he won't care why I'm asking about the runes. The wolf's secret is safe with me. I promise. And the guy owes me a favor, too, so I won't have to mortgage my house to pay for the info."

"Is it safe to assume that, favor or no, you'd still have paid for this information because of the aforementioned embarrassing level of nerdiness over mythical animals?" Deandra asked.

She could hear the smile in his voice when he said, "That's a very astute assumption."

"Well, thank you. Again."

"You bet," he said. "So the rough translation so far is as we expected—a glamour spell that masks the wearer's true form. My contact says the magic in the collar will weaken more and more every time the collar is removed. Once the magic is depleted, the runes will need to be redrawn to reinforce them. He said the craftsmanship and complexity of the runes suggests a sorcerer or someone who went through quite a few years of schooling bespelled the collar."

Whether the creator of the collar and the owner of the dragon were the same person was still a mystery.

"Are there many sorcerers in Axia?" she asked.

"Not that I know of," Cruz said. "In the hierarchy of magic users, sorcerers are at the top. In very basic terms, the amount of schooling you need to get certified as a sorcerer is extensive. Like med school on steroids. Not many people make it to the end of the certification program, so those who do end up as part of a very elite group of magic users with a very niche skill set. The vast majority of them join the magical government—the Collective—and snag jobs in the bigger hubs. Being a sorcerer in a tiny place like Axia would be the epitome of slumming it. The Collective sorcerers here are more or less retired."

Deandra mulled that over. If it *had* been a sorcerer who'd brought the dragon into Axia, could the sorcerer have snuck in without the ruling trio of Collective sorcerers finding out? Surely most people didn't have to check in with the Welcome Center the way Deandra had. Was telepad travel monitored the same way the Welcome Center was?

She supposed it could have been one of Axia's own Collective members who had brought the dragon to this small town. If that were the case, though, why would the ruling sorcerer need to hide or dispose of the dragon in a dumpster? They'd have better resources to keep or get rid of the little guy.

It seemed too careless for one of them to have *lost* the dragon, when they'd know how rare the animal was. It would also stand to reason that the Collective would have informed Parks Management if the personal pet of a government member had gone missing. Ranger Vicks seemed like the type who would jump at the chance to get in the good graces of his bosses. And yet, he'd clearly thought the dragon was the one responsible for the fire. He was trying to get a dangerous animal off the street, nothing more.

So had a sorcerer from another hub sneaked into Axia to stash the dragon? No one, at least from what Cruz had told her, would suspect a dragon *or* a non-Collective sorcerer to be in the sleepy little town of Axia.

But it still didn't explain why the dragon had been in a dumpster. It wasn't the most inspired of hiding places, and it was a truly cruel and crude way to get rid of the animal if the owner had changed their mind about keeping him.

"Sounds like that brain of yours is working overtime," Cruz said.

Deandra flushed. She'd almost forgotten he was still on the phone. "I keep coming back to the rarity of dra—wolves," she said, making the same clumsy save Wendy had earlier. "Someone went to great lengths to either make or commission that collar. Whoever had the wolf before me knew his identity was important to keep hidden. So what happened?"

"That's the other reason for my call," he said. "Preliminary blood work shows he had Quowlaxliquin in his system. I purposefully searched for sleeping agents because I had all the same thoughts you did. The traces of Quowlaxliquin were faint, but they were there. Someone drugged him before putting him in that dumpster."

Deandra frowned, recalling the way the dragon had whimpered when Vicks had jabbed a needle under his foreleg. Someone else had done the same thing to the dragon just days before. No wonder he'd happily thrown his trust at the first friendly face he'd seen when he'd woken up. "Poor guy ..."

"It's one of the stronger types of sleeping agents, too. He could have been knocked out for days. Typically, Quowlaxliquin is used in my office for the larger mythical beings. I even had a hospital contact me recently, asking for an extra supply of it to help them knock out a yeti before surgery. They needed three bottles of the stuff to get her unconscious."

There was a lot to unpack there, so Deandra ignored most of it.

A truck rumbled past her, and she stilled abruptly. "What day is trash pickup here? Does it vary across the town?"

The question clearly threw Cruz off initially, given his confused sputtering. "Uhh ... the town ... um ... is broken into quadrants. Trash day is Tuesday for quadrant one, Wednesday for quadrant two, etcetera."

"What quadrant is the art gallery in?" she asked, eyeing the side of the red brick building she still loitered beside.

"One second ..." he said, followed by the sound of rustling on the other end. "The gallery is in ... quadrant four. Pick-up is on Friday."

Deandra had found the dragon on Thursday afternoon. The gallery was only open Friday to Sunday, so the trash in the dumpster was what the gallery had generated over the *previous* weekend. The posh tusked woman had mentioned the student art fair had been on Monday, and they hadn't finished the last of the cleanup until sometime on Wednesday. Deandra recalled the trash bag she'd thrown aside that had been surprisingly light—a crepe-paper streamer sticking out of the top of the bag, like a tongue.

The art gallery owner had guessed that the destruction of the security cameras had occurred between Wednesday afternoon and Thursday morning—yesterday. But if the arsonist and dragon owner truly *were* two separate people, the dragon owner might not have known the cameras existed at all. They could have crept behind the gallery to dispose of the dragon a day or two before the arsonist had even begun their reign of destruction. There was a chance the footage the police had just seized would clear her *and* the dragon of suspicion, since the dragon had been unconscious at the time of the fire, and Deandra had only been in town for a few hours.

The chances of someone being spotted depositing an unconscious animal into the trash would lessen considerably on a weekday, since the parking lot would be empty of cars while the gallery was closed. Currently, there were at least five cars parked behind the building. Deandra guessed they saw more activity on Saturday and Sunday.

Most likely, the dragon had been placed inside the dumpster sometime between Sunday night after the gallery closed, and early Monday morning, before people started to arrive to set up for the art fair. Had the dragon owner hoped the trash service would pick him up on Friday, or had they planned to be back before then to retrieve him, and something had prevented the owner from returning?

If Cruz was right, and the dragon had been knocked out for several days, that was further proof he couldn't have been the one to burn the building down. She had to hope the cameras had caught the dragon owner making the deposit earlier in the week, but she couldn't rely on that possibility.

"Is Qual ... Quil ... is the stuff easy to get?" Deandra asked.

"No," Cruz said, chuckling. "It's a controlled substance, especially since there are some alchemical ingredients. Every bottle that's going to hit the market has to be tested to be sure the alchemical quantities are within guidelines. A too-concentrated batch could easily be fatal. Without a special certification through the medical or veterinary board, it's very hard to get a hold of the stuff. Doesn't mean someone couldn't steal some, though."

"Have you checked your stash lately?" she asked.

"The moment I found traces of it in the wolf's system. All bottles are accounted for. I'm also the only vet in town with the proper certification," Cruz said. "I already called the hospital to ask them the same thing. They had to put in a rush order to a hub in Michigan just last week because they were the only ones who currently had it in stock."

Which also implied that the Quowlaxliquin, along with the dragon and his possible sorcerer handler, had come from outside Axia. But to what end?

Her head was starting to hurt. "Thank you for your help with all this."

"You said that already."

"It bears repeating."

"Well, you're welcome again. I'll let you know if I learn anything from Parks Management when I stop by there later."

After disconnecting the call, Deandra headed back up the street to track down Wendy, but she was already emerging from the drugstore. A man loitered in the entrance of the store, leaning against the doorjamb, watching Wendy retreat.

Deandra met her at the corner, eyeing the man over Wendy's shoulder. "Any luck?"

Wendy coughed awkwardly. "Depends on the kind of luck you mean. I might have a date next weekend."

Deandra laughed, offering the young man a wave. He grinned, waving back. "He's cute."

Wendy nodded, her cheeks pink, but she didn't turn around. "I'm clearly a very bad detective if, instead of sleuthing, I was flirting."

Looping her arm through her cousin's, Deandra steered them down the sidewalk back in the direction of Wendy's car. She filled Wendy in on what she'd found out. By the end of her story, Wendy was also convinced they needed a new strategy.

"What we need even more than that is an Extra Sensory Pastry," Wendy said.

Deandra wasn't sure that last addition was all that vital to the plan, but who was she to say no to a perfectly crafted pastry?

Chapter 12

Extra Sensory Pastry was packed. Wendy and Deandra had to get in a line that snaked around most of the shop. Though it took fifteen minutes before they reached the counter, they hadn't come up with any new ideas while they waited. Deandra had to hope that Cruz and Dancy were both doing what they could to keep her dragon safe. With any luck, the dragon would remain knocked out for most of the day, minimizing the chances he'd lash out due to fear or anger and blow his cover.

When they reached an exhausted-looking Sebastian—both his sister and a pair of young workers bustling around behind him—he managed a smile for them.

A flash of blue flickered in his eyes as he focused on Deandra, and he muttered, "Oh, interesting," just before his expression went vaguely slack-jawed. "You are still searching for something here in Axia, but what you seek is different than when you were here yesterday. You both are puzzled by the same thing this time. Deandra is more emotionally connected to this particular puzzle, while Wendy is intrigued on Deandra's behalf. You'll both get Clear-Sighted Éclairs, and Serenity shots for your drinks."

As Deandra paid for her order, she felt quietly disappointed that this order was identical to the last, especially when she wasn't sure if the Clear-Sighted Éclair had *actually* affected her yesterday. Maybe the "tinctures" Isabel added to the food had a compounding effect if they were consumed multiple days in a row.

A small table by a window cleared out just as Deandra and Wendy started their search for a place to sit. Wendy happily rambled about the man she'd just met at the drugstore. He was a graduate student at a university in a hub in Massachusetts or Maine—Wendy couldn't remember—but he took a series of telepad rides home most weekends to help his parents at their store. It would be a long-distance situation if he and Wendy ended up liking each other, but since telepad travel was lightning fast, it took a lot of stress out of the whole thing. Wendy kept chatting away as their food and drinks arrived.

The Serenity gently nudged Deandra into relaxing, but the Clear-Sighted Éclair, as far as she could tell, still wasn't doing anything. She wondered if Sebastian and his sister were swindlers, boasting about their abilities but were actually much less skilled than they claimed. Surely the mundane power of suggestion would still work in places like Axia.

Deandra excused herself to use the restroom, ending up in yet another line. This one, thankfully, was much shorter than the one currently snaking out the door of the café. Deandra stared at the back of the woman's head in front of her. Her hair was in two black braids, the part separating her hair into two equal chunks forming a zigzag pattern instead of a straight line.

The restroom door opened, letting out one lady while another one stepped inside. As the woman walked past Deandra, something flapped in her peripheral vision. The wall space just outside the women's restroom had a large cork board directly across from it. "Community Board" was spelled out across the top of the wooden frame with individually cut-out letters, each one in a cheerful pastel color. The board was covered in flyers with pull tabs on the bottom —advertising services for everything from lawn care to dog walking.

Business cards were tacked haphazardly all over the board for things like plumbing, roof repair, custom potion making, lute lessons, and pest eradication—for rats, insects, *and* unruly ghosts.

Deandra was about to turn away from the board when part of a job posting snagged her attention. A feeling she could only describe as a compulsion came over her, and she stepped out of line to get a closer look. Lifting the edge of a poster for an indie rock band playing next weekend in a bowling alley at a retirement home for shifters, Deandra got the full view of the job listing.

Now hiring part-time cashiers at Axia's first Large & Wide!

Though the store won't be opening its doors until the first of July, interviews and training are well underway! We're excited to bring this niche clothing boutique to Axia that will cater to the larger-statured residents of town and hubs across the nation! It's not a requirement to be an orc, troll, ogre, or draken, but experience in the elephantine clothing industry is preferred. Please call the number below and ask for Viola Poppler to set up an interview.

At the sight of the store's name, an image of Callie's face popped up in Deandra's head. Deandra still hadn't sent her friend a check-in text. She couldn't imagine that a "How you holding up?" message from someone she'd met once would offer much comfort a mere day after her uncle had passed away in a fire. A *suspicious* fire in a building that had been abandoned for six months, if Edna and Bea were to be believed.

If there was going to be a funeral or wake for Brian, maybe Deandra could return to Axia to attend. Perhaps Viola Poppler could give that information to Deandra without her needing to bug Callie about such details so soon.

Deandra noted that the faint tendrils of compulsion still kept her standing in front of the job flyer. Was the Clear-Sighted Éclair working its magic on her after all?

"Are you still in line, or ...?"

Deandra turned to find a woman standing outside the bathroom. "Go ahead. I have to make a call."

The woman muttered a cheesy joke about needing to answer *nature's* call, then ducked inside.

The number for Viola Poppler was dialed and the phone pressed to Deandra's ear before she could convince herself not to. She figured if Isabel's gentle magic had guided her toward the flyer, it would be rude to ignore it.

"Hello?" a woman answered after four rings. She sounded harried, the greeting coming out like a bark.

"Hi. I was hoping to speak to Viola Poppler."

"That's me. What do you want?"

Yeesh.

Deandra often didn't know how to react to outright hostility. It made her brain misfire. "Uhh ..." she said eloquently.

Viola huffed into the phone. "I didn't hear a click before you started talking, and I don't hear the sound of a noisy office, so I assume this isn't a telemarketer. You've got ten seconds to tell me who you are. And I swear I will hang up on you and block your number if you're another insurance broker. Don't lie to me."

"I'm not a broker or a telemarketer," Deandra rushed to say. "I was at the soft opening of the Large & Wide and met Callie—you know, Brian's niece?"

"The name's familiar. They weren't exactly close. Not until recently anyway."

Deandra didn't know what to make of that. "We got to talking, and we hit it off and got lunch. At the Dumpling Hut, you know? It's really good." She awkwardly cleared her throat. "Sorry. That's not relevant to you. But I just saw this job-posting flyer today and I thought you might—"

"Might what? Still be holding interviews, even though my business partner died a *day* ago? You thought I'd move your resume to the top of the pile if you dropped Callie's name?"

Yikes. This wasn't going at all like Deandra thought it would. If this was all a result of Isabel's tincture, Deandra wanted her money back. The only thing "clear" about this situation was that Viola was a grouch—whether that was due to grief or a generally sour disposition, Deandra couldn't be sure.

"It's nothing like that, ma'am," Deandra said. "I have a job. It's not even in Axia. I'm only here for the weekend, and—"

"Did Grimshaw put you up to this?" Viola snarled, her voice low. "Tell him to update his harassment spreadsheet. He already had one of his little minions call me today. *That* one was at least a better actor. What happened to Brian was an unfortunate accident. That's it. Let him rest in peace. This isn't part of some grand conspiracy. Grimshaw's a garbage chef and an even worse businessman. Plain and simple."

Deandra had absolutely no idea what was going on now.

"Where did you find my number again?"

"I ... um ... Extra Sensory Pastry. The job listing is on the community board."

Viola grumbled. "I need to find the rest of those and tear them down. Brian put them up, and I can't exactly ask *him* where he left the rest of them now, can I?" Her hardened demeanor crumbled. "Holy realms, what am I supposed to do?"

"I—"

"*Don't.* I don't need pity from people who prey on the bereft," Viola snapped, then the call abruptly disconnected.

Well, that had been an utter failure.

After using the restroom, she flopped into the chair across from Wendy.

Wendy cocked a brow at her. "You okay? You were gone a *long* time."

Deandra explained the odd series of events, hoping Wendy could make sense of what Viola had said.

Wendy sat up a little straighter at the mention of Grimshaw. "Oh!"

Without further explanation, Wendy picked up her cell phone that had been lying on the table beside her empty cup of coffee. Propping her elbows on the table, she began to type furiously into her phone. It took her a minute to finally speak. "Okay, so, the hub system has its own internet. I don't fully understand it, but there are tech-wise witches who have created some corner of the web for hub residents. Anyway! I just Foraged Grimshaw Peabody—"

"You what now?"

"Foraged," Wendy said. "That's the name of the hub search engine: Forage. Anyway, I Foraged him and 'restaurant owner' and got this." She handed Deandra her phone. "I only read the headline and first few sentences."

On the screen was an article in the *Axian Gazette.* "**Failed Restaurateur of Axe & Ale Gets Minced**," said the headline.

Deandra read the article and paraphrased it for Wendy out loud as she went. The article named Grimshaw Peabody as the plaintiff, who was suing a Maxwell Corly for unlawful termination of a commercial lease. Peabody claimed everything from species discrimination to cultural insensitivity to rent gouging. The defendant, Corly, provided photographic evidence of the deplorable conditions of Peabody's kitchen at the now-closed Axe & Ale, as well as several handwritten letters provided by past employees about how much of a tyrant Peabody had been. Corly provided copies of the contract between Peabody and himself that clearly showed Peabody's rent hadn't gone up in the year and a half he'd been there. Apparently, Peabody's consistently delinquent payments had soured the working relationship between the two men.

Even after Peabody had finally vacated the property, he'd pestered Corly for the next six months, calling him at his office at Corly Land Management and harassing his staff. Corly eventually got a magic-enhanced restraining order to keep Peabody away from Corly's workplace. When Peabody ran out of harassment options, he took Corly to court. He asked for his security deposit back, as well as six months of unearned wages—wages he claimed he *would* have earned had Corly not kicked him out of the building prematurely.

As part of his argument, Peabody claimed the termination of his lease was based on a lie. Corly had let it slip to Peabody that he was planning to sell the location to a casual-dining franchise owner from another hub. It was unclear if that had truly been Corly's intention.

Within six months of Peabody's eviction, a new restaurant under a new lease had taken Axe & Ale's place. Peabody managed to talk to the new restaurateurs—a husband and wife team, the McCormicks, who ran Enchanted Frosting—pretending to be someone looking to place his own restaurant in the neighborhood. When Peabody found out the new tenants were paying the same amount in rent as he'd been—and that they weren't franchise owners who'd purchased the building from Corly—Peabody launched into a tirade so intense, the police were called and had to escort him out. The McCormick family, at Corly's suggestion, also got a magical restraining order against Peabody.

The judge ruled in Corly's favor, stating that Corly was within his rights to terminate the lease due to months of unpaid rent. Corly, the judge said, didn't owe Peabody any explanation beyond that, and the harassment Peabody had waged lost him his credibility as a professional businessman. The judge went on to rule that Peabody owed Corly his back rent, attorney fees, and court costs.

Peabody, apparently, went into another tirade of such epic proportions that the judge threw him in the drunk tank overnight because the judge found him "petty and annoying." Deandra was fairly certain that, in the mundane world, Peabody would have been held in contempt of court and thrown in jail and/or fined.

"Is this the same Mr. Peabody who was causing so many problems for you and your boss yesterday?" Deandra asked, handing Wendy's phone back.

"Yep. That guy is the worst. I knew he had a failed restaurant—I don't know what he does for work now—but I didn't know all of *that*. I thought of something while you were reading, though ..." She started typing away at her screen again. "Viola said something about a conspiracy, right? Peabody said something about that yesterday during one of his rants. 'You all think I'm a conspiracy nut, but when I win my class-action lawsuit, you'll all be begging for forgiveness while I'm skipping to the bank.'"

"What a weirdo."

"Oh wow," Wendy said, sitting up a little straighter. "There actually *is* a class-action lawsuit underway. Or, well, Peabody is trying to get one going. He's got a website about it." She placed the phone on the table so they could both look at the screen.

Did your restaurant on 4329 Purl Way close within the past ten years? Sixty percent of restaurants fail in their first year, but how often do they fail in a matter of months, all in the same location? If Maxwell Corly ruined your passion for entrepreneurship and drained your coffers dry while doing it, contact me using the form below. We're stronger together! Don't let the Maxwell Corlys of the world destroy small businesses! We are the lifeblood of Axia!!!

On another page of the website, they found the list of restaurants that had failed at the Purl Way location, along with the dates of their grand openings and when their doors were shuttered. Bea and Edna hadn't been exaggerating about how many restaurants had cycled through the location in a short window of time. Axe & Ale started the list, and it ended with Saucy Wench—a pizza parlor that had had an old-timey tavern aesthetic, complete with waitresses who dressed like barmaids. They'd closed after only eight months, and the location had remained vacant ever since. Now that it had been razed to the ground, *no one* could claim that spot.

"Sounds like any one of these people would have animosity toward that location and Corly," Wendy said. "What if one of *them* burned the building down? Peabody's obviously been going after Corly for a while. Viola accused you of being one of Peabody's 'little minions,' right? He's clearly got several people who agree with him about how bad this Corly guy is. What if one of *them* got frustrated and took matters into their own hands? Corly must be out tons of money because of this. No income from the property for half a year —and now he's got to either foot the bill for a rebuild or cut his losses and sell the land back to the bank. I guess that's where insurance money could come into play, though."

Deandra considered that. "It was a magical fire, right? How many people on that list could have pulled something like that off?"

As they both peered at Wendy's phone, Deandra wished they had a laptop, or at least a tablet with a bigger screen. Without access to the hub-exclusive internet, Deandra's own phone could only perform very basic searches while in the town. Wendy claimed there were too many steps involved to get Deandra connected to Forage today.

At one point, Deandra started scribbling names on a napkin. Wendy got the list of six—including Peabody—knocked down to two, with a bonus name added with an asterisk. The owners of Saucy Wench and Earthen Fare were witches and therefore had access to magic. The species of the asterisked owner hadn't been outwardly divulged anywhere they could find, which Wendy found odd, as most magic-touched talked freely about their abilities and heritage. The name of the café, Elements of Flavor, *might* have suggested the owner had been an elemental witch.

Everyone else on the list had either been mundane or magic-touched in the way Peabody was: a descendant of a species from another realm but who couldn't perform magic in a significant way without the aid of tinctures or talismans. Even Maxwell Corly wasn't on the list of magic-wielding suspects. According to the article, he was a fox shifter.

"I actually know one of the previous owners of Saucy Wench. Well, I know *of* her. She's friends with Heather. The pizza place she works at now is on the same street as the shop I work in," Wendy said. "I bet if we asked her about all this, she'd be able to tell us if there's anything to this conspiracy theory. Plus, Heather said I could pick up my check today. Two birds, one stone."

Shrugging, Deandra agreed, trying to trust in the supposed magic in the éclair, but the Serenity shot was already wearing off. She checked her phone as they walked out of the pastry shop, finding no new messages from Cruz.

Hang on, buddy, she thought, hoping somehow that the dragon would sense her through their bond.

The silence that traveled down the invisible line was deafening.

Chapter 13

The blandly named Pizza Place boasted standard old-school pizza parlor décor: red vinyl booths, a black-and-white checkered floor, and a tiny arcade tucked into a back corner full of old machines with pixelated graphics. There was something charmingly nostalgic about the place, but Deandra would have rather seen Saucy Wench in its heyday.

Wendy led them to the counter where a petite curvy woman stood alone, a bright smile on her face. Her bob haircut had been dyed a vibrant cobalt blue that complemented her pale skin. Her name tag said "Layla."

"Hi there." Recognition kicked in and Layla smiled even more brightly at Wendy. "Oh! You work for Heather, right?"

"Yeah, I'm Wendy. And this is my cousin Dee," Wendy said. "Nice to officially meet you."

"Likewise," said Layla, her gaze shifting back and forth between the pair. When the silence turned a tick toward awkward, her smile faltered a fraction. "Did you come in for pizza, or ...?"

Deandra and Wendy were going to need to sharpen their interrogation skills. Staring dumbly at strangers because the cousins had no idea what they were doing wouldn't instill confidence in anyone.

"We have a random question," Deandra finally said. "You were one of the owners of Saucy Wench, right? Did you ever have any problems with Grimshaw Peabody, the dwarf?"

Layla groaned, rolling her sky-blue eyes. "Yeah. He's convinced our landlord put a curse on the building."

Wendy and Deandra shared a wide-eyed look.

"A *curse*?" Deandra asked Layla.

"Ridiculous, right? Opening a restaurant is risky. My sister and I knew that going in. We had a good eight-month run, but if customers don't come in, we don't make money. It's that simple and that hard. Maybe Saucy Wench was too quirky for a small town."

"I thought your marketing was really clever," Wendy said. "The food was really good, too. It was only open for the first few months I was in town, but the couple of times I went there, the place seemed pretty packed. It had such a cool vibe."

"Thank you. It means a lot to hear that. My sister is still pretty broken up about the loss of the place. I'm not exactly thrilled with my current situation either," she said, gesturing to the pizza parlor at large. "Owning a restaurant had been our dream for as long as we could remember."

Layla chewed her lip, glanced to either side of her, and then leaned forward. Deandra and Wendy inched closer to the counter.

Lowering her voice, Layla said, "The hours and money we put in almost cost Eliza, my sister, her marriage. She and her husband are still having problems because Eliza is buying into the whole conspiracy thing. That's the main reason I know about Peabody—my sister thinks our business failed because it was sabotaged."

Deandra frowned. "Sabotaged how?"

"Well, see, that's why I can't buy into the theory," Layla said. "It was all too subtle, and it was all stuff that one can expect to happen while owning a restaurant. Example ... we had a big Valentine's Day thing there once. We decked the place out in red and pink, made heart-shaped pizzas, hosted a speed-dating event, the whole shebang. The day of the event, the woman running the speed dating got sick and canceled on us, so my sister and I had to fill in last minute. We didn't have any supplies. Then we were short-staffed on top of that, and ... well, the whole thing was a disaster. Got some nasty reviews online. But crap happens. Bad timing, right?

"Another example ... during our second month in business, the pizza oven broke down. The repair guy said there was a piece missing, and it would have to be special ordered. Even with telepads making deliveries faster, it took a week for us to get the piece. It cost us five hundred dollars we didn't have in *addition* to installation. The repair guy said the oven might have been defectively installed, and the piece we needed might have come loose and fallen into some unreachable place in the oven during one of our really busy days where the thing was working double-time.

"We had a big enough menu that we could serve other food, but pizza was where we made most of our money. Eliza swears that the day the oven conked out, the back door hadn't been locked when we got to work. She's convinced someone snuck in in the middle of the night to loosen that piece of the oven."

Wendy asked, "And what do you think? Just a string of bad luck?"

"Everything that can go wrong, will go wrong, right?" Layla said, shrugging. "I think it's easier for Eliza to blame the failure of our dream on outside sources than to consider the possibility that being restaurant owners just wasn't in the cards."

Deandra could tell that the pain of the lost business venture was still raw for Layla, too. She and her sister just dealt with it in different ways.

"Why are you asking about Peabody?" Layla asked after a beat. "Heather said he caused a stink in her shop the other day. Is she planning to get a restraining order against him? Seems par for the course for that guy."

"I'm here *because* of Heather," Wendy said. "She doesn't know I came to talk to you, though. I'm a little concerned that Peabody has her in his crosshairs."

"Do you think he's dangerous?" Deandra blurted. "Is he the kind of person who would resort to violence if he didn't get his way?"

Layla shrugged, her ruby-colored lips pressed into a thin line. "My hope is that he's just passionate. Quick to anger, sure, but I've never gotten the sense that he's violent. Just a pushy, misguided jerk."

Wendy nodded. "Good to know. If you happen to see him around Heather's shop acting weird, could you let me know? I know Heather wouldn't want to set the guy off any further and bring any negative press to the shop. I, however, have no problem stepping in on her behalf if Peabody takes things too far."

Grinning, Layla said, "I knew I liked you. Heather is like a sister to me. I'm glad you're looking out for her, too."

They said their goodbyes and headed back out onto the sidewalk.

As they headed for the shop where Wendy worked, Deandra asked, "Did you know when we walked in there that you were going to spin the 'snooping about Peabody' thing into a 'concern about Heather' thing?"

"Nope!" Wendy said, smiling smugly. "Who says we wouldn't make it as detectives?"

Deandra laughed.

Heather's Elixirs catered to witches in need of supplies for their potions and spells but also to mundanes who could purchase low-level magical tinctures and talismans that allowed them to experience a bit of magic themselves.

They'd only been in the shop for a matter of seconds before they heard raised voices. Deandra glanced over at her cousin long enough to see the tightness of her jaw and the murderous look in her eye before Wendy took off at a jog. Deandra cast a look around the room at the smattering of customers, each one keeping their eyes diverted, or periodically wincing when words like "unacceptable" and "shoddy business practices" slipped into the room from some location in the back.

A bored-looking young woman sat behind a counter nearby, idly flipping through a magazine while blowing bubbles with her gum.

She eventually looked up, raising a dark brow at Deandra. "Did you, like, need something or whatever?"

Deandra didn't need an introduction to know this must be Madison. Last she'd heard, Madison had quit. Had she begged her aunt to let her have her job back, and Heather, hater of confrontation, had caved? Had Madison's parents bullied or pleaded with Heather to reconsider? Without replying, Deandra jogged after her cousin, earning another "okay, whatever" from the young woman.

Wendy stood outside an unmarked door that Deandra assumed was Heather's office.

Though the sound was muffled, Deandra could make out a male voice doing most of the talking. Scratch that—*yelling*.

When the male voice made a disparaging remark about Heather's customer service skills, color flooded Wendy's cheeks. She barged into the room without knocking.

The office was tiny and cramped, a desk taking up most of the space. Heather, a middle-aged woman with hair that had gone almost entirely gray, sat on one side of the desk, while a four-foot-tall man sporting a thick black beard that nearly reached his shoes stood *on* a chair on the other side. He wore a gray pinstripe fedora and a black trench coat.

Wendy's sudden entrance not only startled the man out of his tirade but off the chair. He'd flailed wildly on the way down, taking several stacks of folders with him, sending papers cascading around him like confetti. He screamed a blue streak as he righted himself, attempting to untangle himself from his billowing trench coat, the back of which had flipped over his head.

The man was nearest to Deandra, and when he continued to flail about, she tentatively stepped forward and flipped the trench coat off his head without dislodging his hat. He glared up at her, giving his black, buttoned vest a straightening tug, then adjusted the cuffs of both his coat and the long-sleeved white shirt underneath it. One of his hands was wrapped in a thick white bandage.

"Thank you," he said begrudgingly, his voice deeper than she'd expected. He scanned Wendy from head to foot, his lip curling. "At least *one* of your employees has manners, Heather."

Deandra decided not to correct him, as that would only help further prove his "point."

"What are you doing back here, Peabody?" Wendy asked, arms crossed. "Heather gave you a refund. She gave you a refund *and* you got the nickel-free talisman you wanted. If you hate the products and employees here so much, stop coming back."

The dwarf's face went beet red in a matter of seconds. Deandra wasn't sure if that was impressive or alarming. The guy was going to give himself a coronary. "How. *Dare*. You!"

Oh boy.

Peabody yanked his fedora off his head and winged it at Wendy, who easily dodged it. Peabody's bald head glistened with sweat. This guy needed to take up yoga or something.

"That's enough, Peabody!" Heather snapped, shooting to her feet. "You can berate me with your petty nonsense all you want, but you will *not* threaten my employees. You're no longer welcome here. If I have to take out a loan to afford a charm tailored specifically to keep you out, I will!"

Wendy's mouth hung open as she stared at her confrontation-hating boss. Peabody had finally pushed Heather too far.

"I can take care of that," came a voice from behind Deandra.

She and Wendy spun to find Officer Shannon Sutter behind them. The officer was purposefully exuding her werecat menace this time, and Wendy and Deandra scrambled out of the way, somehow ending up on the other side of Heather's desk in moments. If Officer Sutter was this intimidating in her human form, Deandra could only imagine how scary she was as a giant cat.

Peabody had his hands out, looking especially tiny with a ticked-off werecat bearing down on him. "Easy, Officer Sutter. Easy. We were just having a chat."

Officer Sutter was unmoved. Her blond hair pulled up in another severe bun only added to the steeliness of her demeanor. "According to the young lady working up front who called in a disturbance within a minute of your arrival, I'm guessing it was a bit more than *a chat*."

Huh. I guess Madison can be helpful after all.

"I'll be filing a temporary restraining order on Heather's behalf," Officer Sutter said. "If you're found anywhere near this property during the next three months, you'll be looking at community service for a year and fines sure to cause financial hardship. You've gotten off with too many warnings, Grimshaw."

The dwarf grabbed hold of his own beard with both hands and yanked hard once. Letting out a groan of frustration, he stalked out of the room without giving any of them a backward glance.

"He won't be bothering you anymore, Mrs. Wittly," Officer Sutter said, her tone back to the pleasant rumble she'd used when talking to Deandra and Callie in the Dumpling Hut. With a tip of her head, Officer Sutter left the office, presumably to make sure Grimshaw Peabody didn't knock over every display on his way out the door.

Heather let out a choked sob. "There's really something wrong with him. Thank you for coming in here. He'd still be screaming at me otherwise. I suppose I have to thank Madison, too."

Deandra gazed out the office door, where she could only see a sliver of the shop beyond. She wondered if all dwarves were as hotheaded as Peabody or if his failed restaurant dreams had pushed him over the edge. Her gaze snagged on something near the doorjamb. Peabody's hat.

Struck with an idea, Deandra said, "I'll be right back." She skirted Heather's desk, snatched up the fedora, and headed back into the shop. She wasn't sure Wendy and Heather had even noticed; Wendy was too focused on keeping her boss from crying.

When Deandra made it to the counter, she asked Madison, "Did they both leave? The dwarf dropped his hat." Deandra gave it a little shake to catch the young lady's attention. An eerily familiar odor wafted from the hat—instantly pulling up a memory of burnt plastic and ammonia.

"Yeah." Madison had traded the magazine for her phone. She glanced up long enough to give the hat a lip curl of disgust. "He's so out of pocket."

Deandra admittedly wasn't up to date on slang, but she wasn't sure if the phrase was a common mundane one or a derogatory hub-based one about the dwarf's small stature. *"He's so small he could fit in a pocket!"*

She wondered if there was a version of Urban Dictionary on Forage.

She figured she was overthinking it.

Unhelpfully Madison added, "Fedoras are so cheugy."

Deandra snapped out of her own musings to stare blankly at her, which earned her an eye roll.

With the same level of disinterest she employed to say everything, Madison said, "He was trying to convince another customer to leave because this place is run by 'discriminatory bigots' or something. Officer Sutter picked him up by the back of his jacket and carried him out." Deadpan, she said, "It was hilarious."

"Thanks," Deandra said before darting out the door.

She was worried they'd both be long gone already, but they were only two doors down. Peabody was ranting and raving again from the look of it, Officer Sutter standing before him with her arms crossed as she stared down impassively.

"It's my favorite hat!" Peabody shouted. "I'd get it myself, but your draconian laws prevent it! Just wait until my daughter hears about this! She's a—"

"Lawyer in Luma," Officer Sutter said. "Yes, I know. *Everyone* knows."

Peabody glanced over just as Deandra reached them. "Aha! The only nice employee of that dreadful excuse for a shop was kind enough to bring me my hat."

Deandra placed it in his outstretched hand.

He thunked it on his head, adjusted it so it sat at a jaunty angle, and bowed slightly to Deandra. "It's been a pleasure." Then he sneered up at Officer Sutter before offering a dramatic swish of his trench coat. He strode away.

"I bet he's fun at parties," Deandra muttered.

Officer Sutter snorted. "I'd like to think that's the last time I'll have to haul him out of a place, but I know it won't be."

Recalling the odor that had wafted off his hat, Deandra said, "With his connection to that building that burned down, is he a suspect as the arsonist? Seems like his anger could make him act rashly."

Officer Sutter turned her full attention on Deandra, who did her best not to cower. "You've only been in Axia two days, and you're already getting invested in our justice system?"

Deandra swallowed. "I have a vested interest in the actual arsonist getting arrested. I'm sort of fostering a dire wolf puppy who got accused of the crime. Dire wolves are treated as sapient beings. Did you know that?" She shook her head, still baffled that her "puppy" was basically in a juvenile detention center right now. "I know he didn't do it."

"I heard about that ..." Sutter said. "Didn't realize the puppy was yours." She eyed Deandra a while longer. "All I can say is that, yes, he's a suspect, but more because he's so volatile than anything concrete we can use to pin on him. As much as we'd all like to."

Deandra mentioned his hat. "Seems odd the smell would still linger like that two days later unless he was *really* close to that fire."

Sutter shrugged. "Anyone who was on the same block when that fire erupted probably had to scrub their hair ten times to get the smell out. Certain fabrics soak up scents like a sponge."

Deandra's shoulders sagged. Sutter had discounted her theory immediately.

"That kind of 'evidence' lends nicely to confirmation bias. If you try hard enough, you can force evidence to prove what you *want* to be true. We have to do our due diligence to find the *actual* culprit. Peabody might be odious, but if he's not guilty, we have to accept that."

Deandra supposed she couldn't fault the werecat for having scruples. She wouldn't want someone to pin a crime on her solely because it made *their* life easier, after all. Besides, she hadn't run out here to talk about Peabody. She'd just wanted an excuse to chat with Sutter. Deandra switched tack. "Any idea what caused the fire?"

Sutter smiled at her. "Can't tell you that. But that was a nice try, just easing that question in there."

"Worth a shot." Deandra chewed on her bottom lip. "Have, um, you seen Callie? I don't know if it would be inappropriate for me to reach out. I barely know her, but we got along really well."

The officer's shoulders slumped a fraction. "After you walked her to the station, her family was briefed on what had happened, and then they all went back to Ohio. I'm not sure what they're doing about a funeral or a wake. Axia is where Callie grew up, but her parents moved back to Ohio last year to care for Callie's grandparents. Brian was their eldest child."

Deandra's heart went out to the whole family, hoping the identity of the arsonist was discovered sooner rather than later—not just for her dragon's future, but so Callie's family could have some semblance of closure.

"Were she and her uncle close?" Deandra asked, recalling the phone call she'd had with Viola Poppler earlier. "I wondered why Callie wasn't *with* her uncle for the soft opening. I've heard some rumors that she and her uncle had been on shaky ground."

Sutter stared at Deandra so long, Deandra assumed she wouldn't answer. Callie and Officer Sutter clearly had history. This time, Sutter might opt not to answer a question for personal reasons rather than professional ones.

"Callie's ability got her into a bit of trouble in the past," Sutter finally said. "She figured out that, by reading people, she could manipulate them based on their emotions. She talked more than one family member out of money—sometimes a lot of it—mostly by playing on their sympathy for her. That was why I was reluctant about you and Callie walking to the station together. She'd only just met you, and I was worried she'd already made you a mark since you're new to town."

"A *mark*?" Deandra asked, incredulous. "What, like she's a con woman?"

"It never got that bad, and she *does* seem to have turned a corner on all that," Sutter said. "But she manipulated my brother back in high school. Broke the guy's heart. I don't think he's ever fully recovered. She's apologized repeatedly and is working to make amends with friends and family alike, but I remain cautious around her. I might always be. I know you two hit it off, and I do think she's a good person deep down, but if you decide to forge a friendship with her, keep your eyes wide open until you're sure you can trust her."

Deandra was taken aback by this. She'd liked Callie instantly, but had that been because she was a likable person or because Callie had "read" her and tailored her interaction with Deandra to ensure Deandra would react positively? When she'd first approached Deandra, Callie had mistaken her for her friend Rae, saying they looked similar from behind.

"*Rae grew up here, like me. We were best friends all through high school, but after we graduated she moved to a big hub for a job opportunity she couldn't pass up. We don't see each other as much anymore. One of the hard parts about growing up, right? Friends and family move on and scatter to the wind.*"

Though Callie had stumbled over her reply about Rae initially, Deandra had connected with the sentiment. It had sounded so much like her relationship with Wendy. *Too* much like her relationship with Wendy?

Sutter's phone chimed. She unclipped it from her belt. "I need to take this."

"Wait, just one more question?"

Sutter glanced up, eyebrows lifted in curiosity.

"Did Callie have a best friend in high school named Rae? She might have looked a bit like me—similar hair or skin tone?"

Head cocked, Sutter said, "Not that I know of. My brother was her best friend. They were inseparable in high school. I don't remember the name Rae." Her phone continued to ring. "Sorry, I really have to take this. It was good to see you again, Dee."

Deandra watched the blond werecat stride away, her phone pressed to her ear.

As Deandra slowly made her way back to Heather's Elixirs, she kept replaying Callie's hurried arrival to her own uncle's event. Callie had lied to her when they first met, but why? There *had* been a woman in the picture Callie showed her who vaguely resembled Deandra, but for all Deandra knew, Callie had made up the name Rae.

An even more upsetting possibility settled in her mind: Had Callie glommed onto Deandra *specifically* because she'd sensed Deandra was new to town and therefore wouldn't know Callie's history? Had Callie pegged Deandra as someone who could vouch for her whereabouts and supply her with an alibi?

Chapter 14

Before Deandra reached the door of Heather's Elixirs, her phone rang. A familiar number popped up on the screen. She grinned and answered it, walking across the street where it was quieter. She had a clear view of the shop, so she could wave Wendy down should she come out looking for her.

Back against a tree, Deandra said, "Hi, Grandma."

"I'm surprised you answered," her grandma said. "Been in my town for a full day and you haven't called me. Guess I know distance isn't the reason we only hear from you on birthdays and holidays."

Deandra smiled, rolling her eyes. They both knew Deandra called more often than that, but laying down a guilt trip was one of Grandma January's favorite pastimes. It spoke to Deandra's mother's resilience that she still hadn't been to Axia. "In my defense, you were off doing philanthropic work when I got into town. If you stopped being so selfless, I would have come by yesterday."

"Ooh," her grandma said. "That was good. And last night was less about philanthropic work and more about the Booze and Bingo Extravaganza. That's not the official name of the event, but it might as well have been. Your grandpa hit the vodka a little too hard, and he's sleeping it off in the wind tunnel."

Deandra blinked several times. "Excuse me, the what?"

Her grandma laughed. "It's what we call the padded room in the basement. His magic goes on the fritz when he's hungover. The room is padded in case an involuntary wind spell knocks him onto his behind. The room's covered in spellwork to absorb any powerful magic flying around. He'll be fine. Man is on the verge of turning eighty-five, and I can't convince him to slow down. At least the wind tunnel lowers the chance that he'll break something."

Well, all of that was quite alarming ...

"I'm making dinner tonight. You and Wendy get here by six thirty. Your grandpa should be lucid by then."

There was no negotiating with Grandma January. If she told you dinner was at six thirty, you showed up at six thirty. Dinner probably wouldn't actually be served until well after seven o'clock, though.

"We'll see you then," Deandra said. "Need us to bring anything?"

"Just your beautiful faces," her grandma said. "We'll take a bunch of pictures to send to your mother to make her jealous of all the fun we're having. She's the only one I haven't cracked yet."

"I'll make sure my makeup is on point."

"Good girl."

Deandra was still smiling to herself after she disconnected the call. She was debating whether to head back into Heather's Elixirs or not when a text came in. She didn't recognize the number, but the context of the message quickly revealed the identity of the sender.

UNKNOWN NUMBER

This is my personal cell. Our patient is still knocked out, but his vitals are good. I have a couple of friends at the rehabilitation center, and they have his meds and will administer them even if he's still asleep. They know not to take his collar off. I gave him his most recent dose myself. I'll check in again over the weekend. As long as he stays asleep, he's unlikely to reveal his identity. Also! I think I came up with a way to get him out of there before Monday. I'll let you know if it works

DEANDRA

Officer Dancy said he'll be checking on him tomorrow. He seems like a good guy. He might be able to help you with whatever your mysterious prison break plan is

UNKNOWN NUMBER

Noted

DEANDRA

I appreciate you doing this. Do I owe you anything? Medicine delivery probably isn't in your job description …

She programmed Cruz's number into her phone.

The trio of dots indicating he was typing popped on and off her screen three times before his reply finally came in.

CRUZ

Buy me lunch sometime and we'll call it even.

Her brows hiked. He knew by now that her time in Axia was limited. "Sometime" spoke to some distant date in the future. Perhaps it was a brush-off suggestion, knowing the chances of it happening were slim, but he was keeping the possibility dangling, just in case.

She didn't have time to process it further, however, because

Wendy stepped out of the shop then. Deandra flagged her down, and Wendy jogged across the street to meet her. She had a white envelope in hand.

"How's Heather?" Deandra asked.

Wendy had a mischievous glint in her eye. "So! Turns out that the reason why Peabody was here today had nothing to do with yesterday's fiasco. He was here because Heather's brother—Madison's dad—is thinking about starting a hair salon. Maxwell Corly is one of the top guys in town who manages commercial leases, and I guess Peabody found out that Heather's brother is considering doing business with Corly. Peabody came here to try to convince Heather to talk her brother out of it."

"How did he even find that out? And why not go to Heather's brother directly?"

"Sounds like he did," Wendy said. "You'll be shocked to learn that when Peabody came off as too nosy and pushy, instead of backing off, he doubled down. Apparently Peabody ambushed the guy at a restaurant yesterday while he was out to dinner with his wife and Madison. *That's* why Madison immediately called the werecats when he showed up today."

"So Peabody's on a mission to save everyone from possibly working with Corly, while also trying to get everyone with a failed restaurant from the Purl Way location to rally against him?" Deandra asked.

"Apparently." Wendy excitedly slapped her palm with her envelope several times. "I feel like we're getting close. Who's next on our list?"

Deandra pulled the folded, scribbled-on napkin out of her back pocket. They still hadn't figured out where the owner of Earthen Fare ended up after his restaurant had closed down, but the previous owner of Elements of Flavor, Tor Meller, was last reported to have taken a job at an insurance company. An article had been written in the *Axian Gazette* last year featuring several residents who had made significant career changes later in life. Tor had been one of them.

"Tor works at Unusual Claims Insurance Agency," Deandra said. "We have to go to Grandma and Grandpa's for dinner at six thirty. So this stop will have to be the last one on our sleuthing tour for the day. Also, Grandpa got soused last night and is sleeping it off in something called a wind tunnel."

Wendy was unfazed by this information. "Got it." Taking out her phone, she tapped and swiped at the screen. "All right, looks like Unusual Claims is on Theurgy Lane in the east part of town. To the detective mobile!"

"You're enjoying this entirely too much."

"You forget your roots," Wendy said, heading back in the direction of Oracle Park where her car awaited her. "Don't you remember when we were eight and nine and were on that terrible family vacation to the water park? Aunt Tempest lost her watch there. Who found it? Us!"

Deandra laughed at the memory. She and Wendy had indeed solved the mystery of her mom's missing watch. One of Uncle John's kids had inherited wind magic, much like his father and grandparents, and had taken to using his ability to manipulate the air to become a master pickpocket at a young age. The kid hid his dastardly skills well, and none of the adults had caught on. Even though Wendy and Deandra hadn't *seen* their cousin commit this particular crime, they'd suspected he was the culprit. Their witness was Uncle John's youngest child, who was all of six at the time. Wendy and Deandra had threatened her with a knuckle sandwich if she didn't rat on her brother.

Deandra had her doubts that threats of knuckle sandwiches would work on Tor Meller.

The trip to Unusual Claims took all of ten minutes. Deandra had driven, Wendy calling out directions as she toggled between her map app and the website for the agency. Wendy phoned the office on the way, making sure Tor was in today. She'd had to make an appointment with him on the fly to keep the receptionist from getting too suspicious.

The agency was on the second floor of a squat commercial building in an office complex. It shared the second floor with a dentist who specialized in tusk care, while the entire bottom floor housed an emergency clinic.

A chipper receptionist behind a U-shaped mahogany desk smiled at them as they entered. The décor of the place made Deandra feel as underdressed as she had in the art gallery. Tasteful black-and-white landscape photographs hung on the slate-gray wall behind the receptionist, and a clock with gold accents kept time in the middle, the second hand gliding silently around the white face.

"Hello," the receptionist said. "Are you Wendy Choo?"

"That's me!" she said with a bit too much enthusiasm.

Deandra resisted the urge to elbow her and tell her to take it down a notch.

After Wendy filled out a new-client form, she and Deandra sat in the small, deserted lobby. Deandra could make out the soft din of voices coming from down the hall but hadn't seen anyone other than the receptionist so far. The longer the wait stretched on, the more Deandra questioned this decision. What if Tor got as upset with them as Viola Poppler had with Deandra?

After five agonizing minutes, a bespectacled man in his sixties emerged from a closed door across from the lobby. He was dressed in a white button-up shirt, beige slacks, and shiny brown shoes. His short white hair was gelled and brushed tightly into submission. He smiled warmly, adding a little life to his pale green eyes. "Miss Choo?"

Wendy sprang from her seat as if someone had hit an eject button. The extent of their plan was that Wendy would pretend she was interested in getting a life insurance policy. Deandra swore she'd only heard about life insurance on crime shows when it served as a motive for one spouse bumping off another.

Tor Meller's office was small and tidy, decorated with the same neutral tones as the lobby. The only pops of color came from the row of potted plants that lined his windowsill. The horizontal blinds were kept at half-mast, giving the small purple, pink, and orange flowers plenty of sunlight. The pots were all hand-painted, each one covered in intricately rendered geometric patterns that formed abstract designs. Deandra wondered if those spoke to Tor's being an earth elemental or simply a man with a green thumb.

Wendy and Deandra sat in the pair of chairs positioned across from Tor's desk, while he took the seat before his computer.

He pushed his glasses up the bridge of his nose, then folded his arms on the desk. "What can I help you with today?"

"I'm curious about life insurance," Wendy said, "and I was hoping you could give me a rundown on my options."

"Of course, of course." Tor angled his attention to his computer, jiggling his mouse. He clacked away on a keyboard that sat on a tray below the desk. With his eyes still focused on his screen, he asked Wendy a series of questions.

Deandra wasn't really paying attention to what they said, instead focusing on Tor himself. The man seemed content enough, but she wondered how he felt being in this tiny office when he'd once been a restaurant owner. According to that article in the *Axian Gazette*, Elements of Flavor had been an Asian fusion restaurant that he'd run with his wife who hailed from Korea. Deandra still didn't know if either Tor or his wife were magic-touched, so she was unsure if the fusion part had come from a combination of cultural cuisines or if something alchemical had been at play.

"If I may ask," Tor said, snapping Deandra out of her musings.

She found his gaze flitting between herself and Wendy.

"What made you ask for me specifically?" Tor's keyboard clacking had stopped.

In her peripheral vision, she saw Wendy glance over at her, no doubt shooting her a "Whoops, we didn't rehearse this part!" look.

"I stumbled on an article about you in the *Gazette*," Deandra blurted. "The one about switching careers. I'm thinking of making a big change myself. Even though Wendy really *is* curious about life insurance, I was hoping I could ask you a few questions about the job change?"

Tor's friendly smile faltered minutely. "It's not the easiest time in my life to talk about."

"Because you had to mourn the loss of a dream?"

Now his smile was sad. "Exactly. I opened the restaurant with my wife. We're ... separated now. She needed space from it all. She's not even in Axia anymore."

"I'm sorry to hear that," Deandra said. "Were you both passionate about cooking?"

"Her more so than me. She's a whiz in the kitchen. My passion is gardening."

"Earth elemental?" Deandra guessed.

He eyed her curiously.

"The only personal touches you have in your office are those plants. That plus the 'element' in the name of your restaurant ..." Deandra shrugged.

It took him a few more seconds to speak again. Deandra worried for a moment that he'd tell them to scram. "With my ability, I've been able to cultivate some truly unique vegetables. My wife, Nari, would use those to create some of the most delicious, creative meals. As the restaurant started to fail—our expenses exceeding our income—my magic started to fail, too. It was as if, when I realized the dream was slipping away from me, my magic deserted me. Even after we gave it all up, my magic was never the same. I certainly couldn't make things grow anymore. Nari thought I was making excuses, that I'd given up. But faulty magic aside, I knew I needed to make a change. We'd hemorrhaged so much money trying to keep that place open. I had to build the reserves back up. This job might not be the job of my soul, but it pays well."

Deandra asked, "Do you think you'd ever go back to the old

dream once you have the money for it? Or, when you made the decision to switch careers, did you decide to make it permanent?"

Tor took a while to reply again, staring off into space as he contemplated his answer. "I don't know if I have it in me emotionally to try again. Nari thinks I sold out by choosing a stable career. But when it comes to switching jobs, I believe the thing you have to ask yourself is: Is it financially feasible to keep the job I have? Your feelings have to be taken out of the equation. Your choice needs to be practical, as painful as that is. And I knew that the most practical solution was to find a job that kept a roof over our heads."

"So looking at the books is what let you know it was time to pull the plug?" Deandra asked, noting that he'd never once mentioned anything that even hinted at sabotage as a culprit of his restaurant's demise.

"Oh yes," Tor said. "Nari was the dreamer. Her head was always filled with her next recipe. And they were all brilliant—every one of them. We had signed a two-year lease, but when we hit the end of our first year, I had to tell her it was over. Our landlord was nice enough to let us out of the lease early with only a two-month rent penalty. But the rent was already steep as it was, and we weren't even close to breaking even then."

Wendy chimed in with, "Maxwell Corly was your landlord, right?"

He nodded. "Yeah. He's a good guy. He knows what it's like to hemorrhage money. He's had a heck of a time finding a restaurant tenant who can hang in there for longer than a year or two. That's the way of restaurants, but he's had a string of bad luck."

"So you don't buy into the conspiracy theory that Corly is sabotaging his tenants?" Deandra asked.

Tor barked a laugh. When he realized Deandra and Wendy weren't laughing too, he sobered quickly. "No, of course not. He needs tenants in that place to make owning the space even remotely sustainable. Sabotaging them would be shooting himself in the foot."

Deandra mulled that over, wondering again how much money

Corly had been losing from having that location vacant. "Did Corly own that space outright, do you know? Or if he's paying a mortgage? What other expenses would he have on top of that?"

"Property taxes. Possibly some utilities ..." Tor sat back, arms crossed. "You're not really here about life insurance ... are you, Miss Choo?"

Wendy winced. "I'm not *not* interested in life insurance ..."

"What's this about then?" Tor asked.

"As an expert in insurance, would you say a freak electrical fire could give someone like Corly a way out of financial trouble?" Deandra asked. "The cursed space burns down under unexplained circumstances and then he gets an insurance payment?"

"I'm not answering that," Tor said, his expression shuttered now, all sense of friendliness gone. "I don't know who you are, or who you work for, but I need you to leave."

"We don't work for anyone," Wendy said quickly, hands out.

"If you *do* work for the likes of Grimshaw Peabody, tell him the same thing I told him months ago: I'm not going to testify against Maxwell Corly," Tor said. "We all made bets on our futures, and we all lost. That's not Corly's doing." He picked up his desk phone and hit a button. "Hi, Julie. I'm sending Miss Choo out. Please put a note in her file that I refuse to work with her again. If you don't see them leave the building in the next five minutes, call security."

This escalated quickly.

Deandra and Wendy got to their feet. Wendy called a hasty goodbye and apology, then hightailed it out the door. Deandra lingered in the doorway for a moment. "For what it's worth, I hope you and Nari can work things out. And that your magic returns to how it used to be."

Tor looked a fraction less angry, the tension in his shoulders loosening. "If you *are* here on Peabody's behalf, he at least found someone compassionate to do his bidding this time. I almost believed you meant that." He glanced toward his windowsill, where the row of pretty flowers sat in their pots. Deandra knew she'd overstayed her welcome and had crossed a line with Tor, yet she got the sense he had more to say. "You know what's strange? Yesterday, it suddenly felt as if my magic had ...healed. It was like a shot of caffeine, like I was finally awake after sleepwalking for years. I thought maybe it was a premonition that Nari was coming home. But instead ..."

He lifted a hand, his fingers dancing and twirling in the air in a series of complicated gestures, his fingers almost a blur. It was dizzying to watch.

A flash of green flickered in her peripheral vision and she turned toward the windowsill just as a small green shoot sprang up two inches from a pot already occupied by tiny pink roses. In a blink, the shoot grew two more inches. A bright yellow flower, its petals closed, emerged from the shoot. When the petals unfolded, the bright yellow head angled itself toward the sunlight.

Deandra had never seen anything like it. She was even more curious now about the unique vegetables his magic had helped him create. She swiveled her attention back to Tor. He studied her intently, as if searching for a sign that she'd seen his magic at work—that he hadn't imagined it.

"It's beautiful."

Eyes ringed with silver, he said, "I suppose there may be hope for this old man yet."

"There certainly is."

Chapter 15

"You're quiet," Wendy said from the driver's seat. "Grandma didn't give you too much of a hard time, did she?"

Grandma January had pestered Deandra during dinner—everything from her breakup with Mark, the fact that she was going to be unable to afford her apartment for much longer on a single income, and how stubborn Deandra's mother was. But the pestering hadn't been anything she couldn't handle. She knew her grandma badgered her out of love. Plus, Grandpa Morris had been there to balance everything out with his horrendous dad jokes. She'd had a good time.

But now that they were driving back to Wendy's apartment, Deandra was replaying her conversation with Tor Meller, especially the end of it. Maybe it was because Axia was dark now, the streets mostly deserted; the quiet feel of the town made her contemplative.

"*I suppose there may be hope for this old man yet.*"

"Have you ever heard of a talisman or a potion that can take someone's powers away?" Deandra finally asked.

"Uhh ... I'm not sure. Heather doesn't sell anything like that. That kind of thing has to be high-level magic, if it's even possible," Wendy said. "Why?"

She recounted what Tor had told her before she'd left his office.

"He said his magic had more or less stopped working properly while he worked at Elements of Flavor. I would guess that's at least part of the reason why they had problems at the restaurant, even if he doesn't want to admit that. If part of the draw was the unique vegetables he was able to grow with his magic, and then his magic stopped working properly ..."

"And you think someone used a talisman on him to *cause* his magic to stop working?" Wendy asked. "Hate to say it, but you're starting to sound like Peabody."

"Tor said his magic fully came back to life *yesterday*. As in the day that the Purl Way location burned down," Deandra said. "What if someone *had* sabotaged him, and the talisman that was responsible was still active even when Tor wasn't working there anymore? Maybe someone, I don't know, hid it in the walls or something. If that fire was hot enough to basically melt bone, couldn't it have been strong enough to destroy a talisman?"

Wendy was apparently still thinking about that when she pulled into her parking spot at her complex. The covered spot was dimly lit. She shut off the car and turned to stare at Deandra for a moment. It wasn't until the cabin lights dimmed that she said, "I will amend my earlier statement ... I hate to say it, but this theory almost makes sense."

"Talking to Peabody—even if he's been right all this time about sabotage—is on the bottom of my list of things I want to do," Deandra said. "Especially if I'm down to only two days here."

Wendy offered a very dramatic pout.

"Do you know anything about Maxwell Corly?" Deandra asked.

"Nope. Heather's landlord works at some other land development company. I'd never even heard of Corly until yesterday. He's a ... fox shifter, right? There are the usual stereotypes about them ... smart, cunning, crafty. They usually end up in business-y type jobs. Real estate, banking, marketing. So he already fits the mold on that."

"Well, if Corly's next on our list of who to contact, we have to come up with a better plan than the one we had going in to talk to

Tor," Deandra said. "Getting threatened with security means we messed up somewhere."

Wendy winced. "You're probably right."

They watched an entire season of a ridiculous teen drama on Netflix neither one of them could stop watching, despite making fun of it the entire time. The bottle of wine they consumed helped Deandra feel a little less sad about the fact that the dragon wasn't trotting around Wendy's apartment, sniffing everything in sight or howling forlornly from the kitchen. The supplies they'd purchased for the dragon were still in the trunk of Wendy's car. Deandra didn't have the heart to bring them in.

She hadn't received any new updates from Cruz, so she had to hope no news was good news. He'd claimed to have come up with a potential way to get the dragon out before the weekend was over, but she wasn't going to bank on it. At least she could call Parks Management tomorrow afternoon to get an update from Dancy.

As she drifted off to sleep, she tried to send another message down the invisible line supposedly connecting herself to the dragon.

There was still no answer on the other end.

Deandra had no epiphanies while she slept, nor did her dreams reveal a brilliant suggestion for how to best approach Maxwell Corly. Strolling into his office pretending to be an investor, a building inspector, or a potential new client would no doubt go even worse than Wendy pretending she wanted to purchase life insurance from Tor Meller. All Corly would have to do is ask one question full of jargon she and Wendy didn't understand, and their cover would be blown. Being there under the guise of working as a reporter could backfire immediately, too. One phone call to whatever paper she named—real or imagined—would expose her lies.

The direct approach would probably go badly as well. Did she really expect Corly, a man she didn't even know, to answer her pointed questions? He'd be under no obligation to tell her anything —and would be especially reluctant to do so if he were truly guilty.

"So, did you really sabotage all of your previous tenants at the Purl Way location, Mr. Corly?" she would ask. *"Oh, you did! Can you tell me why? Fascinating. Now, tell me, did you burn the building down as well? Ah, you did! For insurance money, you say? Cool. Let's go tell that to the cops so I can get my dragon out of jail since he's currently taking the fall for your pyromaniac ways."*

Over a breakfast of bacon and oatmeal at Wendy's dining room table, Deandra asked, "Could we go as representatives of Heather's Elixirs and bring him a bunch of stuff from the shop? We could say Heather would be happy to display his business cards on the store's counter if he included things from her shop in his 'congrats on your new lease' gift baskets or something."

Wendy pointed her spoon at Deandra. "We couldn't do that without talking to Heather first, which might open a whole can of worms. But ... that's a good idea. She's got great products in that store, so her reputation alone keeps the lights on, but she's so stinking shy when it comes to marketing herself."

An hour later, they hadn't come up with anything better, so Wendy called Heather. Wendy put the call on speaker, but pressed a finger to her lips, silently instructing Deandra to stay quiet.

"Hi, Wendy ..." Heather answered cautiously. "You're not calling to check up on me, are you? You're supposed to have the day off. Your cousin is going to start feeling neglected."

Deandra stuck out her bottom lip and twisted her balled-up fists near her temples, mimicking bawling her eyes out.

Wendy grinned at her. "Well, this is about my cousin, actually. She's at a bit of a crossroads in her life right now, and we're trying to figure out what career path she should try next. She's got great customer service skills. You have great products. I was thinking we could put together sample packs of your goods, and Deandra could work her magic to convince business owners to put those products in their welcome packages for new clients. Gyms and wellness centers, realtors, maybe even the Welcome Center. Marketing might be the perfect fit for Dee."

Deandra wrinkled her nose. She *was* still clueless about what her life's grand plan might be, but she didn't see herself being a schmoozing marketing type.

Heather was quiet on the other end for long enough, Deandra wondered if the call had disconnected. "I really love the idea, but I don't have room in the budget for—"

"Free of charge," Wendy said. "She's just testing the waters to see if it's something she likes. She'll get some hands-on experience, and you'll possibly get a business partnership out of it. Win-win."

Heather audibly sniffed. "You're a good egg, Wendy. I've been so stressed lately—between Peabody popping up every day to complain, Madison being a royal pain, my husband being so sick—"

"I got you," Wendy said. "It's all good. We're both happy to help. We'll be by in a bit to grab some supplies."

Wendy was looking quite pleased with herself by the time she ended the call, but Deandra was apprehensive. If they screwed this up the way they'd screwed up with Tor Meller, it could reflect negatively on Heather. Which could, in turn, mess up any potential business dealings between Heather's brother and Corly.

But if Corly really had been sabotaging his tenants, perhaps they'd be doing Heather and her family a favor if Deandra and Wendy bungled Deandra's so-called attempts at becoming a marketing guru.

An image of the dragon's gemstone eyes going dull and flat popped into Deandra's mind. She imagined him lying motionless in a cage, Ranger Vicks standing on the other side with a sneer on his dumb face.

She stared very pointedly at Wendy. "Is there a craft store on the way? We're going to need a very large basket."

By the time Deandra and Wendy were armed with a giant basket stuffed with samples of Heather's wares, Deandra's stomach was in knots. She wasn't even worried about falling flat on her face, as far as exerting her marketing prowess went. She was freaking out about dealing with another shifter. The only human-turned-animal she'd witnessed shifting so far was Allegra turning into a giant swan. Allegra's personality, much like a swan's, leaned toward chaotic. Officer Sutter, even while in human form, instilled a sense of fear in Deandra that was purely instinctual—which Deandra imagined was reflective of how'd she'd feel if she encountered a hungry mountain lion while on a hike.

Fox shifters, according to Wendy, possessed the characteristics associated with their animal counterparts—cunning, clever, calculating. Deandra didn't know why she *or* her cousin thought they'd be able to out-fox a fox.

But since the pair was currently walking toward the front door of Corly Land Management, Deandra with a massive basket stuffed to bursting in her arms, she supposed it was too late to back out now, especially since Wendy had already called ahead to inform Corly's receptionist that they were coming.

The scent of something earthy and pungent was wafting out of the basket and tickling Deandra's nose. She tried her best to scratch her nose without using her hands, which she was sure made her look like she'd lost control her facial muscles. Whatever was inside the basket hadn't bothered Deandra while she'd been trapped in a car with it, so she wasn't sure why her eyes were suddenly watering.

Wendy held the front door open for Deandra so she could hustle inside. The office reminded Deandra of a bank. There was a large reception desk directly across from the door, and a good chunk of the remaining space was filled with a handful of freestanding cubicles. The blue upholstery of the cubes matched the cushions on the row of chairs dotting the lobby. Framed blueprints, certificates, and degrees dotted the white walls. A water cooler to the side of the receptionist desk let out a *glug* of greeting.

Deandra's nose twitched as she took in another unintentional whiff of something earthy in the basket. It took every inch of Deandra's self-control to not sneeze all over the samples. The male receptionist eyed Deandra's convulsing face warily. Deandra was reminded of the dragon's sneezing fit and how she'd had to give the little guy's muzzle a hearty series of scratches to provide some relief. Deandra figured such a service was not one the receptionist offered. She deposited the basket on the counter and then hastily took several steps back. The distance helped some, but there was a tickle in her throat now too, and her eyes itched.

"Can I … help you two?" the receptionist asked in a tone that suggested he hoped they'd realized they'd walked into the wrong office.

Perhaps that was due to Deandra rubbing the flat of her palm against her nose. He probably feared she came bearing the promise of a plague.

Without warning, the receptionist violently sneezed in three rapid blasts. Like a contagious yawn, Deandra sneezed, too.

"I think …" Deandra managed before sneezing again, "something in the basket …"

The receptionist leaned toward the giant basket, as if triggered by the same mystifying compulsion people had when presented with the question, "Does this milk smell bad?"

The answer was always yes! Deandra mused.

The receptionist gave the basket a tentative sniff, groaned with regret, and then reared back before sneezing rapid-fire again.

"I can't say this bodes well for your sales pitch …"

Deandra and Wendy whirled around. A strikingly handsome man had joined them. Behind him, Deandra eyed a door as it softly closed. Perhaps that was the man's office.

Before Deandra could issue a greeting, she sneezed. She eyed the water cooler by the receptionist's desk, not wanting to get a drink, but wanting to place her entire face under one of the spigots to wash out whatever she'd unintentionally inhaled. She idly rubbed at her throat. The receptionist issued another trilogy of sneezes, followed by a soft wail of agony.

"Oh gosh!" said Wendy, who, along with the newly arrived handsome man, appeared to be immune to whatever foul object was in the basket. Wendy hurriedly rummaged in the samples until she found a satchel of small, dried flowers.

Deandra's eyes started to leak again as Wendy went running by with the bag of flowers and out the door.

The moment the satchel was out of the office, Deandra felt better. Her throat still felt tight, and her eyes burned, but the urge to sneeze had gone out of her like the tide. She hazarded a glance at the receptionist.

He didn't look much better than she felt. His eyes were bloodshot. "That was *terrible*."

She cracked up, which earned her a smile.

When Wendy returned, her cheeks were flushed, and bits of leaves dotted her hair. "It hit me as soon as I was outside. I sneezed so hard, I fell into a bush." She plucked free a series of small twigs that poked out of her tennis shoes. "It's a blend that's supposed to ward off negative feelings. No one's ever reacted that way in the store before."

Which was saying a lot, considering how often grouchy Mr. Peabody frequented Heather's Elixirs.

"Should I be concerned?" the handsome man asked, but at least he appeared more amused than upset.

All Deandra and Wendy could muster up were awkward chuckles.

He strode forward on his shiny black loafers, hand outstretched toward Wendy, who stood the closest to him. "You must be one of Heather Wittly's employees? I'm Maxwell Corly."

Wendy closed the distance to shake his hand. "Yes, I'm Wendy Choo. I called earlier. And this is Dee Hendricks, the face of Heather's new outreach team."

Deandra fought the urge to kick her cousin in the backside as she also approached the man. As she shook his hand, she said, "It's not as formal as all that. I'm just helping Heather with a few tasks to help her clear her plate. She's been under a lot of stress lately."

Corly tucked his hands behind his back. While the office was a bit plain, bordering on bland, Corly himself was dynamic. Deandra wondered if that was on purpose, or if the man's intrigue was amplified by his shifter magic. Deandra pegged him as being in his mid-fifties, and the bit of stubble on his face had a few streaks of gray. He wore black pinstriped slacks with a white button-up shirt tucked in, accentuating his flat abdomen. The sleeves were rolled to his elbows, revealing lean, tan forearms. There was an effortless style to his rich, dark hair. While it was mostly black, it was shot through with copper. She found herself desperately wishing she could see what he looked like as a fox.

Wendy cleared her throat and Deandra coughed, her cheeks flaming. She'd been ogling. She considered running outside to fling herself into the bushes Wendy had fallen into earlier.

"One of Mrs. Wittly's stressors is Grimshaw Peabody, I hear," Corly said. "He apparently finds me so detestable that he's attempting to stop me from doing business with Mrs. Wittly's brother." His piercing blue eyes, which were even more striking when paired with his tanned skin, slowly roved over Wendy and Deandra in turn. "Have you two been sent here as a peace offering?"

Deandra honestly couldn't tell if he was hitting on them or not. She also couldn't tell if she minded. Sure, he was old enough to be her dad, but he was so ... alluring.

A bell jangled behind her, startling her out of her thoughts. Turning, she found the receptionist holding the black handle of a small bell between forefinger and thumb. His focus was clearly on Corly behind her, though she felt as if the jarring sound had been meant for her, too. Her cheeks warmed. The receptionist eyed his boss as if he were a misbehaving child. "Maxwell ... you're doing it again ..."

When Deandra returned her attention to Corly, his eyes were

closed, and he had the heel of one hand pressed to his temple. The unexplainable draw she felt toward him dropped away. When he opened his eyes, they were still a very pretty blue, but the intensity in them had dulled somewhat. How odd.

"I apologize," Corly said, giving his head a light shake. "I've been a bit under the weather lately, which always makes my innate abilities go a bit haywire. Usually, I actively avoid using my charm skills on clientele. I want to earn my clients based on my hard work and expertise, not my magic. I don't bounce back from illness as well as I used to when I was a pup. Growing older can be the pits."

Deandra thought of her grandpa needing to sleep off his hangover in the "wind tunnel." She supposed both men were lucky to live in a place like Axia, where there was a level of understanding when it came to aging magic. The number of lawsuits in the mundane world filed over allegations of a real estate agent using blatant magical manipulation to get people to sign contracts would be through the roof.

She eyed Corly, wondering if he'd ever used those abilities to gently nudge a client who had wavered on the edge of signing on the dotted line. How tempting would it be to use his magic that way? Who was to say he wasn't using his charm on her right now to make her view him more favorably?

She couldn't forget that just because Mr. Peabody was a hot-tempered tyrant and Maxwell Corly was a suave man in a sleek suit, it didn't mean Corly was the innocent one in this scenario. He could, after all, be every bit the cunning saboteur Mr. Peabody thought him to be.

"I'd be happy to hear your pitch, ladies. I'll keep my magic in check. Thank you for the reminder, Oscar," Corly said, his hand held out to the side. The receptionist, Oscar, apparently understood the gesture, because he rounded the counter, hoisted the basket off it, and hustled over to place the handle in Corly's waiting palm. "Right this way," Corly said, once he had the basket in hand, then headed toward the back corner.

Wendy and Deandra eyed each other warily as they followed the fox shifter.

Corly opened the door for them, leaving the office door open as he made his way to the massive mahogany desk in the middle of the large room. Though the desk was well utilized, covered as it was in folders, notebooks, and office supplies, the rest of the office was dotted with packing boxes. Nothing hung on the walls. The pair of elegant mahogany bookcases that stood to either side of the desk were empty. Deandra wasn't sure if Corly was in the process of moving in or out.

As Deandra took one of the two chairs positioned in front of the desk, she noted that the screen saver on Corly's computer monitor was of a smiling cartoon fox that drifted lazily from one end of the dark screen to the other before it bounced off and floated in a new direction. Corly skirted the desk and a few stacked boxes to make his way to his own chair.

"New digs or old ones?" Deandra asked, glancing around.

"New," Corly said. "The renovations on this office were completed a few months ago, but I couldn't justify splurging on new furniture. We lucked out on a tricky, lucrative contract recently, though, so I finally caved." He gave the desk's surface an affectionate pat. "New coat of paint on the walls. The rug beneath the desk was ludicrously expensive, but I've had my eye on it for years. Waiting on a few more pieces to arrive before I can really set this place up to be my dream den. We've been successful for years, but it really feels like Corly Land Management is on the verge of big things. My wife and daughter assure me it's okay to treat myself sometimes, but I still feel a little guilty about it."

Deandra wondered if the sudden windfall was tied to the Purl Way location burning to the ground. Was a fat insurance check on the way?

Ring!

At the jangle of the bell, Deandra turned abruptly in her seat to stare out the still-open office door.

Oscar stood there, his expression pinched. "You're doing it again, Maxwell."

Corly sighed. "I apologize, ladies. Another symptom of being ill is talking too much. Part of the charm ability is being relatable. My ability allows me to know what to share, and when, to aid in tipping opinions in my favor. When I'm hopped up on medication, that often skews too far in the wrong direction."

Ring, ring.

"Thank you, *Oscar*," Corly said tightly.

Deandra got the impression that the bell had been going off a lot today. She couldn't be sure, but she thought one of Corly's eyelids might have started periodically twitching.

"If you listened to your family, you wouldn't *need* me to ring a bell at you like you're one of Pavlov's dogs," Oscar said, then walked off.

Deandra wondered if Oscar always spoke that boldly to his boss.

"He's my nephew," Corly said, as if he could read her thoughts. "Anyway, tell me about Heather's Elixirs."

Deandra started in on their hastily planned-out spiel, but Wendy soon took over. Despite not being magic-touched herself, Wendy had an impressive level of knowledge about tinctures and talismans. Not just about Heather's products, but about magical items in general. She told him about items that could assist in staging a property, such as candles that changed their scents based on the weather or season, and an elixir that could be added to the water of a flower vase to instantly change the petals' colors to match the décor of a room. There were money-saving items, such as talismans that could help ward off and detect pests, which could be specialized to target everything from termites to pixies to ghosts.

"This would have been very helpful last month," Corly said, closely examining a star-shaped talisman that lay in his palm. "We had a very ornery ghost who scared off everyone who tried to renovate or move into one of our properties. We had to call in a medium to help us out, and she eventually gave us a talisman very similar to this one to ensure the ghost didn't return."

They were in the process of discussing the possibility of Corly Land Management ordering a series of products to use themselves when a phone rang.

"Oh, excuse me," Corly said, sifting through the items on his desk before he found a cell phone underneath a thick folder. "This is my daughter's ringtone. Just one moment."

Wendy shot Deandra an excited smile. They'd come here to use Heather's products as a foot in the door so they could interrogate Corly, and instead, Wendy had managed to snag more business for the store. Maybe it was *Wendy* who needed to consider a career in marketing ...

"Hi, Gracelyn," Corly said. "Can I call you back in a few? I'm meeting with—" He pursed his lips. "Yes, I'm at the office. I'm feeling much better." Pause. "No, I didn't *faint*. It was a minor case of vertigo. I stumbled down a couple of steps, not an entire staircase." Pause. "Well, Oscar has a big mouth. I should fire him for spying on me. He's been following me around with the bell, ringing it every time my magic acts up. Sometimes he rings it for no reason at all. I swear it goes off every five minutes." A deep sigh. "No, I don't want to speak to—hi, honey. Yes, I am, but—" Another deep sigh. "I didn't lie. I planned to swing by the store on my way home from doing a bit of—fine. I'll be home after I wrap this up." In a resigned tone, with his head hung low, he added, "I know. I love you, too. See you soon."

Deandra and Wendy were both pointedly looking anywhere but at the fox shifter by the time he'd hung up.

"Sorry about that," Corly said eventually. "Worried family."

Deandra hazarded a glance at him, noting that color flushed his cheeks. When she'd first met him, she wouldn't have guessed that he'd been ill recently, but now that she was looking for it, there *were* bags under his eyes. "Did you have the flu?"

"I was struck with one of the worst stomach bugs of my life two days ago," he said. "I'm not sure I got more than a foot from the porcelain throne for most of the day on Thursday."

Ring, ring.

"I will *fire you*, Oscar!" Corly called out.

The bell had rung from right outside the door, yet the verbal reply that came next sounded from a considerable distance. "You will not! I'm the one who had to drive your delirious butt to the hospital last night because you were so sick with fever, you were hallucinating!"

Corly sent a long-suffering sigh Deandra and Wendy's way. Deandra tamped down a laugh.

"I hope all of this doesn't dissuade you from working with me," Corly said, addressing Wendy. "I'm very interested in working with Heather, but I also *should* probably get home. I think the meds might be wearing off."

Wendy nodded. "No problem. There's a couple of business cards in the basket. If you have any questions, give us a call."

The pair left Corly's office, bid Oscar a good afternoon, and then headed for the exit. Deandra's eyes started to water the moment she stepped outside, and her throat tightened. Wendy rubbed at her own eyes. They both sneezed violently a few moments later. Wendy pointed out the small hedge she'd fallen into earlier, the satchel of awful flowers lost somewhere in its depths.

It wasn't until they were closed in the car that Deandra spoke. The urge to sneeze had vanished. "Another suspect down, I guess. Corly couldn't have burned his own building to the ground because he was sick the day of the fire."

"Right ..." Wendy said slowly, a distant look in her eye. She had both hands wrapped around the steering wheel but hadn't turned the car on yet.

Her car was parked a row away from the front of Corly Land Management, giving them a clear view of the entrance, while also providing enough distance that Oscar, from his spot behind the counter, wouldn't be able to see them loitering in the parking lot.

Deandra turned in her seat to stare at the side of her cousin's head a little better. "What?"

"The sneezing got me thinking ..."

"We probably should warn Corly about the flowers. That's going to be a problem for anyone who walks in front of the building. How long does the magic on the flowers last?"

Wendy shook her head. She unhanded the steering wheel and turned in her seat, too. "That's not what I meant. Well, I mean, we probably *should* warn him, but that blend is an experiment Heather's been working on. It started off as a custom order for a friend who wanted to use it during one of those murder mystery dinners. You know, the ones where someone pretends to be killed at the dinner, and then the attendees have to figure out whodunnit?"

"I thought you said the flowers were for warding off negative feelings," Deandra said.

"I had to say something believable so as to not tip off Corly that we might be onto him."

"You really need to lay off the true crime shows," Deandra said.

"I can't, and I won't." Wendy grinned. "Anyway, the blend was supposed to make the person sneeze if they were guilty. So at the end of the guessing round, the satchel of flowers would be brought out to reveal the killer once and for all, as the blend is meant to reveal ill intent. In the case of the mystery dinner, the ill intent was that the 'killer' deceived partygoers into thinking he or she was innocent of the crime while lying outright to their faces. Heather was hoping to eventually turn the blend into something she could put in little satchels all over the store to help ferret out potential shoplifters."

Deandra flushed. "Does that mean you, me, and Oscar were acting with ill intent?"

"That's the thing," Wendy said. "Heather's never been able to get the blend to work how she wants. Instead of guilty people sneezing, the *innocent* ones do. Apparently, at that dinner party, as soon as the satchel was brought out and put in the middle of the dining room table, twenty people started sneezing at once. One guy sneezed so hard, he fell out of his chair and whacked his forehead on a piece of furniture. He had to get ten stitches."

"Yikes!"

Wendy nodded. "Turns out 'ill intent' is too general. Someone could have a small ill intent, like planning to steal someone's sandwich out of the office fridge, or have a big ill intent, like running someone's business into the ground or breaking up a marriage. Plus, some people might be planning something shady, but they don't personally view it as ill intent. If they see it as, I don't know, a justified action, then the magic won't react at all. There ares too many variables for the magic to be reliable, and even then, the trial and error needed to specialize the magic to sniff out a specific kind of ill intent is no small feat. But Heather keeps tweaking the blend because she really wants to make one specific to targeting thieves. She included it in the basket because she figured other shop owners would be intrigued by the possibility, should she ever perfect it."

Deandra finally figured out where Wendy was headed. "The only one of us who *wasn't* sneezing was Corly."

"Bingo," Wendy said. "The spellwork interwoven into the blend is far from reliable, but the magic singled the three of us out as innocent of ill intent."

"And Corly as guilty."

Wendy asked, "But guilty of what? Something tame—like him lying to his family about how he was really feeling—or was it something bigger than that?"

The door to Corly Land Management opened then, and Deandra watched as Corly himself stepped out. He'd put his suit jacket back on and was clutching the handle of a briefcase. He stood in the doorway, door propped open with one hand as he presumably spoke to Oscar. Eventually Corly headed for his own car parked in front of the hedge full of the bespelled dried flowers. Deandra didn't detect so much as a sniffle.

Perhaps she'd been too hasty in striking the fox shifter off her suspect list after all.

Chapter 16

Half an hour later, Deandra lay on her back in the grass at Oracle Park, staring up at the clear blue sky. Wendy was pacing back and forth nearby. They'd run out of leads again, now that Corly was firmly in the "maybe" pile.

There weren't many people at the park at this hour, and most were sticking to the walking path that ringed the grassy area. Yappy Charles Barksley and his owner were back. Deandra had hoped the crushing guilt of being at the park without the dragon bounding around would force her brain to come up with something inspired.

As the minutes ticked on, their ideas got more and more outlandish.

"Didn't you say the cameras outside the art gallery were destroyed?" Wendy asked during one of her trips past Deandra's prone form.

"Yeah," Deandra said. "You've asked that six times already."

"What if we go back to the gallery and ask the staff *how* the cameras were destroyed? That could give us a clue about the species of the arsonist," Wendy suggested, but she'd made this suggestion half a dozen times, too. Deandra worried that it didn't speak well of

Wendy's mental state that she kept forgetting she'd made this "point."

A thought struck Deandra, and she sat bolt upright.

Wendy came trotting over. "What? Do you have something? Tell me you have something."

"Pixies!"

"What about them?" Wendy asked, dropping into a squat.

"I bet the pixies who live in that bush next to the alley saw something. Or heard something," Deandra said. "There were at least twenty of them living in there. Should we go talk to them?"

"Sure, why not?" Wendy said flatly. "We'll have to get acorns, though. Some sugar, too."

Deandra stared blankly at her.

"They won't talk without a bribe. They're obsessed with acorns. Let's hit the Zombie Cactus first."

"You know, just when I feel like I'm starting to get a hold on this place, you say stuff like that and I feel like my brain is melting out of my nose again," Deandra said.

Wendy merely smiled at her, hand out. "You know you love it."

The Zombie Cactus turned out to be a specialty grocery store that catered almost exclusively to the magical community in Axia. The store was next door to one of the four telepads in town, in part because some of the unique items from other hubs that were brought into the Zombie Cactus were so temperature or light sensitive, they needed the shortest travel time possible. According to Wendy, a door in the telepad station only accessible to delivery people led directly into one of the Zombie Cactus's storage rooms. Certain parts of the store where items were kept in airtight or chilled containers were blocked off by black-out curtains. Their most popular item, the zombie cactus, was the star ingredient in everything from potions to food. Despite the creepy name, Wendy assured Deandra that the flavor of the cactus was sweet and refreshing, and in summer, Zombie Cactus Iced Tea season put the mundane Pumpkin Spice Latte season to shame.

They purchased a pound of the smallest acorns Deandra had ever seen. The acorns' caps were the usual shade of brown, but their bodies were blood red. The cousins also purchased ten ounces of bright pink sugar and a box of tiny organic bags that, according to the label, were edible.

Armed with their bribery tools, they piled back into Wendy's car. While Wendy drove, Deandra bagged up minuscule amounts of sugar in the edible, silky bags. Each bag was about the size of a quarter, but she supposed to a pixie it would be enormous—like a sack of gold. Wendy told her that if she gathered up the loose end of the bag and squeezed, the heat from her fingertips would seal the tiny bags closed.

Wendy parked a few houses down, then they set off to interrogate the pixies. Deandra hoped the newt hadn't eaten the entire Clarion family.

Now that the stench of ammonia and burnt plastic had dissipated in the area, the sidewalks were more populated. Kids played on lawns, people rode by on bicycles, and others walked by with their dogs.

Deandra felt ridiculous squatting before the hedge, but at least Wendy was there with her. The only consolation was that no one who passed by paid them any mind or looked askance at them. In Axia, it was clearly not at all irregular to stare deeply into a bush with a palm outstretched and dotted with tiny bags of sugar while your pockets bulged with acorns. "Umm ... knock, knock? Miss ... Clarion?" She resisted the urge to literally put knuckles to leaves in an imitation of a knock.

Several long seconds ticked by without even a rustle.

"Maybe they aren't home," Wendy whispered.

Very carefully, Deandra pinched the top of one of the sugar bags and dangled it in front of the bush. "I come bearing gifts."

The sudden appearance of the little face from the depths of the leaves almost made Deandra lose her balance.

"*You*," the pixie said accusingly, but she didn't sound nearly as upset as she had last time. She sniffed the air frantically, like a bunny. She snatched out a tiny hand for the bag of sugar, but Deandra pulled it back just in time. "Is that ... lila sugar?"

"Yep." Wendy fished an acorn out of her pocket and held it up between two fingers. "We've got these, too."

Five pixies darted out of the bushes at once, zipping around their heads like talking mosquitos. They spoke so fast, Deandra couldn't understand a word. It was hard to resist the urge to swat the winged creatures away.

"Whoa, whoa, whoa," Wendy said. "There's more than enough for everyone. We've got questions, though. You answer questions, you get treats."

Five had become ten. The pixies hovered in a single line before Deandra and Wendy, just above the top of the hedge. The pixies' arms were either folded across their chests or their fists were propped on their hips. Wings fluttered so quickly, they were nearly invisible. The lady pixie Deandra had first interacted with floated a bit in front of the rest. Perhaps she was the matriarch of the family. Though they all had blue hair, the group had a wide range of body types, facial features, and skin tones, suggesting this was perhaps more of a found family situation than a biological one.

"What's your name?" Deandra asked the one in front.

"Zora," the pixie said. "What do you want to know?"

"I'm Dee. This is Wendy," Deandra said, but the pixie's hand motion for the universal sign of "let's hurry this up" told Deandra that Zora didn't care for small talk. Jutting her head toward the art gallery, Deandra asked, "Did you see how the cameras on that building got destroyed a few days ago?"

The pixies behind Zora huddled together, talking in furious whispers.

When they resumed their positions, Zora licked her lips nervously. "You're not working undercover for Parks Management or anything? We got a right to live wherever we want. The humans in the house know we're here, and they don't care. We're good tenants."

Deandra and Wendy shared a bewildered look.

"We're not with Parks Management," Deandra said. "They took someone from me, and I'm trying to get him back."

"Any enemy of theirs is a friend of mine." Zora spat toward her own feet. The other pixies all spat, too. "*We're* the ones who messed up the cameras. And we got paid to do it."

"By who?" Deandra asked.

"A fox," Zora said. "Don't know who the fox is as a human, but as a fox, they're black and brown—well, maybe more copper. Real sleek. I'd guess it was a man, since they're typically bigger. He started bringing us acorns. Just leaving them here on the sidewalk in the middle of the night. For a *whole* week, he left us acorns. They were the best acorns any of us had ever had." Several tiny heads nodded vigorously behind Zora. "We got a little addicted to them. Maybe more than a little. So when there was a note with the acorns one day, it was like we didn't even question what he asked us to do. I think we were drugged, but in such small doses we didn't realize it until it was too late. The note had a drawing of the art building with the locations of all the outside cameras. The note said if we chewed through the wires and busted up the hardware, there'd be a reward in it for us. We did it. Next day? The biggest pile of acorns I'd ever seen was right where you're standing. Enough to keep us fed for three months."

Wendy asked, "Do you know what day of the week it was?"

"What do I look like to you, a calendar?"

The pixies behind Zora snickered.

"*Rude*," Wendy muttered under her breath.

Deandra shot a pointed look at the small bag of sugar Deandra still had pinched between her fingers.

Zora bowed her head slightly. "Sorry, Wendy."

Deandra said, "There was an event in the parking lot next door ... young humans putting on an art show."

"Ooh, yeah," Zora said, her blue bangs bouncing against her forehead as she bobbed her head. "We got the note ... hmm ... two days after that. The note said to chew up the wires at night so there was less chance anyone would see."

So the cameras had been destroyed on Wednesday night, just as the art gallery woman had suspected.

"Did you see anyone else suspicious in the parking lot in the last week or so?" Deandra asked. "They would have had a big, sleeping dog with them."

Color crawled up Zora's tiny neck, making her blue hair appear even bluer. "Uhh ... a lot of the last week is kind of a blur ..." She coughed awkwardly. "The fox had already been giving us tainted acorns, making all of us act a bit like addicts, but the effects of that last batch were a doozy. We gorged ourselves on them, which shouldn't have been a problem. It messed us all up, though. We slept off hangovers and stomachaches for nearly two days. We've all had really bad brain fog."

"They gave me more than a stomachache," one of the pixies confessed.

"Me too," said another. "I was awake more than the others, but mostly because I was throwing up so much. I was so sick, I could barely see straight."

Deandra frowned, hoping the plan had only been to get the pixies sick, not that the fox had tried to kill them. "None of you saw anything the day of the fire either?"

Ten tiny heads shook.

One of the male pixies behind Zora flitted forward. "We feel really guilty about our part in this. Zora even more. She thinks she let us down by agreeing to help the fox. But how could she have known there was something wrong with the acorns? It was that fox's fault, not hers. Everyone knows we love our acorns. He wanted us to help him do his dirty work, so he got us good and hooked so we'd comply. Then he got us all drunk or sick afterward to make sure we wouldn't see whatever happened next.

"It's not like we'd tell any of this to the police because it would mean ratting ourselves out. Everyone already thinks pixies are pests. If we confessed to vandalism, we'd be in serious trouble right away. No benefit of the doubt. Since we're so small, the Collective basically considers us animals, which means our complaints are usually redirected to Parks Management. They'd get rid of us all if they could. So we keep quiet. If we stay quiet enough, they forget we exist."

They all fell silent for a moment.

Deandra finally asked, "Do you still have the note or any of the drugged acorns?"

"We got rid of the extra acorns. So much food wasted ..." Zora said forlornly. "But we kept the note."

"Let's swap," Wendy said. "We'll give you the acorns we just bought *and* the lila sugar if you give us the note."

"You gonna tell the cops what we did?" Zora asked.

"We'll leave your names out of it and say we just happened to find the note," Deandra said. "We think we might know who the fox is. Maybe the cops can do a handwriting analysis."

All the pixies' wings went a deep navy blue for a moment, even though they were still fluttering a million miles an hour. Deandra wasn't sure what it meant.

"So we could actually end up helping?" Zora asked, her wings going an even darker blue for a beat. "Maybe the note will help catch the person who did this? The smoke was so bad, we couldn't fly anywhere for hours that day. Many of the animals had to leave for a while. We felt like it was our fault."

"You weren't in your right minds," Deandra said. "The fox took advantage of you."

A pair of the pixies dove into the hedge then, like diving off a board into a pool. They emerged a few moments later with a rolled-up piece of paper. The scroll was a three-by-five piece of scratch paper covered in sketches and little labels, just as Zora had described. The paper was dirty and streaked green from the leaves, but the drawing itself was still in good shape.

Wendy and Deandra handed each pixie a little sack of lila sugar. Once they had their bag, their eyes gleaming, they disappeared back into the bush.

Zora collected hers last, holding the bag to her chest like a pillow. "I'm sorry if I was rude to either of you. It's been a rough few days."

"That's okay," Wendy said, managing a tight-lipped smile.

"Just promise not to take anything else from foxes, okay?" Deandra asked.

Zora laughed—a tinkling sound, like wind chimes. "Deal."

After Zora disappeared into the bush, Deandra and Wendy left the pile of acorns at the foot of the hedge for them to collect later.

Deandra and Wendy set off for the car, the note clutched in Deandra's hand.

Wendy, keeping her voice low, asked, "What do you think the odds are that Corly made *himself* sick? The pixies said they all got stomachaches. Corly said he was down for the count with a messed-up stomach, too."

Deandra nodded absently. "Gave himself an alibi ..."

The longer they walked, the more Deandra's anger at Maxwell Corly mounted. It was unnerving to think she was starting to see where unhinged Grimshaw Peabody was coming from. Corly could have *killed* all those pixies with whatever he'd laced the acorns with. Would he have cared?

She thought of the Saucy Wenches, Layla and Eliza, who had dreamed of opening a restaurant since they were kids. Of Tor Meller, who had built a unique menu with his wife, only to lose his restaurant, his magic, and potentially his marriage due to Corly's potential sabotage. Of the other handful of restaurateurs from Purl Way who may have been cheated out of their dreams, too. Of Brian's family, who was grieving his loss now.

And of a sweet baby dragon who was being wrongly accused of doing something vile and was now trapped in a cage.

She still didn't know how to prove any of it. Maybe this was why Peabody had gone a touch mad: He was convinced of Corly's duplicitous ways but couldn't get anyone to listen.

Chapter 17

Deandra and Wendy had just climbed into Wendy's car when Deandra's phone rang. She hastened to get it out of her bag, hoping not to miss a call from Cruz if he had news. When she saw the name on her screen, Officer Sutter's warning replayed in Deandra's head: "*I know you two hit it off, and I do think she's a good person deep down, but if you decide to forge a friendship with her, keep your eyes wide open until you're sure you can trust her.*"

"Gonna answer that?" Wendy asked, brows hiked.

Deandra hit accept. "Hey, Callie."

"Hey," Callie said, subdued. "Are you still in Axia?"

"Yeah. I'm here until tomorrow."

"Oh good. I wanted to make sure I didn't miss you before you left," she said. "I'm meeting my friend Rae in town for lunch in about half an hour. She just got some really bad news. I don't even know what happened, but I figure an outing would be good for her."

Huh. Rae exists after all ...

Callie asked, "Would you like to join us? We both need some normal hang-out time. Brian's wife and kids are absolutely wrecked, and since I can read their auras and emotions, I'm feeling what they're feeling on top of my *own* emotions. I desperately need a break."

"That sounds really rough."

Callie chuckled darkly. "Understatement."

"One sec ..." Deandra muted the call. "Want to put a pause on sleuthing for an hour or two? Callie wants to grab food."

"Sure," Wendy said, but eyed Deandra curiously. "Everything all right?"

Deandra held up a finger, then took the call off mute. "Hi. My cousin Wendy will be with me, too. Just text me where you want to go, and we'll meet you."

"Sounds good," Callie said. "See you soon."

Deandra disconnected the call, staring at her phone's dark screen for a long moment before telling Wendy about Officer Sutter's warning.

"Is she on our suspect list then?" Wendy asked.

"She sounds so sad. It's hard to believe she would have purposely hurt her own uncle ..."

"Unless she's devastated now out of guilt." When Deandra shot her an incredulous look, Wendy put her hands up in placation. "Just playing devil's advocate. I haven't met Sutter *or* Callie, so I'm biased toward erring on the side of the cop who's had *training* reading people, rather than the lady who used her magic-based ability for evil in high school."

Deandra knew Wendy was being overly dramatic on purpose, but she still saw her point. While Deandra looked forward to seeing Callie again, she'd do her best to stay clear-sighted.

The Haunted Noodle was located downtown and was run out of a supposedly haunted house. Wendy claimed to have been there dozens of times and had yet to see a ghost. Deandra wasn't sure she could deal with wailing spirits on top of everything else, so she hoped the ghosts minded their own business today. Perhaps Callie had chosen the place because she hoped her uncle might pop in for a visit.

Everything Deandra had heard, as little as that was, had suggested the fire had been arson. It still remained to be seen if Callie's uncle had been there on purpose or by accident when the Purl Way location had been engulfed in flames. Not only was Callie dealing with the death of her uncle, she had to consider the possibility that he'd been murdered.

The four ladies met outside the restaurant, and when Callie and Deandra exchanged a hug, Callie hung on for longer than Deandra thought was normal for a friendly greeting. Callie wilted a little during the embrace, as if Deandra was the only thing keeping her on her feet. Deandra wondered if she'd been sleeping.

Officer Sutter's admonition of Callie replayed in her head. "*So you're* using *her?*"

Deandra shook the accusation away.

Rae was a bit older than all three of them by a couple of years. The mint-green silk blouse she wore complemented her tanned skin and dark hair. Deandra still didn't see the resemblance between herself and Rae—partly because there was an elegant polish to the woman. While Rae didn't move with the same fluidity as, say, a werecat, there was something different about her. Elegant was not a word Deandra would use to describe herself. Despite the polish, Rae had bags under her eyes. Makeup was doing its job to mask most of her exhaustion, but Deandra could still see it.

She wondered if her own face looked haggard, worried as she was about the dragon.

It turned out that the other meaning behind the Haunted Noodle's name was because of a culinary challenge spelled out in red letters at the top of the menu. If a brave patron selected The Spiritual Awakening and ate every last noodle, their entire party ate for free. The catch was that the sauce the noodles swam in had been flavored by a generous helping of ghost peppers. Deandra noped out of that one instantly.

A "Wall of Flame" graced the back wall, lined with photos of rosy-cheeked, red-eyed, tear-streaked faces. The same chef was in each one, an arm wrapped around the shoulders of the miserable-looking diner and offering a thumbs-up to the camera. According to the menu, the Haunted Noodle had been open for five years, yet only fifteen people were on the Wall of Flame. All but three were orcs, and even they looked moments from collapsing.

"A guy and I took the challenge on our first date," Rae said. "Let's just say the date ended in the wrong kind of fiery passion."

"Please tell me that was your very traumatic meet-cute, and now you're married with ten kids," Deandra said.

Rae laughed. "I never saw him again. I've been blissfully single for two years now. I just have pets. Much less work."

Callie lifted her water glass to clink with Rae's. "I'd agree with you, but you always have the *weirdest* pets."

Wendy nudged Deandra in the side, giving her an "if only they knew how weird *yours* is" look.

"I hope you ladies don't mind that I'm tagging along," Rae said. "When Cal and I were talking earlier, she mentioned she wanted to meet a new friend for lunch, and I practically begged her to let me come, too. I got the worst phone call of my life an hour ago; I needed to be around friendly faces."

"What happened?" Wendy asked.

Rae hesitated. "I haven't even told Cal yet ..."

Callie put her hand on Rae's arm. "And you don't have to. You don't have to share anything. Not even with me. I can sense that you want to, though. I don't know these ladies well yet, but their curiosity comes from concern. You look as gorgeous as always, but you're also a mess."

Tears lined Rae's eyes in an instant. "My dad was arrested."

Callie reared back slightly, taking her hand off Rae's arm to place over her own chest. "What? Why?"

Rae sniffed hard. "They think he burned that building down. Why would my dad burn down his *own* building?"

Deandra choked on her sip of water. Wendy almost knocked her glass over.

Rae and Callie stared at them, brows raised.

Wendy coughed awkwardly, patting Deandra on the back. "Your dad is Maxwell Corly?"

Rae cocked her head. "Yeah. You know him?"

The drawing of the art gallery was burning a hole in Deandra's pocket.

Corly's daughter had called him while they were in his office. What name had he used when he talked to her? Greta? Grace? Linda? Gracelyn! Was "Rae" short for "Gracelyn"?

"I just know *of* him," Wendy said. "He came up in conversation with my boss because she's been having issues with Grimshaw Peabody."

Rae's jaw clenched. "I'm sure it was *that* weasel who set the fire, and now he's trying to frame my dad."

Callie had, perhaps subconsciously, scooted a few inches away from her friend. "They … they think *your dad* is who … my uncle …"

Rae reached for her, but Callie scooted even farther away. "They have the wrong person. I know it. My dad would *never* hurt Brian. You have to know that. This is a smear campaign by that horrible dwarf. *He* killed Brian. Not my dad."

Callie looked like she was caught between wanting to cry and throw up.

"I told you my dad got really sick the day of the soft opening, right?" Rae asked. "I was already in town running some errands for my mom—" She glanced at Deandra and Wendy in turn. "I live in Kensey—the Washington hub, you know?—but I pop into Axia a lot to help my parents."

"It's cool that telepad travel means you can visit your hometown so easily," Deandra said.

Rae cocked her head. "I didn't grow up in Axia. I'm a born-and-raised Kensian. My parents moved here a few years ago because they needed to get out of the big city."

Deandra's brow furrowed.

So the lie Callie had told Deandra the day they met hadn't been about Rae's existence. It had been about how long the two had known each other. Deandra couldn't fathom why Callie would have lied about *that* of all things.

"Anyway," Rae said, pulling Deandra back into the conversation, "I was running errands when my dad called me to say he wasn't feeling well, and he asked me to pick up some meds from the drugstore. I was literally next door to Dad's empty storefront when it caught fire. Dad couldn't have committed arson if he was laid up in bed with stomach cramps."

The scrunch of Callie's forehead smoothed out as she listened, but Deandra was sure that, no matter how much Callie wanted to believe Rae, she'd be putting in a call to family friend Officer Sutter the moment she was able.

"I've been building a case against Peabody just like he's been trying to build one against my dad." Rae glanced around, checking if any of the nearby patrons were listening, then leaned forward. "Can I show you what I found? I think I almost have enough to nail him. The dumb werecats just got to my dad before I could get to Peabody."

Deandra and Wendy scootched a little closer, but Callie remained stiff-backed and wide-eyed as she stared miserably at her friend.

Rae's shoulders slumped a little. She reached out a hand, palm up on the table. "You know you can sense if I'm telling the truth. Just read my aura."

"It's not foolproof," Callie said tightly. "My magic will only tell me if *you* believe your own truth."

"And your heart will tell you the rest," Rae said. "You trust *me*, don't you?"

Callie tentatively placed her hand in Rae's.

"My dad didn't kill your uncle," Rae said with conviction, staring Callie dead in the eye. "And I have proof that Peabody is an even more terrible person than we thought."

A few seconds later, Callie nodded and let out a shaky breath. "Show us what you found."

Rae clearly had been worried Callie was going to put her faith elsewhere. "Yeah? Oh, thank the realms!" She lunged forward to dramatically throw her arms around Callie. In the process, she bumped her purse off the bench seat beside her, sending it toppling to the ground. It hit the tile with a muted thump. Rae and Callie went to reach for the bag at the same time and managed to thunk their foreheads together.

Callie winced, sitting up straight with her hand on her forehead, while Rae disappeared from view as she scooped up her bag off the floor. "You'd be amazed how many times we've done that," Callie said.

Rae righted herself, plopping her purse back on the bench seat. "This is what happens when friends share a brain." She rubbed a spot just above an eyebrow. "You are literally the most hardheaded person I know."

Callie rolled her eyes good-naturedly.

Rae tapped a few things on her phone, then held it up so they could all see the screen if they craned their necks just right. "This is outside our house a week ago."

It was a photograph of Grimshaw Peabody standing on the sidewalk outside a home.

"Where'd you get this picture?" Deandra asked, impressed by how crisp it was when it had clearly been taken at night from some spot across the street.

"I hired a private investigator," Rae said. "The restraining order keeping Peabody away from the office is still active, but I had a feeling he was coming by our house, too."

Rae cycled through a series of photographs, like a digital flipbook, showing Peabody letting himself through a small gate, creeping across a lawn, and poking around in bushes that lined the front of the house.

"What was he doing?" Callie asked.

Rae placed her phone on the table, then rummaged in her purse again. It took her a moment to find what she wanted. "He was putting this near the house's foundation," she said, holding a cinched-up leather bag the size of a coin purse.

Swallowing nervously, Rae placed the bag in the middle of the table and pulled open the top. She quickly sat back, as if she expected scorpions to pour out at any moment. Nothing happened.

"Oh jeez," Callie said, leaning back as well. "What *is* that? I don't smell anything, but it's almost making me ... queasy?"

Rae nodded. "It's a talisman that gives off some kind of energy that makes magic wig out. It makes me lightheaded."

Deandra and Wendy shot each other a look. An "is that a magic-altering talisman like the one that caused Tor's magic to go screwy?" kind of look. Maybe Wendy and Deandra shared a brain, too.

"Can I?" Wendy asked, gesturing to the bag. "I'm totally mundane," she added a bit glumly, as if she'd just confessed to having a communicable disease.

"Sure," Rae said. "Just keep it as close to you as you can when it's not in the magic-dampening bag."

Deandra wondered how well a magic-dampening bag worked against a magic-altering talisman but refrained from asking.

Wendy picked up the bag and peered into it, angling it so Deandra could see inside too. The talisman was round, about twice the diameter of a mundane quarter. It shone silver.

When Wendy dumped the talisman into her palm, both Rae and Callie hissed in discomfort. Deandra hoped it wasn't actually hurting them.

One side of the talisman was as smooth as glass with no etchings, while the other was covered in what Deandra now knew were runes —the magic language sorcerers used to write out spells. The runes were written in three rings—one along the outside edge of the talisman, one in the middle, and a smaller one that formed a circle about the diameter of a dime. If Deandra took a picture of it, could Cruz pass it along to his contact in Luma?

"This is pretty heavy," Wendy said, testing the weight in her palm. "Dee, feel how heavy this is."

Deandra tried not to let her brows smash together. The slight change in Wendy's tone probably hadn't registered to the other two women, but Deandra noted that her voice was a little too high, her words a little too clipped.

She took the talisman, testing it in her hand the way Wendy had. It didn't feel alarmingly weighty.

"Is that nickel-plated pewter?" Wendy asked Rae in that slightly off tone.

Rae said, "Yeah. Good eye. How does someone who is 'totally mundane' know that?"

"I work at Heather's Elixirs. You gotta learn the stats and ingredients of her products real quick to be able to work there," Wendy said.

"That's so cool. Several of my friends in Kensey make a special trip over here once a month specifically to go to Heather's." Rae jutted her chin at the talisman Deandra held, then added, "That shoddy thing has decent-ish runework, but you can tell a two-bit sorcerer or charlatan who *thinks* they know runework made that. I think it's supposed to negate magic, but it just makes people near it feel sick."

Wendy added, "And pewter is about as cheap as you can get in terms of metals with high magic-conductivity."

"Right? So on top of everything else, Peabody is a cheapskate," Rae said, shaking her head.

Deandra was only half listening. She thought of Peabody's anger over Madison's "irresponsible shelving" that had resulted in him picking up a nickel-plated talisman by accident, causing his entire hand to break out in welts. He still wore the thick white bandage. Peabody *might* have been dastardly enough to leave a magic-altering talisman at the home or workplace of someone he considered an enemy, but he'd be fussy enough to pay more for a nickel-free one to do it.

Wendy's tone and cadence told Deandra that she'd puzzled this out, too. Deandra frantically tried to figure out what to do with this information while remaining calm on the outside. It was only a matter of time, though, before Callie's magic picked up the shift in their auras. Deandra was sure her abysmal poker face would reveal it much sooner.

A sharp pain stabbed her big toe. Thankful for the momentary distraction, she peered under the table. She wasn't sure what she expected to see, but meeting the dark, calculating eye of a jet-black newt covered in glittery yellow spots hadn't been it.

Deandra couldn't imagine how this could be the same newt that had bitten her shoe two days ago, but there was something very familiar about the malice in its eye. It wrinkled its face, and while maintaining unsettlingly intense eye contact, bit down harder.

"Ow!" Deandra yelped, kicking her foot. Newts didn't have teeth, did they? Was this a magic-touched newt blessed with vise-grip jaws? She gave her foot another hard shake, but the amphibious demon hung fast to the toe of her tennis shoe. Deandra could have sworn it smiled. "Get off, you little monster!" she hissed.

That interrupted whatever conversation the other ladies were having. A moment later, Rae's face was peeking under the table, too.

"Sunshine!" Rae said when she realized what was happening. "I thought you were still asleep. Let go and get up here."

To Deandra's surprise, the newt let go of Deandra's shoe in an instant and scurried up Rae's pant leg. When Deandra righted herself, the black newt was perched on Rae's shoulder, nearly blending in with Rae's hair, save for its yellow spots. The newt turned its head to better see Deandra.

Wendy chuckled nervously. "Callie wasn't kidding when she said you had weird pets ..."

Rae reached up to give Sunshine a scratch under her chin. The newt's eyes closed in obvious pleasure.

Deandra's heartbeat started to ratchet up. In a tone that she hoped wasn't as obviously off as Wendy's had been earlier, she asked, "Are you a witch, Rae? I always associate witches with those—eye of newt and all that." She added a laugh that she was sure fooled no one.

Sunshine's eyes snapped open, and she hissed at Deandra, as if offended.

"Nope," Rae said. "I'm a fox shifter, like my dad. I've always been blessed with a connection to animals, though. My mom is a witch, but I didn't inherit much of her powers. I'm pretty handy with potions and herbs. Whether that's nature or nurture, I don't know."

Deandra nodded along as if this were a perfectly normal conversation.

All through lunch, Deandra had been worried about Callie being more than she seemed. But it was Rae she should have been worried about.

Rae was the arsonist, not her father.

Rae, by her own admission, had been right next door when the fire broke out. Rae's trained fire newt had been running loose in the area the day of the fire, harassing the Clarion pixie family. While at the Mythic Pet Kitchen, Deandra had seen firsthand that when a fire newt expelled their magical reserves, their spots went dark. Sunshine's spots had been dark the first time she'd attacked Deandra's shoe.

Rae was the fox who had been visiting the pixies and tricked them into destroying the cameras, not her father. She'd said herself that she was well-versed in herbs—did that include knowing how to lace acorns with a substance that would leave pixies incapacitated for days?

Did that also mean she'd made her father sick to give him an alibi? Or had he been complicit in the plan?

Deandra recalled that, on the day of the fire, several animals had fled the scene, running in the opposite direction of the screaming sirens. In addition to a pair of cats and a murder of crows, a black dog with a fluffy tail had run by. Deandra had thought it was a coyote, but had it actually been a fox?

Rae most likely had lied about the details of why Peabody had been on her property. For all Deandra knew, Rae had lured Peabody there somehow solely to take those incriminating-looking pictures. Maybe he'd been searching for his lost cat. All Deandra knew was that he hadn't planted that nickel-plated talisman there, so it threw everything else she'd said into question. Rae was attempting to frame the dwarf for the crime—for *her* crime.

Had she stood at the counter in the drugstore and let her pet scurry next door to start the fire? Had Rae *known* Callie's uncle was in the building? Was Rae manipulative enough that she could outfox Callie's powers, like a psychopath who could beat a polygraph test? Perhaps Callie, once a manipulator herself, had met her match.

Deandra had to get herself and Wendy out of here. Sunshine's spots were currently a bright yellow, meaning she could ignite whenever she wanted. Whenever Rae commanded it.

"Dee?"

Her gaze swiveled to Callie.

"What's going on? You're so anxious all of a sudden," Callie said.

Deandra placed a hand on her own stomach. "I don't think I'm as tolerant of spicy food as I thought. I should probably get home and take something to settle my stomach. I'm just ... a little embarrassed, I guess."

Callie smiled sympathetically.

Deandra hazarded a glance at Rae, finding both the fox shifter and her fire newt watching her intently. "Really sorry to cut this short," she said, hastily pulling some cash out of her wallet and dropping it on the table. Wendy did the same.

Callie disentangled herself from the bench seat and hurried over to give both Deandra and Wendy a hug. "We'll all keep in touch, okay? It was great to meet you, Wendy."

"Yeah, you too," Wendy said.

Rae didn't get up. "Nice to meet you both," she said flatly.

Deandra and Wendy waved, then speed-walked out of the Haunted Noodle.

The moment they were inside Wendy's car, Wendy yelped, "Rae is the killer, isn't she?"

"Yes! Get to the police station!"

Wendy didn't need to be told twice. She started up the car and nearly peeled out of the lot. Deandra hoped the werecats would believe her when she told them that they'd arrested the wrong fox.

Chapter 18

"We're almost there," Wendy said. "I don't know how we're going to convince them that—"

Deandra jerked forward in her seat, the seat belt like a vise across her chest. She whipped her head to the side to ask Wendy what had happened, but she found her answer a moment later. A jet-black newt covered in yellow spots was perched atop Wendy's steering wheel. It wore that almost-smile again, its head cocked as it regarded Wendy and Deandra in turn.

Thankfully, they were driving on a road not currently occupied by other cars, so they avoided adding a fender bender to this mess. As Deandra glanced around, she noted that they were surrounded by several new commercial buildings that were either closed for the evening or had "For Lease" signs in their windows. For lease by Corly Land Management.

Wendy's wide eyes were focused on the newt. Her hands gripped the wheel so tightly at ten and two that her knuckles had gone white. "I don't know what to do."

Deandra didn't either. The brightness of those spots was doing nothing to comfort her nerves. This demonic little amphibian could erupt like a miniature bomb whenever the fancy struck. The fact that it had shown itself now, while they were on a stretch of road lined by buildings owned by Corly, wasn't lost on her. Rae had somehow commanded the newt—who must have chased after them and jumped into the car just before they'd peeled out of the Haunted Noodle's lot—to stop them here. Rae had to be nearby. Would the newt engulf everything in the car in one great burst, or would its blast only be big enough to leave Wendy horribly scarred?

"Slowly take your hands off the wheel," Deandra said. "No sudden movements."

Wendy let out a choked sob but eased one hand off the wheel. Sunshine cocked her head to watch more closely. Wendy pushed the button to release her seat belt, carefully sliding the belt into its holster up by her head. The newt's too-observant gaze snapped to Deandra as soon as she started to remove her own seat belt.

When Wendy's other hand went from wheel to door handle, though, the newt hissed, her body flashing such a bright orange that Deandra had to shield her eyes. It reminded her of the video sent into Parks Management of the dire wolf's fur erupting in flames.

Wendy screamed, throwing her arms over her head.

When the smell of burning flesh or hair *didn't* reach her, Deandra unshielded her face. The spots on the newt still glowed a vibrant yellow but were perhaps a little dimmer now. Part of the steering wheel had melted, but Wendy was unscathed. At least physically. Sunshine stood on the dashboard now, body pumping up and down as if she were doing preparatory push-ups before the real altercation began.

"We have to get out of this car, Wendy," Deandra said, grateful that her body hadn't chosen to shut down on her. Perhaps she was instinctively taking the practical route because Wendy was very much not.

Sunshine opened her mouth in that semblance of a smile again, like a dog panting. She'd stopped doing push-ups, but the few yellow spots Deandra could see on her legs and head appeared to be as bright as they'd been in the Haunted Noodle, as if her energy stores had already been replenished.

Shakily, Wendy said, "It's like my limbs don't work."

"That's the fear talking." Deandra cast a quick glance in her side mirror and the rearview. No other cars. "When I say go, you fling yourself out the door no matter what, okay?"

"But—"

"No matter what," Deandra repeated. "If your car turns into a puddle of goo, I'll figure out how to buy you a new one. Given the state of my bank account, though, it might have to be a skateboard."

Wendy spluttered a laugh.

Something dark darted by in the side mirror. "What was *that*?" Deandra whisper-hissed.

Wendy only had eyes for the newt. "What was what?"

Deandra scanned the glass. "Nothing. Okay. On three. One, two—"

The passenger door flew open.

Wendy and Deandra shrieked in unison.

"Hi, ladies," Rae said, squatting beside the open door, hands on her knees. "Wendy, I'm going to need you to give me those car keys. Otherwise I'll have Sunshine melt this car with you both still in it."

What was more chilling than the words was the chipper way Rae had delivered them.

"What do I do, Dee?" Wendy asked, voice tight.

Deandra wondered how far they'd make it if Deandra head-butted Rae and Wendy hit the gas. Probably not far.

"Fire can't kill a fire newt," Rae said, as if she could hear the growing list of possible escape plans flying through Deandra's head. "Well, I suppose she wouldn't survive if I tossed her into an active volcano, but not much would, would it? If Sunshine goes nuclear, she'll walk away unscathed and you two won't walk away at all."

Deandra said, "Give her the keys."

With a heavy sigh, Wendy turned off the car and passed the keys over. Deandra watched as the keys disappeared into the pocket of Rae's slacks.

Rae draped an arm on top of the open door, peering in, stance casual. Rae's pupils were blown wide. The brown of her irises—what little Deandra could still see of them—had gone an unsettling shade of red, like the pile of red acorns gifted to the pixies. A predator lay beneath the posh, put-together exterior, and Deandra couldn't let herself forget it.

"Hands back at ten and two, Wendy," Rae said. "Sunshine, my sweet, if she attempts to get out of the car, make her regret it."

Sunshine hissed in reply.

Rae refocused on Deandra. "Why did you two run off so quickly? We were just getting to know each other."

Deandra tried to mimic Rae's outward calm. "I wasn't feeling well, remember?"

Rae tsked. "You can't trick a trickster, girl. I might not be able to read people the way Cal does, but I can still read them. Wendy's reaction to the talisman was my first clue you two weren't just mundane ladies Cal met on a whim. Dee's reaction to Sunshine confirmed that." She jutted her chin at Deandra. "Now, I'll ask you again, where were you two running off to?"

Her gut told her to be direct with Rae. Being "tricky" only seemed to annoy her, and since the fox shifter was clearly unhinged, Deandra didn't trust Rae not to hurt Wendy out of frustration. "To tell the werecats they arrested the wrong person for arson and Brian's murder."

Wendy stiffened.

Rae's brilliantly white teeth made a quick appearance. "See, that wasn't so hard, was it?"

If Deandra was right that Rae bore some characteristics of a psychopath, she might want to boast about how clever she'd been, reveling in the pain she'd caused. "Was it your dad who was sabotaging everyone's restaurants or you?"

Rae's nostrils flared. It was a very ... animal-like reaction, and

Deandra wasn't entirely sure what it meant. "It was my dad's scheme."

"Peabody's *actually* been right this whole time?" Wendy asked, incredulous.

Offering a chuckle of surprise that she hoped sounded natural, Deandra said, "Peabody's smarter than I gave him credit for ... than anyone does, really. A hotheaded dwarf shrewder than a fox. Hear something new every day."

Scoffing, Rae said, "He's *not* more shrewd. He got lucky. Peabody ran his own restaurant into the ground without our help. He did so much damage to the place that Dad had to spend thousands just to get it presentable again. That location was always a money pit, but it got even worse after Peabody trashed it. Dad heard about this scheme on the news where a mundane landlord weaseled tenants out of a lot of money. Dad got inspired. He figured if a mundane could do it, he could do it even better.

"He locked new tenants into a really affordable commercial lease in exchange for robust security deposits that were promised to be returned at the end of a lease's term. Then, *all of a sudden*, things started to go wrong for the tenant. Expensive machinery broke down. Employees experienced car trouble or illnesses at inopportune times ..."

"Magic started to glitch," Deandra offered.

Rae nodded. "That one was my idea. Subtle enough to drive a magic wielder slowly insane without them realizing what was going on."

Poor Tor ...

"Tragically, month after month," Rae, without a shred of sympathy, said, "there were fewer customers in the restaurant for one reason or another. Money started getting tight for them. When my dad offered to let them out of their lease early, or if they begged him to break it before their term was up, Dad would graciously agree. As long as he got two or three months of rent and could keep the hefty deposit fee, they could break their lease with no further penalties.

Dad made a lot more money that way, a lot faster. The faster he got the cash, the sooner he could get out of the red. Plus, when something went a little sideways with equipment, Dad was always there with a recommendation for a really great handyman."

"Who would offer your dad a kickback if the tenant went with your dad's suggestion?" Deandra said.

Rae tapped her own nose. "Right on the money. And it was all quite lucrative ... until it wasn't."

Wendy spoke up. "Let me guess. Peabody, obsessed with being wronged and letting everyone know it, plus all the 'bad luck' tenants experienced, suddenly made people too scared to lease the place?"

"More or less," Rae said. "By the time Saucy Wench opened, I was well aware of what Dad was doing. We agreed that one should run its course for a while. People would be much less suspicious if one of the restaurants actually thrived."

Deandra's phone vibrated in her purse by her feet.

"Don't even think about it," Rae snapped, the red ring around her pupils glowing bright.

"So what happened?" Wendy asked.

Rae slipped back into her conversational tone just as easily. "Brian Coburn happened."

Deandra turned in her seat so she could more fully stare up at Rae. Rae who had looked Callie in the eye and had told her that her uncle hadn't been killed by Maxwell Corly. Rae *had* been telling the truth, yet the awful truth was that *she'd* killed Brian.

"*You know you can read if I'm telling the truth,*" Rae had said.

"*It's not foolproof. My magic will only tell me if* you *believe your* own *truth.*"

"*And your heart will tell you the rest,*" Rae had said. "*You trust* me, *don't you?*"

Rae had looked her friend right in the eye, defied Callie's magic, and lied to her face.

"What did Brian do?" Deandra asked. "Was he more shrewd than you and your dad, too? Wasn't Brian a lowly mundane?"

While Deandra knew goading the shifter wasn't smart when the woman was both a predator and quick to anger, the jabs at her intelligence made her chatty. If she talked for long enough, maybe Wendy could figure out how to get away.

"Yeah, Brian figured out what Dad was doing and threatened to go public with it," Rae said, disgusted. "The only way Brian would keep quiet about it was if Dad agreed to a thirty percent reduction in rent for the Large & Wide location that couldn't be increased for two years—*and* no security deposit. Dad agreed. That was almost a year ago. Around then, I'd overheard a conversation between Brian and Dad about Brian having a niece in town. Dad and I thought Cal and Brian were thick as thieves, so I decided to befriend her to see if she knew whether Brian was really going to keep his word. I didn't need the ability to read auras to know Cal was lying through her teeth about Brian's promise to keep quiet. Dad thought I was giving Brian too much credit, but I know a schemer when I see one—mundane or not. He was trying to have his cake and eat it too."

Deandra asked, "Did you lure him to the Purl Way location on the day of the soft opening?"

Rae grinned. "Yep. He might have been a schemer, but he never suspected Maxwell Corly's daughter was a threat. Not even Dad knew my plan. He really *was* at home sick with a stomach bug—thanks to a potion I mixed into his morning tea.

"I told Brian I was helping Dad with paperwork and that, since I was only in Axia for a few hours that day before I had to close a deal in Kensey, we could wrap up the final details an hour or so before he had to be at Large & Wide. I left a key for him under the mat and a note on the door that said to let himself in to sign the papers. The note said I'd be back in a few minutes, after I picked up some medicine for my dad from the drugstore next door." She stared wistfully into space. "I saved up my pennies for six months to buy that alchemical powder from a black-market website. Days before, I'd lined the inside edge of the building with the powder. I bought an even more expensive flame-retardant powder from the same alchemist and ringed the *outside* of the building so it wouldn't burn down the drugstore or the apartment complex."

"How thoughtful of you," Wendy said, deadpan.

"I thought so," Rae said. "I actually hadn't even thought of that step, but the alchemist recommended it. I figured he knew best. Turns out that was a good call. I only wanted to get rid of Brian and that money-pit of a building."

Deandra clenched her jaw. This woman was completely off her rocker. Deandra looked away from Rae long enough to address Sunshine. "Once the powder was in place and Brian was in the building, you set the fire?"

Sunshine hissed, smiling.

Rae said, "Shifters don't have familiars the same way witches do, but I have some powerful potions that can create a familiar-like bond for a short window of time. When we're bonded, we can practically speak telepathically. She'll do whatever I tell her, no questions asked."

Deandra eyed the newt again, *refusing* to feel sorry for her.

Mostly.

Rae said, "My plan went off without a hitch. I thought it was pretty brilliant." She smiled wistfully again. "I set up a trip wire that ran the length of the room, just in front of the table where I left Brian's paperwork. When he triggered the wire, it released the door on Sunshine's terrarium. She'd been stuck in there for three days with little food to purposefully make her madder than a hornet. When she was released, I knew she'd go nuclear almost immediately. The alchemical powder all over the floor, plus an open flame, equals ... kaboom. No more money-sink of a building, no more blackmail from Brian Coburn, and Dad will get a nice check from the insurance company any day now. Win-win-win."

"Callie's your *friend*." It was all Deandra could think to say.

Rae flapped a hand. "I'm trying to make a name for myself in this industry. I'm poised to open my own branch of Corly Land Management in Kensey. I can't have someone like Brian Coburn ruining that before I even get started."

"What about Peabody?" Wendy asked. "He's been close to figuring this all out for a while."

Deandra thought that if the dwarf could have gotten his raging temper in check, he would have deduced all this himself. But his anger seemed to override rationality more often than not.

"Peabody is a nuisance, sure, but he's harmless," Rae said.

Deandra asked, "Yet you're still planning to make him go down for all this?"

"Yeah, obviously," Rae said, as if she thought Deandra were simple indeed. She leaned down an inch to get a better look at Wendy. "Has she not been listening?"

"She doesn't know how to react in the presence of utter lunacy," Wendy said.

Rae was unfazed by the comment. She reached into a pocket and produced a small leather bag. She grabbed a pinch of something from inside and tossed it into the car. A faint whiff of ammonia and burnt plastic assaulted Deandra's nostrils. Her chest constricted.

"This can't possibly be your plan," Deandra said. "If you keep setting fires, someone is going to find a pattern. It'll get traced back to you."

"Eventually, maybe," Rae said. "But while the werecats are investigating this mysterious fire, I'll have plenty of time to point their feline noses toward Peabody. And, lo and behold, when the pest is locked up, all of a sudden the mysterious fires stop!" She tossed a small handful of the alchemical powder into the car now instead of merely a pinch. It landed on Deandra like fine sand, dotting her clothes and arms with specks of maroon. Sand that made her itch. Sand that ... *burned*. Deandra slapped at her arms and at the spots on her jeans being eaten away by the malicious powder.

Wendy cursed, removing her hands from the suggested ten and two so she could swat at her arms and face. She dove for the door, only to have Sunshine land on the glass, igniting in a flash of bright orange. The air filled with the scent of burning plastic. Sunshine hissed. Wendy screamed and reared back. Flecks of powder that had touched the upholstery above the door burned bright like embers. Seconds later, the fabric of Wendy's roof was on fire. Wendy ducked, shielding her head.

"No matter what!" Deandra said. "Go!"

Wendy flung herself at the driver's side door and spilled out just as the flames licking the roof jumped to the headrest of her seat. Deandra lunged toward Rae, hoping the sudden movement would startle the woman. Deandra hit the ground, Rae nowhere to be seen. Deandra didn't know where Sunshine had gone either, but she could hear Wendy's retreating footsteps. At least she'd get away.

Deandra struggled to her feet, swatting at her arms and neck and finding small welts rising there. She'd only stumbled a few steps from the car when a wall of heat slammed into her back. The roof on the passenger side was now engulfed too.

A snarl sounded, and she whirled to find a black-and-copper fox the size of a mountain lion standing a few feet away. Its eyes glowed an eerie red. Deandra swallowed hard, taking a step to the right. The fox mirrored her, perfectly in sync, as if she anticipated the move Deandra was going to make before she'd made it. Rae's fluffy black tail gently swayed back and forth, as if taunting Deandra.

I'm waaaiting, the sway seemed to say.

Running from wild animals was *not* the thing to do, right?

The fox unleashed the most unsettling screaming cry—like a woman in agony—and that was it. Instinct took over and Deandra ran. She'd never run as fast in her life as she did then. Her mind had gone blank. She was pure adrenaline now.

The fox huffed behind her, her teeth snapping. Deandra imagined Rae trying to bite her ankles.

Deandra ran faster.

She ran, and ran, and ran. Her lungs burned even more painfully than the welts on her arms and legs, where the powder had eaten through denim.

She veered to the right, running pell-mell down the sidewalk instead of in the middle of the street, hoping to find some kind of shelter she could duck into. She'd just run past a space between two buildings when something huge and beige flashed in her periphery. The crash of bodies sounded a breath later. She skittered to a stop and whirled to find a massive puma pinning a black fox to the ground. Both animals heaved. The fox, on her side, tried to wriggle free, but the puma had her firmly held down with two giant paws. Half a dozen other big cats appeared then—leaping off roofs, careening around corners, and loping down the middle of the road.

Deandra swayed and stumbled until her back hit the brick wall behind her. Her legs ached. She placed her hands on her knees and watched as the big cats morphed into people in uniform, a circular symbol adorning the breast pockets of each. The last of the animals to return to human form were Rae and Officer Sutter—the puma who'd pinned the fox to the asphalt. Officer Sutter hauled Rae to her feet.

"You okay, Dee?" Office Sutter called out.

Deandra managed a thumbs up.

A muted explosion in the distance told Deandra that Wendy's car was likely no more. Several werecats seamlessly shifted back into cats and took off to investigate.

"Dee?"

Deandra heaved out a relieved breath and pushed away from the wall, staggering toward the street to see Wendy jogging toward her. They met in the middle of the road and crashed into a tight hug. Now that Rae was in the hands of the werecats, some of Deandra's fear was fading. Which meant the pain from the welts marring her skin was loudly making itself known. Still, she didn't let Wendy go for a long time.

When they finally broke the embrace, it was clear Wendy had been crying. "You told me to run, so I ran, but I didn't know if you got away, too. It all happened so fast."

"I'm glad you ran," Deandra said. "Don't feel bad about that."

"You ladies sure you're okay?"

They turned to find Officer Sutter approaching. The woman looked no worse for wear. Rae was in the custody of two other were-cats, who were hauling the woman away. Deandra didn't see any squad cars nearby, but she supposed when you could turn into a massive cat, you didn't always need one.

There wasn't a speck of dirt on Sutter's crisp uniform, and not a blond hair had slipped free from her tight bun.

"I think so," Deandra said. "But ... how did you know where we were?"

"Callie called me," Officer Sutter said. "She could tell her friend Rae was lying, though she wasn't sure about what. She could tell that the things Rae told you two made you both become instantly nervous. When Rae made an excuse to part ways shortly after you two left the restaurant, Callie worried Rae was going after you."

Remembering the note in her pocket, Deandra hastily scrounged around until she pulled out the crumpled drawing of the art gallery. She handed it to Officer Sutter. "Rae drew that, got a bunch of pixies addicted to drugged acorns, and then convinced them to destroy the cameras around the gallery."

Officer Sutter let out a knowing, "Ah," as she took the mangled piece of paper. "That was the one piece of the puzzle we couldn't parse out. We all assumed magic was used in the vandalism, since we couldn't physically see anyone on screen, but there were no magical signatures of any kind on the cameras, nor was there any magical interference in the feed." She paused. "Do you think the pixies would be willing to come in for a statement?"

"I'm not sure," Deandra said. "They're very bitter about ... everything. I promised I wouldn't divulge names."

"Fair enough," Officer Sutter said. "If a statement is necessary, I may ask you to be an intermediary for us with the pixies."

Wendy chuckled. "Pixie liaison! Now there's a career change."

Deandra ignored her. None of this explained how the werecats had known exactly where Deandra and Wendy were. Could they smell the ammonia and burnt plastic with their heightened feline senses?

Officer Sutter craned her neck to glance around Deandra, peering toward the alley Sutter had barreled down just before tackling Rae to the ground. "You can come out now."

A high-pitched chirp sounded, and Deandra spun to find Cruz emerging from the alley. And he had company. The dragon shrieked in delight when he saw Deandra, pulling so hard on his leash that Cruz was nearly yanked off his feet. Cruz let the leash go and the dragon galloped toward Deandra, crashing into her and knocking her onto her backside, just like the first time they'd met. Her tailbone twinged, the bruise probably flaring to life again, but she didn't care. The dragon knocked her all the way over, the back of her shirt instantly damp. But she didn't care about that, either. The dragon, with his feet on her shoulders, furiously licked her face and neck. The welts stung even more, but she was so happy to see he was okay that she hardly felt the pain.

Once they'd both calmed down, and the dragon allowed her to sit up, she found Wendy, Cruz, and Officer Sutter standing around her in a semicircle, all of them sharing a bemused smile at Deandra's and the dragon's enthusiastic reunion.

Deandra addressed Cruz first. "How'd you get him out? I know you said you had a possible lead, but I hadn't heard anything since then."

"You didn't get any of my messages?" he asked.

"If they were sent in the last half hour, no," Deandra said, remembering that her phone had gone off at least once while they'd been held hostage.

Wendy idly scratched at a welt on her neck. "Rae went on a villain monologue and then almost burned us alive in my car, so we weren't really checking our phones."

Cruz seemed unfazed by Wendy's sarcasm. "I got in contact with Dancy like you suggested. When I showed him the test results that revealed the ... wolf had Quowlaxliquin in his system—meaning the chances of him even being conscious when the fire happened were slim—he called in a favor and got the release approved in a matter of hours. I got your boy out about half an hour ago. I was planning to keep him at my place until I could talk to you, and then ... he just ... freaked out. Kept pulling me down the sidewalk like he knew where he was going. I think he sensed you needed help."

Deandra, who had the dragon clutched in her lap, hugged him a little closer and kissed the top of his head. "Were you trying to find me, buddy?"

He chirped, then tipped his head back and licked her chin.

"After talking to Callie," Officer Sutter said, "we were attempting to figure out where you all were. Dr. Caddel literally went running by with the puppy, who was running so fast, Dr. Caddel was practically flapping in the air behind him like a banner. We quickly figured out we were all looking for the same person, so we let the puppy guide us to you."

Cruz said, "Once we got over here, he thankfully listened to me when I told him we had to hang back and let the cats do their thing. I think he calmed down because he knew you were safe."

Deandra hugged the dragon a little tighter.

Officer Sutter offered one of her rare smiles. "You two are lucky to have found each other."

The dragon peeped in agreement.

Chapter 19

Deandra and Wendy spent Saturday evening sprawled out on the couch, covered in poultices and creams supplied by their grandparents and Heather to treat the welts covering their arms, legs, faces, and necks. Cruz had dropped the pair at Wendy's apartment with a promise to check on them in the morning. When Deandra had gotten a good look at herself in the mirror, she had a sneaking suspicion that Cruz's invite to lunch would be forever rescinded, if only because her frightful state would haunt his nightmares until his dying day.

He'd sent her a cryptic text later, though, to say he was still working on how they were going to get past Ranger Vicks eventually demanding Deandra supply Parks Management with proof of her "dire wolf's" registration. She supposed she'd cross that bridge once Vicks was actively trying to throw her off it.

Their grandparents managed to pry most of the story out of the ladies—except for the little detail about the dragon's true identity, of course. Deandra figured the tale would be the talk of the town by morning. She could only imagine how the next conversation with her mother would go.

Deandra's technical final day in Axia was decidedly calmer than the days preceding it. She and Wendy had a nice breakfast with their grandparents; Deandra learned from Officer Sutter that Maxwell Corly had been released, while his daughter had been charged with arson and the murder of Brian Coburn; and Cruz and Wendy agreed to look after the dragon in rotating shifts until Deandra made a decision about whether she wanted to keep him.

No one had made a claim on him—either as a dragon or a dire wolf.

Callie came over to Wendy's apartment on Sunday evening, and they cried and lamented over Rae's role in Brian's death. Deandra wasn't sure which was eating Callie up more: the fact that her uncle had been killed, or that she'd been friends with a woman who had spent months plotting Callie's uncle's death while she'd been none the wiser. Callie had clearly always put great faith in her ability and was now wondering how much she should rely on it.

"I'm sorry I wasn't totally truthful about Rae when I first met you," Callie told Deandra. "I was picking up on your feelings and memories about Wendy ... and your truth became mine. I said Rae and I had been friends in high school, but I've only known her for a year or two. It honestly felt like I'd known her all my life when I first met her. Connections like that don't happen very often for me, since

I can read most people right away. Takes the mystery out of almost everyone. It was different with Rae." She frowned. "Turns out Rae had been using her shifter abilities on me the whole time. Charmed her way into my life without me realizing our friendship had been built on a lie."

Deandra could tell Callie found that admission embarrassing.

Callie continued, "Maybe this is karma. I don't know. It's a bad habit of mine to let my reading of people dictate what I say, especially in initial interactions. Their truths and feelings become *my* truths and feelings, and the line where they stop and I start can be blurry."

What Callie had initially said about her friendship with Rae had sounded so much like Deandra's own friendship with Wendy that it had felt like she'd made an instant connection with a stranger. Instead, Callie had done to Deandra what Rae had done to Callie, but on a much smaller level.

"It's like my ability forces me to perpetually tell little white lies," Callie said. "I didn't fight it when I was a kid. I'm trying to fight it now."

Callie hadn't supplied details of the things she'd done in her past to get her estranged from several of her friends and family members, or how she'd broken Sutter's brother's heart, but it was evident Callie was struggling with her demons. Maybe one day she'd be able to forgive herself.

While the trio stayed up into the wee hours watching the trashiest shows and movies they could find, the dragon lay on the floor in front of the couch, his head on Deandra's feet.

Since Deandra's and Wendy's purses had gone up in flames along with Wendy's car, Deandra realized she needed to stay in Axia at least another day or two to get some of her affairs in order. They had to request replacement driver's licenses, credit and debit cards, and purchase cell phones. Deandra's replacement ID would be sent to her apartment in Los Angeles. Hopefully she wouldn't get pulled over on the way back home. *Sorry, officer, but I don't have my driver's license because an unhinged fire newt roasted the car my purse was in* would no doubt be even less believable than the old "my dog ate my homework" excuse. Thankfully, Deandra had left her car keys in Wendy's apartment and hadn't needed to get those replaced, too.

The phone issue she took care of within hours, and she was able to contact her boss to let her know she'd be stuck in Axia for a few more days. Deandra had built up enough good grace with her boss that she didn't give Deandra much grief about it.

By the time Wednesday rolled around, Deandra had a temporary license, some cash from her grandparents in her newly purchased wallet, and very few excuses for continuing to stay in Axia. The dragon seemed oblivious to the fact that Deandra was leaving the following morning. She had to admit that the theory that they shared a special bond rang true, but even so, he was a baby with a short attention span. There were too many butterflies to chase for him to concern himself with more difficult things for long.

Every morning that week, she awoke to find him on his back next to her, his head on a pillow, his limbs splayed out, and his tongue lolling out of his mouth. He looked so vulnerable when he slept—every bit the baby he still was. It hurt to watch him when he was like that. She knew the more attached she got, the harder it would make it to say goodbye when she finally returned to her life in Los Angeles.

Early Wednesday evening, she and Wendy took the dragon to Oracle Park for one last group walk. Deandra did her best not to burst into tears every time the dragon peeked over his shoulder, as if he needed constant reassurance she was still there.

Wendy claimed she didn't want a pet, but Deandra knew she'd take good care of him. Cruz would too. It would be fine. Deandra could try visiting once every few months. The drive wasn't *that* bad, and when she finally downsized to a smaller apartment she could actually afford, she could occasionally spring for plane tickets into Fresno, then rent a car for the rest of the journey.

At the end of each walk, the three of them would settle in the grass, and Deandra would work on teaching the dragon a few tricks. He was a quick study, so he already knew "sit," "shake," "down," and "speak." Today, they were working on "roll over." The dragon thought dried mealworms were the greatest snack in the world, and since they were small, they made for great training treats. It had taken Deandra a while not to squirm every time she had to pluck one of the dead worms out of the bag. Wendy sat leaning against a tree, staring up at the sky just starting to show signs of approaching dusk.

The dragon either wasn't understanding the "roll over" command, or he was too easily distracted, because every time he got halfway through the action, he would give up and merely flop onto his side, sniffing the grass. An offered mealworm was usually enough to get him to refocus.

Sighing at her dragon—who was very aggressively sniffing a white flower in the grass instead of listening to her—she stuck her hand in the oversized bag of mealworms, grabbed a fistful, and pulled out ... a newt. She screamed. Wendy lurched upright. Deandra dropped the amphibian, who had a good dozen mealworm tails sticking out of her mouth. Sunshine gobbled the worms down and then lunged at the bag again, limbs splayed wide like a flying squirrel. Deandra grabbed the bag and yanked it out of reach.

Sunshine hit the ground, then scuttled back a few inches. She hissed at Deandra. The hiss was lackluster, though.

Wendy jabbed a finger at the newt. "You've lost the privilege of hissing, little lady! You almost killed us!" Sunshine jumped at Wendy's finger as if it were an offered mealworm, but even that attempt didn't hold the same malicious intent as it once did.

Perhaps the newt was slightly less murderous when she wasn't under the thrall of one of Rae's familiar-bond potions.

Sunshine cocked her head, angling an eye toward the bag of worms. She glanced up at Deandra, then back at the bag. The dragon lay on his belly with his chin in the grass and merely watched this interaction, his big pink eyes tracking everyone's movements. Deandra supposed if the newt posed a threat, the dragon would have attacked, or at least scared her off.

Reluctantly, Deandra opened the bag of worms and took one out.

Sunshine scurried forward, hissing.

"Nuh-uh!" Deandra said.

Sunshine scuttled back and closed her mouth.

Deandra held the worm out to her. Every time Sunshine lunged at it too aggressively, Deandra would snatch the worm back. Eventually, Sunshine waited, practically vibrating with anticipation, for the worm to come to her. She gently took it from Deandra's fingers. "See! You can be nice when you want to be, Sunshine."

The newt hissed, which had the vibe of "*Yeah, maybe*" rather than "*I will kill you!*" and then she darted away, diving into a shrub near the parking lot.

"Should we be worried that an orphaned, psychotic fire newt is running loose in town?" Wendy asked.

"Definitely."

After ten more tries, the dragon successfully completed his first "roll over." The celebration Deandra and Wendy threw rivaled fans cheering for an underdog team who'd just won the Super Bowl for the first time in forty years. The dragon was so pleased with the display of praise that he rolled over five times in a row, his scales turning a shade of pink that matched his eyes. Deandra could only guess what that had looked like to everyone else.

When they finally settled down and Deandra and Wendy started packing up, Deandra heard someone clear their throat. She found a middle-aged woman standing nearby, eyeing the dragon warily. If this woman was about to give Deandra grief for not having his leash attached to his harness, despite the fact that he hadn't left her side in an hour, she would go postal.

"Are you a pet sitter, ma'am?" the woman asked.

Deandra stared dumbly at her.

"Or an animal trainer, perhaps?" The woman wrung her hands. "I don't sense any magic on you, so I'm guessing you're not a zoolinguist like Dr. Caddel. But you have a gift with animals. I've seen you work with this dire wolf puppy every day this week. And then with that fire newt just now. I have an unruly frilled dendrune at home, and it would make my life so much easier if someone could come walk him and clean out his cage once a day."

What in the world was a frilled dendrune?

"She's still working out the kinks in her animal care business, but if you give us your number, she can contact you soon," Wendy said.

Deandra resisted the urge to elbow her cousin—in the face.

"Oh, excellent!" The woman scurried away long enough to get a pen and paper out of her purse where she'd left it with her husband. He sat in a lounge chair with his nose buried in a book. She wrote down her name and number and handed the paper to Deandra. "I look forward to hearing from you."

Once the woman was out of earshot, Deandra whirled to glare at Wendy. "You can't promise people stuff like that. I leave tomorrow."

The dragon let out a low, soft howl. She thought he might be hungry for more mealworms, but when she glanced down at him, he was watching her with big, sad eyes. He army-crawled toward her on his belly before resting his chin on her knee. Her shoulders slumped.

Perhaps he'd known exactly what was going on after all.

She ran a finger back and forth across his forehead. "You'll be having so much fun with Aunt Wendy and Uncle Cruz that you'll hardly know I'm gone."

He huffed a small plume of smoke out of his nose.

Yeah, she didn't believe herself either.

Chapter 20

Two weeks later

Deandra's new apartment was smaller than her last one, but it was cheaper, so it had that going for it. She'd been on a month-to-month lease at her old place, so she'd been able to jump ship quickly. She'd sold most of her furniture when she moved to give herself an extra influx of cash. The state of her bank account had been rather bleak, and it needed all the help it could get.

She'd thought a lot about her time in Axia over the past two weeks. The experience almost felt like a fever dream now—one populated by centaurs, orcs, pixies, and humans who could shift into animals. It was a place where dragons existed. Once she'd been away from it, she'd realized how dangerous the town could be. There were greedy, manipulative people in the mundane world, too, but at least in the mundane world, there wasn't magic complicating things even further.

Her time away from Axia had even made her consider picking up the phone to call Mark. Maybe she'd told him "no" out of fear. What if she'd let something good and stable go simply because she'd had cold feet?

Her mother had nearly fainted when Deandra had recounted her exploits in Axia, and she was relieved Deandra had come back to the mundane world where one didn't have to worry about pyromaniac fox shifters.

The mundane world was definitely safer.

Happy with the path she'd chosen for her life, even if it was currently sparsely furnished, Deandra stepped out of her bedroom and into Wendy's hallway.

A happy chirp erupted from the living room, and the dragon bounded over.

"Awake from your nap finally, I see?" Deandra asked him, bending to give him a scratch behind a horn. "Want to go for a walk?"

The dragon twirled in a circle, then got distracted by the end of his own tail.

Wendy padded down the hallway. "Everything moved in?"

"Yeah. Thanks again for letting me stay here. I'll find my own—"

"Stop already," Wendy said. "There's no rush. Having a roommate will be nice, actually. And if Nathan and I end up working out, we'll just work out a system of socks on doorknobs or whatever."

Deandra laughed. "Gross."

The dragon got so dizzy from chasing his own tail, he toppled onto his side. He huffed out an exhausted breath, which sent a dust bunny floating across the floor. He scrambled to his feet to chase it down.

"Time for a walk since he's out of his ever-loving mind?" Wendy asked.

"Yeah. One sec, though. I picked up something on my way into town." Deandra ducked into her room, rummaged around in the shopping bag on her bed, and fished out a small trinket. She walked back out into the living room and handed the item to Wendy.

The dragon had the dust bunny stuck to the middle of his muzzle and was ineffectively trying to dislodge it with his too-short forelegs.

Wendy smiled down at the bone-shaped tag in her hands. "Havoc, huh?"

"He's wreaked all kinds of havoc on my life, so I thought it suited him."

"*Good* havoc, though, right?" Wendy asked.

The dragon—Havoc—sneezed, dislodging the dust bunny and releasing a tiny fireball the size of a pea at the same time. It left a small scorch mark on Wendy's otherwise stark-white wall.

Deandra sighed. "Definitely the good kind of havoc."

After attaching his new tag to his collar, where it rested against the tag that had a flame etched on one side, Deandra got the wiggly lizard into his harness.

Havoc chirped, then galloped toward the door.

Deandra and Wendy walked down the sidewalk, talking about everything and nothing, while Havoc trotted along in front of them, stopping every few seconds to sniff the flowers, chase a butterfly, or glance over his shoulder to check that Deandra was still there.

She smiled to herself.

Turned out she *could* uproot her life in Los Angeles and move to Axia simply because a baby dragon adopted her ...

Join Deandra and Havoc on their next adventure in A Mythical Case of Murder! You can also join Melissa's mailing list to be notified about upcoming releases.

Also by Melissa Erin Jackson

A Mythical Case of Murder

Job hunting is a deadly sport.

Deandra "Dee" Hendricks is settling into her new life in Axia. She's got her trusty baby dragon, Havoc, by her side, is sharing an apartment with her best friend and roommate, Wendy, and even has her first pet-sitting client. Things are looking up!

Shortly after launching her new website, Dee receives an invitation to a pet-sitter happy hour where she meets Sarah, the owner of Axia's largest pet-sitting operation. Other attendees include sole proprietors, like Dee, and a few of Sarah's employees. Everyone is welcoming and willing to share advice—mainly to steer clear of their notorious fellow sitter, Lydia Monroe.

They accuse Lydia of everything—from magically manipulating her animal charges and poaching clients from Sarah to making false claims about possessing "zoolingual" abilities. The sticking point is Lydia's questionable acquisition of a lucrative gig offered by Oleander Basnet, a yeti whose son needs one-on-one care. Sarah's company fought hard for the opportunity, only to have yet another job snatched away by Lydia.

The peaceful get-together is interrupted when a late arrival informs the group that Lydia had been found murdered. Worse still, the time of death doesn't exonerate anyone at the event. Dee fears she just shared discounted apps with a murderer.

Later that night, a job offer from Oleander hits Dee's inbox. Dee's wallet desperately wants her to take the job, but could there be someone in town so desperate to beat the competition that they murdered Lydia? And could Dee be next?

While waiting for the next book in the Mythical Pet Sitting Mystery series, you can check out the Witch of Edgehill series. There are five books—and the series is complete! (They're all in audio, too!)

Book 1 is *Pawsitively Poisonous.*

Every town has its secrets, but no one has a secret like hers.

Amber Blackwood, lifelong resident of Edgehill, Oregon, has earned a reputation for being a semi-reclusive odd duck. Her store, The Quirky Whisker, is full of curiosities, from extremely potent sleepy teas and ever-burning candles to kids' toys that seem to run endlessly without the aid of batteries. The people of Edgehill think of the Quirky Whisker as an integral part of their feline-obsessed town, but most give Amber herself a wide berth. Amber prefers it that way; it keeps her secret safe. But that secret is thrown into jeopardy when Amber's friend Melanie is found dead, a vial of headache tonic from Amber's store clutched in her hand.

Edgehill's newest police chief has had it out for Amber since he arrived three years before. He can't possibly know she's a witch, but his suspicions about her odd store and even odder behavior have shot her to the top of his suspect list. When the Edgehill rumor mill finds out Melanie was poisoned, it's not only the police chief who looks at Amber differently. Determined to both find justice for her friend and to clear her own name, Amber must use her unique gifts to help track down Melanie's real killer. A quest that threatens much more than her secret ...

Acknowledgments

As always, I offer a hearty thank you to my beta reading team. I'll keep sending y'all my stories as long as you let me! Thanks, Mom, Jennifer, Margarita, Garrett, John, Emilie, Kayla, and Cyndi.

Thank you, Molly Burton, for the wickedly cute cover! I was so worried my idea was too weird or, worse yet, impossible, and then you sent me something so adorable, I almost burst into tears. I mean … c'mon! Havoc is in a *harness*. I can't. (I'm perhaps living out my dream of having a dragon for a pet through this series.)

Thank you, Justin Cohen, for the proofreading and the friendship.

Thanks to Annie, Lesli, Cecilie, and Lauren for being another set of eyeballs for me.

Thank you to Sarah Waites who took my chicken scratch of a drawing and my rambling notes and somehow created such a cute and detailed map. I'm so glad I kept that portfolio pamphlet from years ago!

Thank you to the gang over at Etheric Tales for all the drawings of Havoc. The drawings I sent you were even worse than the ones I sent Sarah!

I send out a monthly newsletter, and in one of those emails, I asked my subscribers to give me ideas of unique pets that our girl Deandra might have to deal with over the course of the series. Gwenyth Jones wrote back and told me about her ornery newt. The email cracked me up so much that it resulted in the creation of

Sunshine, the misunderstood (and lightly homicidal) fire newt. Thank you, Gwenyth, for the idea!

And, finally, thank you to Sam for keeping me sane. It's not an easy task. I kinda like you a lot.

See you all back in Axia soon!

About the Author

Melissa has had a love of stories for as long as she can remember, but only started penning her own during her freshman year of college. She majored in Wildlife, Fish, and Conservation Biology at UC Davis. Yet, while she was neck-deep in organic chemistry and physics, she kept finding herself writing stories in the back of the classroom about fairies and trolls and magic. She finished her degree, but it never captured her heart the way writing did.

Now she owns her own dog walking business (that's sort of wildlife related, right?) by day ... and afternoon and night ... and writes whenever she gets a spare moment. She alternates mostly between fantasy and mystery (often with a paranormal twist). All her books have some element of "other" to them ... witches, ghosts, UFOs. There's no better way to escape the real world than getting lost in a fictional one.

She lives in Northern California with her very patient boyfriend and way too many pets.

You can find out more about her upcoming books and join her newsletter at: https://melissajacksonbooks.com

Printed in Great Britain
by Amazon

50110142R00138